MONTANA MAVERICKS

Welcome to Big Sky Country, home of the Montana Mavericks! Where free-spirited men and women discover love on the range.

LASSOING LOVE

After years away, some of Bronco's most memorable sons and daughters have returned to the ranch seeking a fresh start. But there are some bumps along the road to redemption. Expect the unexpected as lonesome cowboys (and cowgirls) discover if they've got what it takes to grab that second chance!

For Mike Burris, rodeo is just a job. Ever since he can remember, he's wanted to study medicine. For Corrine Hawkins, rodeo is *life*. She always thought she and Mike would wind up together, but their goals are taking them in different directions—and to different locations. When the timing is all wrong, can the good doctor still be her Mr. Right?

Dear Reader,

Welcome back to Bronco, Montana, home of famous rodeo stars the Burris brothers. They've been falling in love recently. First Geoff and then Jack. Now it's Mike's turn. He's given up life on the rodeo circuit in favor of medical school. His studies keep him busy, so to his way of thinking, there's no time in his life for romance. But his heart has other ideas and won't be lassoed.

Corinne Hawkins, a third-generation rodeo star and member of the well-regarded Hawkins sisters, became friends with Mike when he was still competing on the circuit. *Good* friends. But Mike's life is in Chicago now, while Corinne is living in Bronco and traveling from rodeo to rodeo. She's not thrilled to just be friends, but she needs more attention than Mike can give her. And she's not willing to settle for less.

Can these two make a romance work with so much stacked against them?

I hope you enjoy *Falling for Dr. Maverick* as much as I enjoyed writing it.

I love hearing from my readers, so feel free to drop me a line at my website, kathydouglassbooks.com.

Happy reading!

Kathy

Falling for
Dr. Maverick

KATHY DOUGLASS

HARLEQUIN
SPECIAL
EDITION

Special thanks and acknowledgment are given to
Kathy Douglass for her contribution to the
Montana Mavericks: Lassoing Love miniseries.

HARLEQUIN®

SPECIAL EDITION™

Recycling programs
for this product may
not exist in your area.

ISBN-13: 978-1-335-59426-6

Falling for Dr. Maverick

Harlequin Enterprises ULC
22 Adelaide St. West, 41st Floor
Toronto, Ontario M5H 4E3, Canada
www.Harlequin.com

Printed in U.S.A.

Kathy Douglass is a lawyer turned author of sweet small-town contemporary romances. She is married to her very own hero and mother to two sons, who cheer her on as she tries to get her stubborn hero and heroine to realize they are meant to be together. She loves hearing from readers that something in her books made them laugh or cry. You can learn more about Kathy or contact her at kathydouglassbooks.com.

Books by Kathy Douglass

Harlequin Special Edition

Montana Mavericks: Lassoing Love

Falling for Dr. Maverick

Sweet Briar Sweethearts

How to Steal the Lawman's Heart
The Waitress's Secret
The Rancher and the City Girl
Winning Charlotte Back
The Rancher's Return
A Baby Between Friends
The Single Mom's Second Chance

The Fortunes of Texas: The Wedding Gift

A Fortune in the Family

Montana Mavericks: The Real Cowboys of Bronco Heights

In the Ring with the Maverick

Visit the Author Profile page at Harlequin.com for more titles.

This book is dedicated with love to my husband and two sons. I appreciate your unwavering love and consistent support.

Prologue

Two months ago...

Mike Burris sat beside his parents in the beautifully decorated ballroom at the Bronco Convention Center and looked at his brother Jack. Mike couldn't believe that Jack was getting married—and as part of the Bronco Summer Family Rodeo no less. Jack must have felt him staring because he looked over at him, the wide smile that had been permanently affixed to his face all week even broader. Mike flashed his brother a thumbs-up. He'd never seen Jack this happy. And why wouldn't he be? He was marrying the love of his life. Audrey Hawkins and Jack might have butted heads while their families competed in the Battle of the Sexes in last year's inaugural Bronco Summer Family Rodeo, but it had been clear from the beginning that the two of them were perfect for each other. Clear, that was, to everyone but them. They had stubbornly resisted the attraction. It had taken Jack losing Audrey for him to finally admit that he was in love with her.

Now that Mike thought about it, this was the perfect place for Jack and Audrey to get married. The rodeo had played such an integral part in their relationship. If they hadn't been forced to spend time together doing promotion as the Rodeo Sweethearts, they wouldn't have gotten past their initial rough start and gotten to know each other. Since the entire town of Bronco, Montana, had been emotionally invested in the relationship, Jack and Audrey had decided to share their big day with as many members of the community as possible. Although the ceremony was private, there had been plenty of press about the nuptials. Jack and Audrey had even made a brief appearance at the rodeo earlier today.

A string quartet had been playing softly as guests took their seats. Now a soloist started to sing about love and devotion, signaling the beginning of the ceremony. Mike turned his attention toward the center aisle where the bridesmaids and bride would be making their entrance. But he wasn't looking for his future sister-in-law. He was waiting to see Corinne, Audrey's youngest sister and the woman Mike was sort of involved with.

Mike and Corinne's relationship had once been so uncomplicated. They'd been instant friends who'd enjoyed hanging out with each other whenever they were home in Bronco or competing in the same rodeo. They'd kept in touch when they'd been apart, texting and talking on the phone.

But that was before he'd started medical school last year. His first year had been busy, leaving little time for a serious relationship. Corinne and Mike had agreed that although they liked each other—*really liked each other*—it would be for the best if they were just friends.

At the time, the decision had seemed reasonable. It had prevented problems and reduced their stress. Since she was busy competing with her sisters, and his time was spent either in class or studying, it had been the wrong time to even consider a romantic relationship. Being friends was the best way they knew to remain on good terms.

Corinne couldn't feel neglected if Mike didn't have time to talk to her every night. She couldn't expect him to share the big and small events of his day with her. Mike wouldn't feel guilty about not finding time to see her. Nor would he have the right to be jealous if she spent time with other men. Friends didn't have those rights. He'd hated the thought of Corinne dating other men, but he reminded himself they were free agents who could see whoever they wanted. He couldn't have it both ways. Until he was in a position to fully commit to a romance, friendship was the way it had to be.

He only hoped Corinne was still a free agent when that day eventually came. Not that he had any right to think that way.

That plan had worked well until this past summer. School was on break and Mike was once more on the rodeo circuit. He and Corinne had spent lots of time together, picking up where they'd left off. And going even farther. They'd kissed a couple of times—more than a peck, but less than a make-out session. Even so, those kisses had rocked Mike's world. Only knowing that he would be returning to school had kept him from going too far.

Mike felt a sharp elbow in his side and glanced at his mother. She mouthed *pay attention*. He nodded.

The soloist sang the last note of her song, and instantly the air became charged with excitement. People shifted in their seats, turning to watch the procession. The quartet began playing as the first bridesmaid started down the aisle. Although Mike wasn't the groom, and Corinne wasn't the bride, she hadn't wanted him to see her before the ceremony. He'd agreed because it had been important to her. Corinne stepped into view and his mouth fell open. She was an absolute vision in her deep pink gown. The long dress was modest, yet Corinne looked sexy as hell.

It wasn't the dress that captured and held his attention. It was Corinne. She was just so beautiful. With clear brown skin, large dark brown eyes and high cheekbones, her face was exquisite. She looked straight ahead as she processed, but when she was standing across from him, she glanced over and smiled. His heart lurched and he smiled back.

Once all of the bridesmaids were standing at the front of the room, Audrey entered, holding her father's arm. Mike had only met the man once—yesterday— but he liked him. He seemed a decent man who loved his daughters. They loved him in return, which was all that mattered. Audrey's father kissed her cheek and then he stepped aside, leaving Audrey standing beside Jack.

Although Mike told himself to pay attention to the ceremony, he couldn't keep his eyes from straying to Corinne. Unlike him, she was paying rapt attention, hanging on every word the minister uttered and being swept away by each song the soloist sang. When Jack and Audrey recited their vows, Corinne's eyes floated closed as if she were drifting into a daydream of her own. Mike couldn't help wondering what she was thinking at that moment.

Before long, Jack was kissing the bride. Afterward, the bride and groom jumped over the broom, and the minister formally introduced the newlyweds to great applause. Mike wasn't a big fan of weddings, but he had to admit that this had actually been pretty nice.

There was a lot of commotion as the wedding guests congratulated the bride and groom before moving to the section of the arena that had been transformed into another beautiful space for the reception. The dirt and barrels that had been there for the rodeo earlier had been replaced by linen covered tables and pink and white roses. Mike loved nothing more than a party. With his brothers and close friends in attendance, this would be a great one. But it was Corinne's presence that was the icing on the cake. Mike and Corinne might not currently be involved romantically, but she was the person he wanted to spend his time with.

"Wasn't that a beautiful wedding?" Corinne asked as she approached. Her face glowed with happiness. She'd been posing for pictures with her sisters, and Mike had grown increasingly impatient as the photographer had insisted on taking one more picture. "I didn't think that getting married in a conference room would be romantic, but it was."

"It was a bit nontraditional," Mike agreed.

"But I suppose it was fitting," Corinne continued. "After all, they were the Rodeo Sweethearts last year."

Mike laughed. "Whatever you do, don't mention that to Jack. You know how much that whole situation annoyed him."

Corinne nodded. "Audrey was just as irritated. At least in the beginning. Once she admitted that she was in love with Jack, she didn't mind the attention."

"Speaking of attention, everyone is looking at you. You look positively stunning."

"Thanks. It's this dress." Corinne ran a slender finger across the fabric. "Anyone would look good in it."

"The dress is nice, but it's all you."

The smile Corinne flashed him easily outshone the sun. He hadn't been exaggerating. Corinne looked even more gorgeous up close. Before they could continue their conversation, the wedding planner announced that dinner was about to be served.

"Do you need to sit with the wedding party, or can you eat with me?" Mike mentally crossed his fingers.

"I need to sit with the wedding party. But after the cake is served, I'll be free to party."

"In that case, I'll see you later."

Corinne turned and walked to the head table. As he went, Mike couldn't tear his eye away from her round bottom, admiring the gentle way it swayed with each step.

"I thought you were just friends," his brother Ross said, coming to stand beside him.

"A man can still look."

"Is that right?" Ross turned to look at Corinne and Mike nudged his shoulder.

"This man. Not you."

Ross laughed. "Just checking. Come on, let's sit down. I'm ready to eat."

Mike and his brother were seated at a table with some of their closest friends, and they laughed and joked throughout the meal. Though he had fun kidding with the others, Mike was glad when the wedding cake had been eaten. Now he could hang out with Corinne.

He was getting out of his chair when Ross grabbed his arm. Mike looked at his brother. "What?"

"The first dance." He nodded to where Jack and Audrey prepared to sway to their chosen song.

Mike sighed and turned his chair to face the dance floor. Dang, all of these traditions were conspiring to keep him and Corinne apart.

He glanced at the head table. Corinne's hands were clasped to her chest as she watched Jack and Audrey slow dance together. She might not have been able to look away from the newlyweds, but Mike couldn't tear his eyes away from her.

After the traditional dances, the lead singer of the band announced that the dance floor was available for everyone. Finally. Mike rushed over to Corinne and held out his hand. She took it without hesitation. Her fingernails were painted to match her dress, which Mike found incredibly sexy.

After two dances, one of the Jack's friends tried to cut in. Corinne shook her head, saving Mike the trouble of telling the other guy to find another girl. He and Corinne didn't see each other often enough and he wasn't willing to share her with anyone.

"It's so good to see you," Corinne said as they moved to the ballad. He'd forgotten how good she felt in his arms. "I've missed you."

That was so Corinne. She'd always been direct and honest. He'd always appreciated the way she didn't play silly games, trying to make him guess what was on her mind. Her openness made him respond in kind, and he'd revealed things to her that he'd intended to keep to himself. "I've missed you, too."

"Nothing is the same," she continued. "I've been trying to convince my sisters that we need to coordinate our schedule so that we're competing at the same rodeos as you and your brothers. They haven't been all that eager to do so in the past, but now that Jack and Audrey are married, she should be on my side. That means we could be seeing each other more often."

"Not necessarily so," Mike said. "I'll be going back to school soon. I was able to compete and take classes while I was in undergrad, but medical school is an entirely different beast. My first year was rough and I expect this year to be even more challenging. I don't think I'd have even one weekend a month to travel. And I definitely wouldn't have time to practice."

She looked surprised. "So, are you saying that you're quitting rodeo for good? That the rodeos you compete in this summer will be your last?"

Mike hesitated before he answered. The idea had been floating around his head for a long while, but he hadn't made a firm decision yet. Although his brothers had always intended to make a career in rodeo, that had never been Mike's plan. He'd always wanted to be an orthopedic surgeon. From the time he been a kid, medicine had been his goal. Rodeo had simply been a means to an end.

Now that he was getting closer to making his dream a reality, he was surprisingly reluctant to leave his cowboy days behind permanently. Rodeo had been a part of his life for as long as he could remember. He'd made a lot of friends and had many great experiences. Quitting was harder than he'd expected it to be. But if he wanted to succeed in medical school, he couldn't compete in rodeo every few months.

"Yes. I knew the time was coming when I would have to end my career. Even so, it's been a hard decision. I've given it a lot of thought. And it's time. I need to spend my time studying. Trying to be a full-time medical student and part-time competitor just isn't workable."

"So I won't be seeing you on the circuit anymore?" She sounded crestfallen and he felt like a jerk.

"That's not true. I'll still try to catch shows whenever I can. I'll just be a member of the audience instead of another competitor."

"So, what does that mean for us?" They'd been having such a good time that he hated to have this conversation now. But he knew that he couldn't avoid it forever. As hard as it was, he knew Corinne deserved better than that.

"I've been thinking about that," he said, struggling to maintain eye contact with her. "I think it would be best if we stick to our plan to just be friends. I know that we crossed the line a time or two, but I think things work best for us when we don't try to have a romantic relationship. I'm focused on school now. And you're focused on your career."

Although Corinne's expression remained unchanged and she didn't move a muscle, Mike felt the change in her. The lightness of spirit that he had come to associate with her faded, taking her earlier happiness with it. He'd ruined the moment and he felt like a heel, but he'd done it for her.

"Oh. Okay." She took a step back.

He reached out and took her hand, unwilling to let the moment end on a sour note. "Can we go outside and talk?"

She pulled her hand away and tucked it behind her back. "Why? You just said what you meant. I understand completely. More talk won't change anything."

"I'm not pushing you away. Far from it," he said honestly as Corinne began walking away. "I just want to go back to the way things were when we were just friends. It was easy and fun."

Corinne paused and his heart stuttered to a stop. Giving her less than she deserved would only lead to disappointment. Resentment. Anger. And the end of their friendship. And that he could not accept.

Finally she nodded. "Okay, Mike. We can do that, if that's what you really want."

It wasn't. But he had no choice. And he regretted his decision the instant he watched her walk away...

Chapter One

"If you look better, you'll feel better," Corinne said to herself as she wrapped her favorite shawl around her shoulders. The orange print fabric was both warm and fashionable. Though she'd never been overly concerned with her appearance—she was a mascara and lip gloss girl at heart—for the past few weeks, she'd spent more time on her looks. She'd upped her makeup game to include blush and eyeliner, and added stylish new pieces to her wardrobe. She still wore comfortable jeans most of the time, but instead of an old T-shirt with a snappy saying and well-worn cowboy boots, she now paired her jeans with cute tops and colorful boots. She glanced in the mirror. She did look good. Sadly, the good feeling hadn't kicked in yet. But the day was still young. Maybe it was just running late.

"You look nice," Remi said, poking her head into Corinne's room. When they'd moved to Bronco, Montana, last year, all four sisters had shared the house. It made sense to sign the short-term rental since they competed as the Hawkins Sisters on the rodeo circuit. When the lease was up, they'd moved on. Then they decided to remain in Bronco permanently. At first they'd planned to find their own places so they could have their own space. Once they'd discovered the house was still vacant, they'd rented it again. It had felt like home. Over the past year, Audrey had gotten married and moved out. Although Brynn and Garrett were only engaged, she had moved in with him on his ranch. Corinne missed having her two oldest sisters around, and she was glad that Remi still lived here.

"Thanks."

"Are you going someplace special?" Remi asked, a hopeful look on her face.

"No. It's such a nice day. I didn't want to waste it inside. I thought I'd walk around downtown and do a little window-shopping. Do you want to come?"

Remi nodded. "I'll grab a jacket and meet you downstairs."

Corinne nodded and jogged down the stairs, grateful to have the company. Although quite a bit of time had passed since Mike had told her he definitely only wanted to be friends, she still felt the ache of his rejection. Their attempt at a romantic relationship had been brief, so it shouldn't hurt this much. But that had been the best time of her life. Now she knew it had been an illusion. She'd been falling in love, and he'd been searching for an escape hatch.

Whenever she was alone, his words echoed through her head, and she tended to brood, which was the last thing she wanted to do today. If Mike was happy with just being friends, then she would make herself happy with that relationship too.

Just thinking about Mike made her heart ache and she told herself to knock it off. He wasn't thinking about her. He was off in Chicago, focused on his studies, making new friends…maybe finally moving past what they'd had. It was time for her to move on and start living too.

"I'm ready," Remi said, coming to stand beside Corinne.

Corinne drove the short distance to downtown. Bronco, Montana, could be described as two towns in one. There was the tony Bronco Heights part where the wealthy and well-connected lived. Several of the modern mansions had been featured in glitzy magazines. Bronco Valley was where the middle-class families— including Corinne and her sisters—lived. The houses were older and smaller, but Corinne loved the sense of belonging she felt in the community. The moment she'd stepped inside the cozy rental house last year, she'd felt at home.

The small downtown was filled with nice shops and upscale boutiques where she was able to enjoy one of her favorite pastimes—window-shopping. There were also good places to eat such as the Gemstone Diner and Bronco Burgers, one of her favorite places to get shakes.

"Did you want to go any place in particular?" Remi asked after they'd parked and were standing in town.

"Not really. I just have a bit of wanderlust."

"And walking downtown will satisfy it? I don't think that word means what you think it means."

Corinne laughed. "Good point."

Remi pointed in the direction of the diner. "How about we walk that way? I saw a cute skirt in the window display in Cimarron Rose that I want to try on. And when we're done, we can get an early dinner."

"That sounds good to me."

The leaves had begun to turn and were now varying shades of red, orange and yellow, creating a beautiful setting. A few had already fallen from the trees and crunched beneath their feet as they walked.

"I love this time of year," Corinne said after a while.

Remi laughed. "You say that with the change of every season. In a few months, you'll be waxing poetic about the beauty of winter and saying how much you love snow."

"I suppose you're right. There is something wonderful about playing in the snow and then drinking hot chocolate beside a fire."

"To you. The only thing I like about winter is the end."

"I forgot. You're a summer baby."

"Yep. And all of the short days and chilly nights are making me miss it already. I'm hoping to squeeze in a visit to Arizona soon. Want to come with me?"

Corinne shrugged. "I don't know. I'm feeling kind of at loose ends these days."

"I wonder why that is," Remi said, pausing and dramatically putting a finger up to her cheek. "Oh, I know. It has something to do with Mike Burris."

Sarcasm aside, there was no sense denying Remi was right. Her sister knew her too well to be fooled. Besides, Corinne wanted to talk about her feelings. "I kind of miss him."

"So call him."

Corinne shook her head and they started walking again. If only it were that simple. "No. We agreed to be just friends."

"Friends talk to each other."

"I know. But we just talked last week. He's busy with his classes and study group. Medical school is hard and requires serious commitment. If he wants to get good grades, he can't be distracted. And a relationship with me would be a distraction, which is why we're just friends. And why I can't call him."

"If you say so. But if you agreed that you're only friends, you need to move on. Maybe you should see other people."

Corinne shrugged. "I thought about it but I'm not interested in anyone else."

Remi gave her a long, searching look before stopping in front of a boutique. "This is where I saw the skirt. They have a lot of pretty clothes. You might find something that you like."

"Maybe." That was quite a shift in the conversation, not that Corinne was complaining.

They stepped inside and looked around. The clothes were of good quality and were reasonably priced. Remi went directly to the skirts, pulled one off the rack and held it up to herself, turning so Corinne could take a look. Corinne smiled. "I like it."

"I just need to find a top to go with it. Then I'll try on everything just to be sure."

"You know you'll look great in it. You have a knack for knowing what clothes will accentuate your body." Remi had an uncanny fashion sense. She never missed.

"And I know what looks good on you, too." Remi shuffled through a couple of dresses and then pulled out a hanger and offered it to Corinne. "You'd look sensational in this."

"Where will I wear it?"

"Anywhere. Maybe a date."

She should have known Remi wouldn't let the matter drop that easily. She'd just been biding her time. "I told you, I'm not dating anyone."

"Do you think Mike is spending all of his time in class or studying? I don't. He's attractive and charming. Trust me, I'm sure that plenty of his female classmates have noticed that. They might be from big cities, but they will also appreciate the appeal of a country boy. Especially one who's a rodeo star."

The thought of Mike spending time with another woman and possibly falling in love with her made Corinne's heart ache. She wasn't exactly jealous, but she couldn't put a finger on what she felt. All she knew was that it was unpleasant, and she wanted to be rid of the emotion as soon as possible.

Her relationship with Mike had once been so easy. They'd been instant friends who'd gotten close very quickly. They'd spent all of their free time together, doing all kinds of fun things. They'd gone to dinner and movies. Other times, they'd spent the afternoon horseback riding across the open acres of hills, stopping to enjoy an impromptu lunch.

She smiled as she recalled the time he'd tried to teach her how to fly a kite. The day had been windy, and he'd gotten the kite up into the air easily. It hadn't been the same for her. She'd spent close to an hour trying, yet she hadn't been able to keep the kite in the air more than a handful of seconds. It had looked easy, but it hadn't been. After a while she'd admitted defeat. So they'd lain on their backs, their hands beneath their heads, and stared up at the kite she'd gotten caught in a tree. Of all the times they'd spent together—and there had been plenty of them—that had been her favorite. She carried the memory in her heart, taking it out from time to time to look at it and smile.

And when she took out that memory, she always pictured him. With clear brown skin, short-cropped hair, and neatly trimmed facial hair, Mike was easily the most handsome man she'd ever seen. He had the muscular body of an athlete and the face of an angel. For all of his good looks, his personality was even more attractive. No doubt, his female classmates had noticed.

"I suppose he might be dating occasionally," she said when she realized Remi was waiting for a reply.

"I think you should start, too."

"I'm not looking for a relationship." Remi looked like she might protest, but Corinne wanted to be done with this conversation, sooner rather than later so she added, "But I am looking for a dress." She grabbed the hanger from her sister's outstretched hand.

Remi got the message and nodded. They picked out a few more outfits and then headed to the changing rooms. Although there were numerous shoppers bustling about the store, the changing area was empty, so Remi and Corinne chose rooms across from each other. Corinne slipped out of her jeans and top and then slid on the dress. Although she hadn't planned to buy anything, she had to admit that Remi had been right about this dress. It was fire!

The red, orange and yellow pattern made her brown skin glow. The dress was sleek with a fitted skirt that clung to her every inch without being too tight. Corinne lifted her long black braids from her shoulders and twisted them into an impromptu updo. After checking her appearance in the mirror, she stepped into the aisle separating the rows of changing rooms. Remi's door opened at the same time. When she caught sight of Corinne, she clapped her hands and crowed. "I knew you'd look great in that dress."

They headed for the three-way mirror at the far end

of the changing area. Corinne stepped onto the platform and checked her appearance from every angle. "I like it."

"So, you're getting it?"

"Yes, although I still have no idea where I'm going to wear it."

"If you buy it, he will come."

Corinne laughed. "I know you didn't just misquote *Field of Dreams* to me. You hate baseball movies."

Remi shrugged. "Is that where the saying is from? I've never seen the movie. But I do agree with the sentiment. Now that you're all glamorous, Mr. Wonderful is going to come along and sweep you off your feet."

"Didn't I just tell you that I'm not interested in a relationship?"

Remi sighed and shook her head in a hopeless gesture. "Unless it's with Mike. The man who's put you on a shelf where you're gathering dust."

Corinne didn't take offense. Still, she protested, "That's not exactly accurate."

"What part? You guys were inseparable until he started medical school. Now suddenly he doesn't have time for you, so he ended things. And instead of getting on with your life, you're sitting around waiting for him to squeeze you into his busy life."

Corinne threw her shoulders back, determined to set her sister straight. "We were more friends than anything."

"Save that line for someone who doesn't know you as well as I do. You were falling for Mike. It wouldn't have taken much on his part before you practiced writing your signature as *Corinne Burris*."

"First of all, if and when I decide to get married, I'm not changing my name. Hawkins women don't change our names."

"Noted."

"And second, I wasn't imagining myself as Mrs. *Anybody*. I was just enjoying our friendship."

"It's me you're talking to," Remi said, her voice soft and understanding.

That tenderness was all it took for the strong facade Corinne had erected to start to crumble. She felt tears sting her eyes and she blinked them away. "Go on."

"I know that you were hoping for more than friendship from Mike." Corinne started to cut in and Remi raised a hand, stopping her. "And there's nothing wrong with that."

"Maybe," Corinne said, unwilling to concede more. Not that she thought Remi would react poorly but rather because she wasn't willing to examine her feelings too deeply. She didn't know what she would find and honestly, she wasn't sure she could handle the truth. The disappointment she couldn't shake was a heavy enough burden on its own.

"Then if you want my advice, get out there and date. You don't need to have a great romance, or a romance at all. But you're a social person. You thrive around people. So go out with a guy or three. Not at the same time, unless that's your new thing," she teased, trying to force a smile from Corinne. She didn't succeed. "Sitting around the house waiting for him to call isn't good for you."

"I'm not sitting around the house. I'm out with you."

"And you're constantly checking your cell phone."

"True. But not because I'm waiting to hear from Mike."

Remi frowned and shooed Corinne off the platform so she could stand in front of the mirror. She glanced at her reflection and the caught Corinne's eyes in the mirror. "What do you think of my outfit?"

"You look gorgeous, as we both knew you would. Do you have a man in mind?"

"Nope. But if I wear it—"

"—he will come," Corinne finished and they laughed together.

They tried on a few more outfits and then chose to buy the first ones. After they purchased their clothes, they wandered down Commercial Street, stopping to look in windows with displays. The one in Sadie's Holiday House was especially beautiful, and they stared at it for a while before continuing down the street. They didn't go inside any other stores. The temptation to buy would be great and they were sticking to their budgets.

They were near the diner when they spotted an orange tabby walking down the center of the street as if it didn't have a care in the world. It didn't appear to have on a collar. Corinne looked around for its owner but didn't see anyone.

"Here, kitty," she said. She placed her bags on the ground and stooped down.

"What a pretty kitty," Remi said softly. She stooped beside Corinne, and they tried to coax the cat to come to them. Their efforts had the opposite effect and the cat turned and raced down the street.

"I wonder who that cat belongs to," Corinne said. She hoped it stayed safe.

"I don't know. I heard that a cat has been seen around town, but I don't know who it belongs to."

"I hope it makes it home," Corinne said, picking up her bags and she and Remi continued down the street.

When they reached the diner, they went inside for a delicious meal. They talked and laughed as they ate, and Corinne was in a better mood when she returned home. Even so, the words her sister had spoken earlier echoed in her mind and she forced herself to face them.

No, she didn't think Mike was spending all of his time in class or hitting the books. No matter how much studying he needed to do, he'd probably found time for female companionship. Knowing that, why was she spending all of her nights watching reruns on TV? The next time a man asked her out, she was going to say yes.

She just wished that man could be Mike.

Mike closed the textbook and then rubbed his weary eyes. It had been a long day, as usual. His day had started with a quick breakfast at 7:00 a.m. followed by classes. In between sessions, he'd met with his study group to go over the new material that had been covered. He'd squeezed in a sandwich and chips while reviewing his notes. Somewhere between classes, studying, reading and reviewing, he'd swallowed hospital cafeteria food, this time meat loaf and mashed potatoes that was nowhere near as good as his mother's. Like most of the students, he ate a lot of his meals at the hospital attached to the medical school, choosing convenience over taste. He was counting the days to the next break so he could enjoy his mother's cooking again. And see Corinne.

He opened his eyes and checked his watch. It was past midnight. Too late to call her. Although Bronco's time zone was only an hour behind Chicago's, Corinne was an early bird and would have been asleep for hours. Though he longed to hear her voice, he wasn't going to be selfish. If they were going to talk, it would have to be at a time that was convenient to both of them. Lately those times had been few and far between. He considered sending her a quick text to let her know that she was on his mind for her to read in the morning but decided against it. The sound the phone made could disturb her.

He blew out a breath. This was so much harder than he'd expected it to be. They'd been friends before and he'd thought they could easily step back into that relationship. After all, they'd only tried dating for a short time. Going back should be easy. He'd been wrong. Going back was torture. But it was for the best. They hadn't seen each other as often as either of them would have liked last year, and the opportunities to spend time together were going to be even fewer this year. He'd had a front-row seat to the decline and eventual demise of his classmates' relationships and wanted to avoid the same fate. They'd all followed the same predictable pattern.

As the intensity of the studies became more demanding and time-consuming, it took a toll on life outside of class – life with one's partner, one's children. He'd seen several classmates break up, even one friend who came back from summer break divorced. All they had left were bitterness and anger and a whole lot of coursework. Most of those relationships hadn't been long-distance like his and Corinne's.

Her job required her to zigzag across the country as she competed in rodeos and performed in exhibitions. He certainly didn't expect her to give up her life just to sit in his apartment and wait for him to shoehorn her into his ridiculously busy life.

Corinne meant too much to him to ever ask her to do that. She was fun and happy, finding joy in the simplest things. But he knew that disappointment in their relationship could steal that joy from her. He didn't want to be responsible for turning the sweetest person he'd ever met into a bitter woman because he'd been too selfish to let her go.

Not that he wanted the break to be permanent. He hoped it wouldn't be. There were only two and a half more years of medical school. He knew internship and residency would be busy, too. But eventually he'd have his degree and his hours—and his life—would settle down a little. And Corinne wouldn't be in the rodeo forever. Eventually she wouldn't have to travel as much. There would come a time when they could see if their relationship could progress from friendship to romance.

But in the meantime, he needed to consider Corinne's needs. And right now, she needed her sleep. So instead of texting, he scrolled through his phone's photo gallery, stopping on his favorite picture of the two of them together. It was a recent one, taken at Audrey and Jack's wedding. Corinne looked so glamorous in her fancy dress, and he'd looked pretty good in his suit if he said so himself. They'd been slow dancing in the candid photo taken by his brother Ross, smiling at each other. There were people in the background, but Mike hadn't been aware of them at the time. Even now, they faded into nothingness.

He was staring at the picture when there was a knock at his front door. Giving Corinne's gorgeous face one last look, he closed his phone, crossed the small room and opened the door. His friend and next door neighbor, Andy, was leaning against the wall. "I was hoping to get the notes from study group that I missed."

"No problem. Come on in."

"I appreciate it," Andy said as he stepped inside. "I'm sorry for missing the group."

"Don't give it a second thought. We all understand." Andy's girlfriend, Layla, had recently broke up with him. Via text. He'd gone to see her in an attempt to convince her to give their relationship a second chance, It hadn't worked. Mike had expected them to beat the odds. Their breakup only solidified Mike's belief that relationships and med school didn't mix.

Mike had printed a copy of the notes earlier, and he handed them to his friend. "How are you doing?"

Andy shrugged and tried to smile but it looked more like a pained grimace. After a moment, he gave up the effort. "I'm doing as well as can be expected. I really thought we had something special. Apparently, I was wrong."

"Med school is intense."

"I know. But I don't think that was the problem. At least not all of it. Layla told me she got tired of being ignored. Now she's dating some lawyer at the firm she clerked at last summer."

"Ouch."

"I wonder how long she's been seeing this guy behind my back."

"Nothing good can come from thinking about that."

"You're right. But still…a lawyer. I can't think of anything worse."

Mike huffed out a laugh. "Neither can I."

"When you told me that you were going to keep things with your girl friendly, I thought you were out of your mind. But now I understand why you did it. Breaking up sucks big-time." Andy headed for the door. "Thanks again for the notes. I'll see you later."

Mike didn't feel right shoving his friend into the night when he was obviously still hurting. "Are you going to be okay?"

Andy shrugged and looked back at Mike. His normally ruddy skin looked pale and his eyes were filled with sorrow. "I'm going to have to be. Truth be told, I should have expected something like this to happen. I was a fool to think we could make it work."

"There's nothing wrong with being hopeful."

"It's better to be practical. Like you," Andy said before he turned and walked down the stairs.

Mike closed the door behind his friend. He didn't have a choice other than to be practical. He just didn't see a way to maintain a relationship with Corinne now. Not for the long haul. Eventually one of them would become disappointed and hurt. The demise of Andy and Layla's relationship only confirmed that his decision had been the right one. Mike would rather have friendship with Corinne than no relationship at all.

No matter how much he missed her, this was the way it had to be.

Chapter Two

"So, you found a place to wear that dress after all," Remi said a few days later. She'd been leaning against the doorjamb of Corinne's bedroom. Now she came inside, dropped onto the chair beside the window and propped her stockinged feet on the windowsill. She had a smug smile on her face. "That didn't take long."

"I'm kind of surprised myself. I wasn't expecting anyone to ask me out, but Dante Sanchez did. And since I'd promised you that I would say yes to the first guy who asked, I had to follow through."

"How did it happen?"

"I ran into him when I was grabbing a shake at Bronco Java and Juice. Dante was there and we started talking. He's easygoing and I felt really comfortable with him. When he asked me if I wanted to continue our conversation over dinner, I said yes."

Remi grinned. "That sounds promising. This could be the beginning of a beautiful relationship."

"You are incorrigible," Corinne said, laughing. "Nothing is going to happen. And please stop misquoting movies to me."

"Maybe. Maybe not. But even if nothing develops, you'll still have enjoyed a nice evening with a gorgeous man. That's not a bad way to spend a Thursday night."

"How are you spending your night?" Corinne asked, staring at her sister. "You're so busy worrying about my social life that you're neglecting yours."

"Wrong. I'm going to the movies with some friends. And who knows, I might strike up a conversation with an attractive man who wants to date me."

"You know, I can always ask Dante if he has a friend."

Remi shook her head, sending her hair flying over her shoulders. "No thanks. I believe that the right person comes into your life when it's time and not a moment before."

"Really?"

"Yes. And when the two meet, everything clicks, and it's smooth sailing."

"I would like to believe that, but experience has taught me otherwise." She held up her hand, palm out, to stop her sister's remark. "I wasn't just thinking about one person in particular, but all of my past romantic relationships. Everything always starts out just wonderful. Just when I start to think he could be the one, the guy backs off. He's not ready. Or the time isn't right. Whatever the excuse du jour happens to be. I don't have it in me to get my hopes up only to hear how it's not me, it's him. That I deserve a man who can give me more than he can."

"And that's the truth," Remi said. She crossed the room and placed her hands on Corinne's shoulders. "You deserve the world. And if a man knows he can't give it to you, then he's right to step aside."

"Now *you're* talking about Mike."

"I'm talking about all of them." Remi glanced at her watch. "I need to get going. You look fabulous by the way. And I'll expect all the details about your date as soon as you get home."

"There's not going to be much to tell."

"Don't be so sure," Remi said before dashing out of the room. A few moments later Corinne heard the front door close behind her sister.

Corinne checked her appearance and then went downstairs to wait for Dante. It felt strange to be waiting for a man other than Mike to pick her up, but Remi was right about one thing. Corinne couldn't waste her life sitting around until Mike finished school. There was no guarantee that in two years he'd have any more room in his life for her than he did now.

She didn't for a moment believe that he had ended their relationship in order to date another woman. Mike was nothing if not honest. If he said that medical school was eating up all of his time, then Corinne believed him. If she thought that he was lying, she wouldn't want to be with him. Her past relationships had been unsuccessful, but even she knew that trust was vital to make a romance work.

The doorbell rang the minute she stepped into the living room, and she automatically checked her watch. Right on time. It was a small thing, but she appreciated that Dante was prompt. It showed that he respected her time.

She inhaled deeply and then slowly blew out the breath. Time to get this show on the road. She opened the door to find a smiling Dante standing there. He embodied the tall, dark and handsome cliché, but when Corinne looked at him, she felt...nothing. Her heart didn't skip a beat and the blood didn't rush in her veins. Shivers didn't dance down her spine. He might be wildly attractive, but Corinne didn't feel even the slightest attraction to him. Obviously this date wouldn't be the beginning of a romantic relationship. But she did like him as a person, so they might be able to become friends.

Corinne grabbed her coat, locked her front door and then accompanied Dante down the stairs. They made small talk as they drove to the restaurant. Once they arrived, they were immediately shown to their table. Pastabilities was a casual nice restaurant that Corinne liked.

After they'd placed their orders with the waiter, Dante leaned against the back of his chair and looked at her. "How was your day?"

"It was a good one. We're in between rodeos so I took care of my horse and did some chores that had been piling up. Then I relaxed."

"Sounds good." He nodded. "I only know a little about you, and even less about your rodeo career."

She laughed. "Do you want to know more or would you rather I smile and change the subject?"

He gave her a slow, sexy grin that should have curled her toes, but didn't affect her at all. "I'm actually interested in knowing more about you and your career. How did you get started?"

"Well, my sisters and I are third-generation rodeo riders. Our grandmother, Hattie Hawkins, was a big star in her time. She's a legend. She adopted four daughters and raised them on the rodeo circuit. They were the original Hawkins Sisters. My sisters and I picked up the mantle when our mother and aunts retired. We chose to use their name. Back then, I thought it was a good idea. You know, a tribute to the previous generation."

"But now?"

She sighed. "Now I realize just how big the shoes that we have to fill are. When I perform, it's not just Remi, Audrey and Brynn that I'm representing. It's our entire family, especially my mother and aunts."

"Believe me, I understand the pressure of living up to a family name. I have a family of my own with a good reputation, too." He took a bite of his chicken parmesan, and then met her eyes. "I have no doubt that you're doing your family proud."

"According to my mother, she and her sisters are pleased by the reputation we've earned, which is a relief. The last thing any of us want to do is bring shame on the family name. And some of our cousins are also on the rodeo circuit, upholding the Hawkins name."

"It really must be in the blood."

Corinne laughed. "In some ways. My mother and her sisters aren't the only members of our family who are adopted. Remi and I are adopted, too."

"I didn't know."

"Our birth mother worked at the rodeo. She was killed in an accident when we were still in diapers. I was one and Remi was two. I have no memories of my biological parents or of my life before I became a part of the Hawkins family. My parents have pictures of my birth mother and they've given Remi and me copies. The funny thing is that they are actually in a couple of them."

"Your parents and your birth mother?"

"Yes. My mothers were actually friends so adopting me and Remi was a no-brainer."

"What happened to your biological father?"

"He was killed in a car accident before I was born."

"I'm sorry."

He sounded sincere, and she touched his hand. Again,

not the slightest spark or tingle. "Thanks. I don't have any pictures of him, though. But one thing I know for sure—family is who you choose to make it with. Remi and I are not related to our other sisters by blood, but I love Audrey and Brynn just as much as I love her. And I know they feel the same about us. We're just family, you know?"

He nodded.

She realized she'd droned on – perhaps because it felt odd to be with a man other than Mike – and forced herself to get back on track. "But you were asking about the rodeo. I enjoy it, but it's a lot of work and takes a lot of practice in order to master the skills. I'll never be as good as Audrey no matter how hard I try, but that's okay. I'm not as competitive as she is either."

"Do you ever get tired of the travel?"

"No. I like seeing different places and meeting new people. There's a whole big world out there and I want to see as much of it as I can. Of course, we don't often get to glamorous places. But wherever we go, I try to discover what makes that place different from the others. You know, determine what makes it special."

"And do you find it?"

"Most of the time I do. It may take more than one visit, but if I look hard enough, I'll find it."

"And that's important to you?" He took a swallow of his drink and then twirled the ice in his glass.

"Yes."

"Why?"

"Because everyone deserves to have something that sets them apart."

"So what was notable about Bronco?"

"Well, there's Doug's and the haunted bar stool." She gave him a grin and a wink.

He laughed. "Don't tell me you believe that nonsense about bad luck attaching to anyone who sits on the stool."

"Not at all. After all, my cousin is engaged to Bobby Stone so I know he didn't die after sitting there as legend had it. But still, it's something unusual."

"I'll give you that. Anything else?"

"I made friends here." She swallowed some of her drink and then turned the question back at him. "Don't you think Bronco is special?"

"Well, we have the two first families of rodeo living right here in town so…"

"Can there be two first families?" Corinne asked with a smile. "That sounds mathematically impossible."

Dante chuckled. "Hey, this is my list and I say it's possible."

"Good enough." She inclined her head. "Continue."

"Geoff Burris is the biggest star in rodeo, with his brothers coming in right behind him. And then we have the lovely and talented Hawkins Sisters, stars in their own right. Both are first in my book."

"Not all of Geoff's brothers are still in the rodeo. Mike is in medical school. He doesn't even live in Bronco anymore."

"There isn't a medical school in town, so he had to leave if he wanted to pursue his dreams." Dante's words were logical, but they did little to diminish the disappointment Corinne still felt.

"I know. And he's seriously smart. He plans on being a surgeon."

"It sounds as if you know Mike pretty well." Dante gave her a knowing look.

"I do. He's one of the best men I know. He always tried to do well in competition, but he didn't brood if he didn't win. He was content as long as he'd done his best. He would be genuinely happy for the winner. Everybody liked that about him. You didn't have to worry if he was being sincere when he congratulated you. And if he saw something that you were doing wrong, he would tell you and help you correct it."

"Really? Not too many people would try to help their competition."

"That's just how he is."

"I don't know him, but I bet you could tell me a lot of good things about him."

"I could."

Dante smiled and she felt her face grow hot. "I take it you and Mike are more than friends."

She took a sip of her ice water to cool down. There was no need to be embarrassed, she told herself. "No. We hung out a lot the summer of last year when we were both in Bronco for the rodeo. That's actually how we met. When we went back on the circuit, we performed in the same rodeos a lot, so we were able to see each other. As friends, mind you."

"Of course."

"But like I said, he quit rodeo to focus on his studies."

"Which means you won't be seeing him on the circuit anymore."

That still hurt, but she pushed aside the pain. "No. And I understand. There are only so many hours in the day, so choices needed to be made."

"That has to be disappointing."

She frowned. "You have no idea."

"Actually, I think I do. You were falling for him." He sat back, his drink in hand. "Does Mike know that you still care for him?"

"What makes you think that I do?" Her voice trembled slightly.

He grinned. "The first time you mentioned him was at salad. We've just finished our entrees and we're still talking about him."

"Oh."

"Yeah. Oh."

"Sorry."

"Don't be. It's not as if we're in the midst of a hot and heavy relationship."

She looked down at her hands, entwining them in her lap. "It doesn't matter how I feel. He's made it clear that he doesn't want to be in a serious relationship. And I respect his decision."

"Commitment can be scary. When you put yourself out there, you run the risk that the other person isn't as invested as you are. That's a recipe for a broken heart. Or you can discover that you aren't as compatible as you thought. You might not end up heartbroken, but you will still be disappointed."

"Maybe."

"I understand how he feels. I'm not in any hurry to settle down either. My brother Felix and my sisters, Camilla and Sofia are either married or engaged."

She looked up at him. "But it's not for you?"

"No. I like the single life. I like adventure and meeting new people. Going where I want, doing what I want when I want. I can't imagine giving all that up just to be with one person. It just doesn't seem like a good trade-off to me."

Corinne smiled. "I understand what you mean. I didn't think I was ready to settle down either. I'm only twenty-five after all. But then I met Mike and my thinking changed. Being with him didn't seem like a bad deal. We were good friends and had fun together. Before I knew what happened, I found myself thinking about him as more than a friend. I thought he felt the same. I honestly believe he was starting to fall for me. But timing is everything and ours was off. Hence the end of our romance before it had a chance to start."

"I'm no expert, so I don't know if that's true or not. But I do know if both people are not on board and willing to do the work to maintain the relationship, it doesn't have a chance of succeeding. And in the end, the person who put in the most effort will feel angry and hurt."

She sighed. "I know. And I value our friendship too much to risk it. Especially with the odds being against us. Since our siblings are married, we're going to be a part of each other's lives forever. We need to keep things cordial between us for their sakes as well as our own."

"And as long as things are good between you, there's a chance that something romantic might develop," he said sagely.

"Do you think that's silly?"

"Not at all. There's nothing silly about caring for someone and hoping that they feel the same way about you."

"So you think there is a chance that things can work between me and Mike?" She didn't know why she was asking him this, but she couldn't make herself stop.

"Based on what you told me." He paused and then looked into her eyes. "Yes."

Corinne blew out a relieved breath. "Thanks for that."

"Sure. So what are you going to do?"

Corinne picked up her glass. Mike might care about her, but he'd been clear they couldn't have a relationship now. Maybe they wouldn't be able to make one work in the future either. "The only thing I can do. I'm going to continue living my life."

Dante lifted his glass in a toast. "Here's to living your life. And to making new friends."

It was clear that Dante and Corinne were on the same page when it came to any future relationship, which was good. Corinne didn't need complications in her life.

She and Dante had just finished drinking their toast when Corinne glanced up. Mike's parents were standing at the hostess station. And Mike's mother was looking straight at Corinne. Then she looked at Dante. When Mike's father saw where his wife was looking, he followed her gaze. Then as one, Mike's parents smiled and waved. Corinne did the same.

The hostess led Mike's parents to a table on the opposite side of the dining room. Thank goodness. Corinne leaned back in her chair, closed her eyes and sighed.

"What's wrong?" Dante asked.

"Mike's parents are here."

"Is that a problem?"

Was it? They'd always been kind to her. Corinne had no reason to believe that would change. "No. It's just weird. Which is an odd thing to say considering we live in the same small town."

"Do you want to leave?"

"Without dessert? Perish the thought. I said that it was weird, not that I was doing anything wrong. I'm sure they know that Mike and I are just friends. We're free to go out with other people. Besides, you and I are just friends, too."

"As long as you're sure."

"I am. So let's get our dessert."

Although the weather was getting chilly, it was never too cold for ice cream. Corinne ordered her favorite dessert—a hot brownie topped with two scoops of chocolate ice cream and lots of whipped cream. Dante ordered a slice of cherry pie.

"You're going to be so jealous when your pie is gone and I'm still eating my dessert."

Dante laughed. "You mean you won't share?"

She shook her head. "That's a no."

"Not to worry. I'll just order another piece of pie."

They talked and laughed as they ate their dessert— Dante did indeed order a second slice of pie, earning endless teasing from Corinne. After dinner, they walked around town for a few minutes before Dante drove her home. He parked and then walked beside her up the stairs.

"I really had a nice time, Corinne."

"So did I. I feel like I made a good friend."

"Me, too. And remember, it you ever need a man's point of view, give me a call."

"I'll remember that."

She watched as Dante walked down the stairs and then drove away. She'd had a good time tonight. It wasn't as much fun as she would have had with Mike, but she was doing what she needed to do.

Putting him behind her and moving on with her life.

Chapter Three

"So, how was your date with Dante?" Audrey asked the next morning. She and her sisters were having a family breakfast so they could finalize their upcoming schedule, arrange practice for their joint rodeo events, and generally catch up with each other's lives. Although Brynn and Audrey hadn't lived here for a while, the four sisters fell into their old roles, working in sync to cook breakfast. It hadn't taken long for them to get food cooked and on the table.

"How did you find out about that?" Corinne asked, shooting Remi a dirty look. "As if I didn't know."

"You're kidding, right? We're sisters," Brynn said, adding a teaspoon of honey to her decaffeinated green tea.

Corinne frowned. "I don't see how you can drink that stuff. It tastes like dirt."

Brynn took a sip of her tea and gave an exaggerated murmur of pleasure. "Mmm. Delicious. And don't try to change the subject. We don't keep secrets."

"Especially when Remi is around."

"Was it supposed to be a secret?" Remi asked, feigning innocence. "All I did was tell Brynn and Audrey how happy I am that you stopped moping around about Mike and decided to go on a date."

"We could wait for you to tell us something, or we could just jump right in and ask," Audrey said.

"You don't know how to be passive, Audrey."

"Exactly. So how was it?"

"It was fine. But don't start thinking there's a romance on the horizon because there isn't. Dante and I are only going to be friends."

"How do you know that?" Remi asked. "You only went on one date. He might be interested in something more."

"I know because we actually talked about it. He's not interested in a relationship. And to be honest, I'm not either. Unless it's with Mike." That last bit slipped out before she could stop it. "Forget I said that."

"Yeah, right," Audrey said. "Like that's going to happen."

"I thought the decision to be friends was mutual," Brynn said.

"It was Mike's idea, but I agreed."

"You might not want to hear this, but are you sure you're in love with Mike?" Brynn asked softly.

"What do you mean? You think I don't know my own feelings?"

"I think that of all of us, you're the one who has always been swept away by romance. You've read hundreds of romances. You've watched every romantic movie ever made at least twice. I think your brain is oversaturated with thoughts of love." Brynn gave her a gentle smile in what Corinne knew was an attempt to remove the sting from her words.

"What are you saying?"

"She's saying that you might be more in love with the idea of being in love than you are with Mike," Audrey said.

"I know my feelings. And they're real."

Her sisters exchanged glances. Audrey shrugged. "Okay."

"Don't patronize me. I know the difference between love and infatuation. Not that it matters."

"Don't say that," Remi said, covering Corinne's hand and giving it a gentle squeeze. "Of course it matters."

"Not to Mike."

"Well then put him out of your mind. Move on," Audrey said. "There are plenty of men in the world who would love to be with you. Just give one a chance."

"If things didn't work out between you and Jack, would you have just walked away from him?"

Audrey raised an eyebrow. "You have a short memory if you're asking me that."

"True. You did walk away from him. And you were miserable," Corinne said.

"And you made the rest of us miserable, too," Remi added with a laugh.

"I get your point. And I'm not saying it will be easy to put Mike in the past. It won't. But medical training is long. He's only in his second year of med school. Do you really want to sit around for years hoping that today will be the day he calls?" Audrey asked.

"No. But I don't want to lead anyone on either. That would be unfair."

"Well, you can't keep putting your life on hold, hoping Mike will decide he wants to be with you," Brynn said.

"I'm not doing that," Corinne protested. "I'm still

living my life. I went out with Dante, didn't I? And if I find another man interesting, I'll go out with him, too. I just don't want to pretend that I don't feel what I feel."

"That makes sense," Audrey said. "The last thing you want to do is lie to yourself."

"Thank you. If you don't mind, I would like to move on to other issues. Like our upcoming schedule. It's the reason we're having breakfast together."

"Not the only reason," Remi said.

"It certainly isn't. But if you're tired of talking about yourself, we can talk about me," Audrey said.

The sisters laughed.

"Go ahead," Corinne said.

"Jack and I have finally decided on the color we want to paint the living room. He's picking up the paint right now. We're going to tackle it this afternoon."

Audrey and Jack had closed on their house shortly before the wedding. It was in Bronco Valley, not far from the house Corinne and Remi were renting.

"That debate has been going on for weeks. Are you sure?" Corinne asked.

"Yes."

"How did you finally reach agreement?"

"We each chose our favorite color and then we rock, paper, scissored it."

"I take it you won," Corinne said.

"What makes you say that?"

"Because you would still be in the negotiating stage if you hadn't," Remi said with a laugh. "We know how much you hate to lose."

Audrey shook her head. "Maybe the old Audrey had to win at everything, but I'm a new and improved woman."

"Really?" Corinne asked, not bothering to keep the skepticism from her voice.

Audrey managed to maintain her serene expression for a minute before bursting into laughter. "Sort of. Jack and I are trying to be less competitive with each other."

"And...?"

"We're works in progress."

Audrey and Jack were the most competitive couple Corinne had ever met. Even with each other. Neither would willingly give an inch. But they loved each other fiercely, which in her mind made all the difference in the world. They fit together in a way that they never could with anyone else.

The way Corinne had hoped she and Mike would fit together. Too bad it hadn't worked out that way.

Mike parked the car in front of his parents' house, grabbed his duffel from the backseat and then jogged up the stairs and glanced around. None of his brothers' cars were parked nearby, but that didn't slow his pounding heart any. Now that he wasn't competing on the circuit, he didn't keep track of rodeo as closely as he had in the past, so he didn't know if his brothers were in or out of town. No, that wasn't entirely accurate. He still kept up with the Hawkins Sisters, or more accurately, Corinne. No matter how busy he was with school, he always made time to check on her scores and watch any internet videos he could find of her rides.

Mike shook his head. Why was he thinking of Corinne right now when he was worried about his parents? His mother had left him a cryptic message Thursday night telling him to call home right away. Although she hadn't said anything was wrong, she hadn't sounded like herself. She'd sounded...stressed. He'd called her back as soon as he'd listened to the message but hadn't gotten an answer. Unable to sleep, he'd thrown some clothes into a bag, grabbed his books and headed for home. He'd made good time, only stopping once in a rest area for a quick nap before hitting the road again. Still, after over twenty hours on the road, he was beat and stressed.

Although he lived in Chicago for school, Mike still had keys to the Bronco house. His parents had insisted that this was still his home. Mike's hand trembled as he fit the key into the lock, but he managed to unlock the door after only two attempts.

On the ride home, his imagination had run wild as he thought of everything that could possibly be wrong, so he was surprised to see his parents sitting in the living room, sipping coffee and sharing the newspaper as they did every Saturday morning.

Jeanne looked up and smiled. "Mike. What a nice surprise."

"We didn't expect to see you today," Benjamin added. "Is everything okay?"

Mike slumped into the nearest chair and blew out an exhausted breath. "Are you kidding me?"

"No," his dad said seriously.

"I got Mom's message Thursday night telling me to call home. She sounded as if something was wrong, but when I called back, there wasn't an answer," Mike told his father before turning to look at his mother. "You didn't answer your cell either. I was worried so I decided to come home to make sure that everything was fine."

"As you can see, we're just fine. Everything is all right," his father said. He walked over and put a comforting hand on Mike's shoulder. As always, Mike drew strength from his father.

"Everything is not all right," Jeanne contradicted. She pressed her lips together, frowning at Mike. She looked perturbed and seemed to be directing that irritation in Mike's direction. But that couldn't be right. He hadn't been around to do anything to get on her bad side.

More importantly, his mother never got upset with him. Perhaps it was because he was the youngest. He and his brothers always joked that they were each their mother's favorite, but he knew that it was actually true in his case.

"What's wrong? Are you sick? Is someone sick?"

His parents exchanged a glance. They'd been married for so long that they didn't need words to communicate. Mike, however, did. "Will someone *please* tell me what's going on?"

"This is all you," Benjamin said to Jeanne. He gave Mike's shoulder a squeeze before returning to his chair, picking up the sports section and beginning to read again.

"You're making the biggest mistake of your life." Jeanne crossed her arms over her chest.

"What?" This was not at all what Mike had expected her to say.

"You heard me. You're making a big mistake."

"With what?" He had absolutely no idea what she was talking about.

"With Corinne. Your father and I went out to dinner at Pastabilities on Thursday night and we saw her."

"Okay." He'd driven all this way for this?

"She was with another man," Jeanne said, drawing out each word. "And she seemed to be enjoying herself."

"That's it? That's your emergency? You scared me out of my mind because you saw Corinne at dinner with another man?" Deep down, he felt a slight pang of jealousy, and did his best to bury it.

"Yes. You and Corinne are perfect for each other. And you're blowing it."

"How?"

"With this whole just-being-friends thing you suggested."

He wasn't surprised that his mother had heard about that. She knew everything. "We are friends, Mom. I care about Corinne. A lot."

"You have a funny way of showing it."

"What would you have me do? Tell her we should have a relationship, but it's going to be long-distance? And only on my terms? I live in Chicago now. My life is literally class and studying. That's it. I barely have time to eat or sleep. Is Corinne supposed to sit around and hope that I can fit her in for a couple minutes a week?"

"Of course not. But you could be doing more than you're doing."

"I don't see how. I care about Corinne. More than I've ever cared about a woman in my life. But right now, I don't have the ability to be in a relationship with her or anyone else. And it would be unfair of me to ask her to wait until I do."

"I just keep thinking about how good you looked together at Jack's wedding. How happy you were."

Mike kept thinking of that, too. Nothing compared to how good it'd felt to hold her in his arms as they danced. The whole night had been magical, and they'd spent every moment they could together. Until he'd ruined it by telling her they should just be friends.

There'd been times when he'd regretted saying that, but he knew in his heart that it had been the right thing. The fair thing. But that didn't mean it was easy or that he was happy with the situation.

"Mom, Corinne and I agreed that now wasn't the time for us to try to be more than friends. I'm busy with school and she's busy on the rodeo circuit."

Jeanne waved a dismissive hand. "Please. That girl would give up the rodeo to be with you if you asked."

"Maybe. But I'm not going to ask. I'm pursuing my dreams. She has a right to pursue hers."

"It's pretty presumptuous of you to assume what her dreams should be and what sacrifices she should make."

Mike blew out a breath. He was tired and wasn't in the mood to have this discussion. They would just have to disagree. "I may be making a mistake, but it's my mistake to make."

"That has to be the most ridiculous thing I've ever heard."

"Mom, please. Let me live my life the best way I know how. You and Dad raised me to be honorable. That's what I'm trying to do."

"Of course we want you to live your life on your terms," Benjamin said, setting the paper aside. "But we wouldn't be good parents if we didn't tell you when we thought you were making a mistake."

"I know. And I'll consider everything Mom has told me."

"That's all I want," Jeanne said.

Mike huffed out a breath. That wasn't all she wanted and they all knew it. She wanted him to go to Corinne and tell her they should date. "Then we're all happy."

"How long can you stay?" Jeanne asked.

"I don't have classes on Monday. Since it's Saturday, I may as well stay the night and leave early tomorrow morning. That is, if it's okay with you," Mike joked.

"Always glad to have you home. I'll make your favorite dinner."

"Everything you make is my favorite." He kissed his mother's cheek. "I think I'll take a shower and then walk around town. Chicago is a great city, but I miss Bronco."

He hugged his father and kissed his mother's cheek before taking a quick shower. He'd tried not to show it, but when his mother said that Corinne was dating another man, he'd felt pain in his heart so sharp he'd barely managed to breathe. There was no reason for him to be jealous since being friends had been his brilliant plan. But he was jealous. He was green with it. He hated the idea of Corinne spending time with another man. Smiling and laughing with him. The very idea of a man holding Corinne in his arms and inhaling her intoxicating scent or kissing her sweet lips nearly buckled his knees.

The only thing that hurt more was thinking of Corinne putting her life on hold. He cared too much about her to be that selfish. So he would just have to find a way to cope with the knowledge that she'd moved on and hope she didn't fall in love with someone else before he was in a position to give her everything she deserved.

Rejuvenated after his shower, Mike headed downtown. He didn't have any particular destination in mind. Just being in his hometown was enjoyable. After driving around, he spotted Doug's and decided to stop. Doug's was a hole-in-the-wall dive bar that was popular with Bronco residents. The building was nondescript and there wasn't a sign, so if you didn't know it existed, you would never find it. Doug's served some of the best burgers and fries in town and Mike decided to treat himself. The food would take the edge off his hunger but wouldn't leave him too full to eat the feast his mother was preparing for dinner tonight.

He had just reached the door when he heard someone calling his name. Mike immediately recognized the voice and his heart sped up. *Corinne.* Smiling, he turned and waited for her to reach him, unable to tear his eyes away.

Corinne had always been beautiful, and today was no exception. In fact, she was more stunning than he'd ever seen. Dressed in a deep green knit sweater dress that hugged her curves and hit her midthigh, black tights and boots, and a short black leather jacket, she was positively gorgeous. A black-and-green band held her long braids behind her shoulders, giving him an unobstructed view of her face.

And what a face it was. Her clear brown skin seemed to glow from within. Her eyes shone with both intelligence and humor. Her full lips enticed him as she smiled. When she was close enough to touch, he automatically reached out and pulled her into his arms for an embrace. As he held her, she wrapped her arms around him, and he inhaled her sweet scent. His eyes closed as he let the moment stretch as long as socially acceptable before he eased back, reluctantly releasing her.

"I didn't know you were in town." Her voice was happy, but he heard a hint of disappointment. Did she think that he had planned this visit and hadn't told her?

"It wasn't scheduled. I got a message from my mother and she seemed upset. I couldn't reach her, so I came straight home."

"Is everything okay?"

"It's fine. She overreacted to something she saw. And I overreacted to something I heard."

She laughed. "I guess it runs in the family."

"Looks like." They stood silently for a moment, at a loss for conversation. That had never happened before. Despite the awkwardness, he didn't want this time with Corinne to end yet. "Are you busy? Do you have time to get a burger?"

"Do you have time?"

That was an odd question considering he'd just invited her to eat. "I do. I was just going to grab one now."

After a moment she nodded. "I would love a burger."

He held the door for her and they stepped inside. Everything was wonderfully familiar. The tables were still scarred, and the floor was still uneven. There were a few people playing pool and others sitting at the mismatched tables, enjoying lunch.

Doug, was behind the bar, polishing it so that it shone. He might be nearly ninety years old, but he moved incredibly well, and his mind was as sharp as a tack. The bell over the door jingled when Mike had opened the door but Doug didn't look up. "Take a seat anywhere. Someone will be over to take your order."

"Sure thing," Mike said.

At the sound of his voice, Doug paused, rag in hand, looked up, and smiled, his ever-present toothpick in the corner of his mouth. "Is that you, Mike Burris?"

"It is."

"How's medical school going?"

Being a member of a famous rodeo family not only made him recognizable in his hometown, but his personal life was also common knowledge. Not that he had a problem with people knowing he was in medical school. His mother was proud of him and had told everyone she knew and the few people she didn't. It had even been reported in the sports pages of the *Bronco Bulletin*. Still, he'd kind of gotten used to flying under the radar in Chicago, a place big enough that nobody knew his name much less anything else about him. "It's going well. Thanks for asking."

"Good to hear. We're all wishing the best for you."

"I appreciate it." Mike led Corinne to a table in a

secluded corner where they could talk in private, held her chair as she sat then took one across from her. As promised, a waitress took their orders and returned in a minute with their drinks. "How have you been?"

Corinne smiled. "I have no complaints."

Not a day had passed that he hadn't thought of her, counting the moments until they'd be together again, so he was a bit disappointed by that bland response. He wanted to know how she *really* was. How she kept busy. What brought her joy these days.

And if she was serious about the man she'd gone out with Thursday night.

"That's good to hear."

"How have you been?"

He sighed. He didn't want to talk about *himself.* But if he wanted to have a real conversation, he needed to take the first step and hope she followed his lead. So he answered honestly. "Tired. Drained. Medical school is exhausting. I've been tired after rodeos, but that was purely physical. Now I'm physically and mentally worn out. There's so much to learn and I feel guilty if I'm not spending every waking minute studying."

"Guilty? Why?"

"Because being a doctor is serious business. People will be relying on me. Trusting me. If I miss something or make the wrong decision, someone could die. Or suffer longer than necessary. How can I risk slacking off my studies with so much on the line? Knowing that, I have to be willing to make whatever sacrifices are necessary in order to be my best."

Corinne heard the tension in Mike's voice and it shocked her. Then it saddened her. In rodeo, he'd tried his best in competition, but when his event was over—

win, lose or draw—it was over. Listening to Mike, she realized the same couldn't be said for medicine. He was so serious that she didn't recognize him as the same person she'd known so well. The person she'd had so much in common with. She couldn't bear to see him stress himself out this way. He might be the medical student, but she knew from experience that stress could wreak havoc on the body and spirit.

"Medicine is serious, but there has to be more to life than your studies. You need to have fun. You'll burn out otherwise. Then when you start seeing patients, you won't be any good to them."

He flashed an unexpected smile. "I actually see patients now."

"Really. Already? That's wonderful."

"Don't be too impressed. It's only for a couple hours, three days a week. Everything that I do is checked by at least two other doctors."

"That's still a big deal. What do you do?"

"First I take a patient history and do a little workup. You know, listen to their heart, take blood pressure. That kind of thing. Then an intern checks my work and does a more thorough exam. And then my and the intern's work is reviewed by a resident. Even so, it's thrilling to have some hands-on experience. It makes me feel like a doctor. At the same time, there is some comfort in being supervised and knowing that someone is making sure to ask the right questions, order the right tests, make the correct diagnosis and come up with a treatment plan."

"Like a security blanket?"

"Exactly. But one day I won't have anyone standing over my shoulder and giving me directions. I'll be alone with no one to lean on. Which is why I need to soak up every bit of knowledge that I can. I don't want to let even one opportunity to learn pass me by."

"Learning all that you can doesn't mean that you can't take a few moments to just relax." She understood that he needed to study, but she still couldn't believe that there wasn't place in his life for pleasure. *For her.* But he didn't see it that way. He'd sacrificed everything in his life—including their relationship—for his education. Free time was just the latest thing he'd given up.

He took a bite of his burger, chewed and swallowed. "Enough about me. I've been following your scores on the rodeo. You and Remi are at the top of the leaderboard in team roping. And you're moving up in barrel racing."

Surprise surged through her. "You're following me?"

"Of course I am. Why do you sound so shocked?"

"I don't know. I just didn't think that is something you would do." Not after he'd ended their romance before it could really start.

"Not to sound like a broken record, but why not? Did you really think I wouldn't be interested in how you were doing?"

"I wasn't sure," she said slowly. She picked a bit of crust from her bun and set it on her plate, stalling for time. "You just said how busy you are and how much studying you have to do."

"That's all true. But I make time to check your scores and watch videos of you whenever they're posted. I love watching you compete. I just wish I could be there in person."

"It would be nice to have you there. But I know you don't have the time. I'm surprised you're in Bronco now."

He sat there for a moment, as if taking in her words.

She didn't think she'd said anything to offend him, but maybe she had. Last year, they'd gotten close very quickly and had spent all of their free time together. Perhaps that closeness had only been a mirage. The only true way to know the strength of a relationship was to test it. Theirs had been tested by time and distance. Sadly it had failed.

Perhaps she didn't know him as well as she believed. Maybe they weren't as compatible as she'd once hoped. No doubt Mike had figured that out more quickly than she had. Being as kind as he was, he would never hurt her feelings. He was more inclined to wait until she reached the same conclusion. That sad thought left her fumbling for something to say.

"I guess I should be honest about what brought me running back to town," Mike said.

"You mean your mother didn't call you?"

"Oh, she called me all right. She left a frantic message for me to call her back. I did and when I didn't get an answer, I raced home. That's all true. But the big emergency was...you."

"Me?"

"Yes." He huffed out a laugh that sounded strained. Almost embarrassed. Not like himself at all. He smiled, but only with his lips. "Yes. She saw you on a date the other night and was concerned that you were getting involved with someone else."

"Dante. I had dinner with Dante Sanchez Thursday night." So *that's* why his mother had called him. Corinne didn't like people meddling in her personal life, but she would make an exception in this case. If Mike's mother was around, Corinne would give her a big hug.

"You don't owe me an explanation. I'm glad to know

that you're enjoying yourself. I don't want you to sit around and wait for me to have time for you."

He was saying the right things, but the words sounded forced. As if they had been pulled from him. "Really?"

"Dante is a lucky man." Again, the right words but the wrong tone. He sounded just as miserable at the prospect of her dating another man as she felt envisioning him with another woman.

"I don't know whether he's lucky or not. But if he is, it has nothing to do with me. We're just friends. There is absolutely nothing romantic between us."

He smiled, and this time it reached his deep brown eyes. Warmth flooded her stomach and her toes curled inside her boots. Her mind had reluctantly accepted that she and Mike were only friends, but now her body joined her heart in rebellion.

When Mike spoke, his voice was lower. Deeper. She was barely able to control the shivers that tripped down her spine in response. "I know I don't have the right to be jealous since I'm the one who said that we should only be friends, but I am. Ridiculously so. I can't help it. I miss you every day. I miss talking to you. I miss seeing your smile. Hearing your laughter. I miss everything about you. I want to share my day with you and hear all about yours. I'm so lonely without you."

She'd ached to hear him say this for the longest time. Sadly, his anguished words didn't change a thing. He still lived in Chicago and was devoting every free moment of his time to his studies. And she lived in Bronco. "I miss you, too. I wish we could spend more time together."

"So do I."

She looked him in the eyes. "Be honest. If we didn't

both have a craving for Doug's and end up here at the same time, would you have let me know that you were in town?"

He sighed. "That's a tough one."

"Not to me. It's a yes-or-no question."

"But it's not. The part of me that misses you like crazy and wants to be with you wants to say yes."

"But?"

"But the piece of me that knows it's selfish to keep you hanging on when I can't give you the time and attention you deserve says no. If I hadn't run into you here, I might have left town without letting you know I'd been home. It depends on which side of me was strongest, and that's something that I don't know."

"At least you're being honest."

"I'm trying." His eyes were sincere. He covered her hand with his. "I don't want to be a selfish jerk."

"I don't want to be selfish either. More than that, I don't want you to force a feeling that isn't there."

"You think that I don't care about you?"

"When I'm at my most insecure, yes. Other times, no. I suppose it would be more accurate to say that we shouldn't try to force a relationship right now. We agreed to be friends for reasons. Those reasons haven't gone away."

"So you still think that being friends is the best thing for us?"

"Yes." She blew out a breath. It broke her to say that, but she wouldn't weaken and beg him to at least try. She had some pride.

His chest rose and fell as he inhaled and then blew out the breath. "I suppose you're right."

"I know I am. And we don't need to talk about this again. There's no point. We're just going around in circles. We both know that we're going to end up back here. Being friends is the right thing for us."

"We need to stick to the plan we agreed to."

She nodded and changed the subject. "So…back to the rodeo. My sisters and I will be competing in a couple of new ones in the Midwest. We've added events in Indiana, Illinois and Wisconsin to our schedule."

"That's great. Let me know the dates and I'll do my best to come to one of them. It would be a shame for us to be so close and yet not be able to spend at least a little time together."

He said that now, right after admitting that he'd considered leaving town without letting her know that he had been here. So color her skeptical that he would make the extra effort to see her when she was a few hours away.

A part of her was willing to drive to Chicago if his schedule didn't allow him to make it to one of the rodeos. Although the Windy City was a place she'd like to visit, she'd never been there. The idea of seeing the sights and dining at a fancy restaurant appealed to her. Especially if Mike would be by her side. But she couldn't be the one who put in all the effort—even in a friendship. She'd had a one-sided romance before, and it hadn't been fun. It had been degrading and wasn't something she would repeat.

It had hurt to know that although she had put her former boyfriend first, he hadn't done the same. His wants and his needs had always come before her. Coming in second had done more than broken her heart. It had devastated her. And she had stuck around way longer than she should have. She'd given him the benefit of the doubt when she should have walked away. She had to be on her guard to be sure she didn't fall into that type of relationship again. No matter how much she cared about Mike. She had to be wiser and keep her eyes open.

Once the subject of her rodeo schedule had been put to bed, they discussed other topics. Before long, they were laughing and talking as easily as they had before he'd started medical school. They'd long since finished their food when Mike glanced at his watch and Corinne did the same. She couldn't believe how much time had passed.

"I guess we need to get going," Corinne said, rising slowly and grabbing her jacket. Mike took the jacket from her and then held it for her to put on. His hands lingered on her shoulders for a blissful moment before he released her.

"I know. I wish we had more time."

It was late afternoon and the sun had begun to set, taking with it the warmth that had been present earlier. The wind blew and Corinne wrapped her jacket around her more tightly.

"Cold?"

"Not really. Just a little chill."

The wind blew hard again and Mike angled his body to shield Corinne from the worst of it. Of course he had. Mike had always been concerned with her comfort. She yearned to stay this way, the heat from his body wrapping around hers, but she couldn't. Not after they'd confirmed their decision to be friends.

Corinne was affectionate by nature, but she didn't think hugging Mike was the way to say goodbye. But she couldn't just say *see you later* and walk away either. That would be too cold. Not knowing what else to do, she held out her hand. "I'm parked down the block. Have a good visit and a safe drive home."

Mike looked at her hand a second before he took it

into his and shook it. The instant their palms touched hers, electricity shot through her body and her knees actually weakened. Although the chilly wind blew again, her body was suddenly hot. The air crackled with sexual tension and her eyes flew to his. She knew that she should break contact and step away, but she wasn't that strong.

The street was deserted, not that it made a difference. Their surroundings faded into nothingness until the only thing Corinne was aware of was Mike. Ever so slowly he lowered his head and she lifted hers to his. Their lips brushed softly and her eyes drifted shut. Rational thought fled and all she could do was feel. The warmth of his touch. The strength of his arms as they held her near. His gentle lips as they moved against hers. The desire that she'd denied for so long broke free, and she moved even closer. He wrapped his arms around her more tightly as he deepened the kiss, and she sighed in pleasure.

This was what she'd been imagining from the moment she'd seen Mike going into Doug's. This was what she'd missed. What she'd hoped for. She could kiss him forever. The thought had barely formed in her mind when she felt him easing away, ending the kiss. She wanted to pull him back so she could enjoy a few more seconds of pleasure, but instead she stepped back as well. They were panting and several moments passed as their breathing slowed to a normal pace.

"I'm sorry," Mike said. "I didn't mean to do that."

Although his words broke her heart and were the last thing she wanted to hear, she couldn't let him take all of the blame. She'd wanted to kiss him. Once she'd felt his warm hand on hers, it had been all over. She'd been powerless to resist. "Don't apologize. You didn't do anything I didn't want. And honestly, the kiss only revealed what we both want. It spoke the truth."

"And that is?"

"Neither one of us wants to be just friends. We want more. The question is—are we going to be bold enough to go after what we want."

Chapter Four

Mike watched as Corinne blinked and shook her head as if she couldn't believe what she'd just said. If he were being honest, he was a bit shocked himself. He wasn't sure if it was because she'd asked him to enter into a relationship that they both knew would be difficult to maintain, or because he was actually considering it. Knowing the damage a failed relationship could do to their friendship, he should have dismissed her statement out of hand. And yet he hadn't. Couldn't.

Not when the sweetness of her kiss still lingered in his mouth. Not when she was standing so close that he inhaled her enticing scent with every breath he took. And certainly not when he still felt the intense desire to kiss her again. And again. He settled for asking a question. "And how exactly would that work?"

"The same way it did before. We weren't always together, but we managed to make it work."

"You aren't talking about the same thing. Back then,

we ran into each other often and had time to spend together. Not only that, except for a few kisses, we were basically good friends. Now, though, there's little chance of us being in the same state, much less the same city, for weeks if not months on end. When you're not competing, you're either traveling to or from a rodeo, or practicing. I know how grueling that schedule is. And we've already talked ad nauseam about my schedule."

"So you're saying you don't want to try."

"No. I'm saying we *shouldn't* try. The odds are stacked against us."

"Surely you aren't the first medical student to be in a relationship."

"No. But none of the ones that I've seen recently have been successful. And when they ended, they ended badly. I don't want that for us."

"So, we're going to remain just friends. I don't like it, but if that's what you want, it's what we'll do. After all, it takes two people to make it work."

The smart part of his brain, if there actually was one when it came to Corinne, was suddenly silent. Or perhaps it was overwhelmed by his heart screaming not to let her get away. "I know that's the wise thing to do, but I can't. I miss you and I feel so empty without you."

"So what are you saying?" Her voice was barely above a whisper and there was hope in her eyes.

He blew out a breath. He was going to follow his heart and make them both happy. "It's going to take a lot of work and sacrifice on both of our parts. And a whole lot of understanding. But if you're willing to accept the risks, I think we should go for it."

The look of pleasure that flashed on Corinne's face warmed Mike's heart and quieted his misgivings. Just because his classmates hadn't been able to make their relationships work didn't mean that his and Corinne's was doomed to failure.

"Good. I know we can make it." She looked at her watch and frowned. "This is bad timing, but I really do need to go."

"So do I. Let me walk you to your car." This felt so odd. They'd just agreed that they were going to date, but now, instead of spending more precious time together, they were going their separate ways. Of course, he did need to get home. His mother was expecting him for dinner. Corinne had things that she needed to do, too.

They didn't speak as they walked to her car, but it wasn't unexpected. He imagined that she was just as astonished as he was at the change in their relationship. It would take a bit of getting used to. He'd always wanted to have a romantic relationship with Corinne. The time had never felt right. Truthfully, he wasn't sure now was the right time either. But he also knew that if he didn't take this step, he might lose her forever. Her date with Dante had proven that she wasn't sitting at home waiting to hear from him. She had a life. He'd do well to remember that.

Besides, life didn't happen according to his schedule. Love came when it wanted and it was up to him to make the most of it. He had to make room for Corinne in his life. And he would. He just didn't know how.

Mike arrived home just as his mother was putting dinner on the table. The wonderful aromas floated on the air and Mike's stomach growled. The burger and fries were a distant memory.

"Just in time," Jeanne said, setting mashed potatoes beside a pot roast.

"When has this boy ever been late for dinner?" Benjamin asked, placing warm rolls beside a bowl of mixed vegetables.

"You raised me with better sense than that," Mike said. "Can I help with anything?"

"No. Just wash your hands and sit down."

Mike complied. He sampled everything and closed his eyes. Delicious.

"Did you have a nice time?" Jeanne asked.

Mike couldn't help but grin. "I had a great time. I stopped by Doug's for a burger."

"Of course you did. And you're eating again," Benjamin said. "You must have a hole in your toe."

That had been his father's favorite line when Mike and his brothers were growing up. Someone was always hungry even after they'd eaten, so Benjamin had sworn that the food was leaking out through their toes.

"While I was there, I ran into Corinne."

"Really?" Jeanne tried to sound casual, but Mike heard the excitement in her voice.

"Yes. We ate lunch together and then talked for a while." Mike took a bite of his roast, chewing slowly and following it down with water, dragging out the moment. Surely his mother would ask what they talked about or how things went. When one minute stretched into the next, Mike knew that he'd been bested. His parents knew how to use silence to get their boys to talk, but they were both immune to the tactic themselves.

"We decided to date."

"That's wonderful. I'm glad that you have finally come to your senses," Jeanne said, a broad smile lighting up her face. "If ever two people belonged together, it's you."

"Hold your horses, Mom. I just said that we were

dating. We haven't come anywhere near to making a lifetime commitment."

"Okay."

"And to be honest, I'm not one hundred percent sure that dating is the right thing for us now."

"Then why are you?" Benjamin asked, raising an eyebrow. That one gesture spoke a paragraph.

"Because I miss her. My life is empty without her."

"That's not a good reason to be with someone."

"That's not the only reason. I care about her. But we're just dating. Not planning a future." Mike glanced at his mother as he said that. Jeanne simply lifted more mashed potatoes to her mouth. Now that she'd gotten her way, she had nothing more to say on the subject.

After dinner, Mike called Corinne. He would be leaving town early and wanted to talk to her before he left. They didn't stay on the phone long, but just hearing her voice was all he needed to quiet his doubts. They agreed that she would come to visit him on an upcoming weekend. Although it was a few weeks off, the anticipation of seeing her again would be enough to get him through some rough days.

Corinne blew out a pent-up breath as she drove down the street. Chicago traffic was even more congested than she'd expected it to be. At first, she hadn't minded driving slowly and getting caught by red lights every couple of blocks because it gave her time to take in some of the sights. And there were plenty to see. But the interest she'd had in looking around initially gave way to irritation as she neared Mike's apartment. She was minutes away from seeing him again and she wished the other cars would just get out of the way.

It had been three weeks since she'd seen him in person. Over that time, they talked on the phone, texted and FaceTimed, so they'd been able to keep abreast of what was going on in each other's lives. In a way, he had an advantage when it came to understanding her life. He'd traveled the rodeo circuit for years and knew what her days were like. She had no idea what it was like to be a medical student. She'd paid close attention while he'd told her about his day, but she knew she was only capturing part of what he was trying to tell her. Her imagination could only take her so far. She was looking forward to getting a firsthand look.

Corinne wanted to meet his friends and visit his school. No matter how frequently they talked or how open he was, she still felt like she was on the outskirts of his life. For a few days she would be a real part of his life, which could only bring them closer together.

She turned onto his block and her heart began to pound. She was seconds away from being reunited with Mike. There was an empty parking spot, and she pulled her car into it. She was checking the address on a building when she heard him calling her name. He was smiling and waving as he dashed across the street, pausing to let a car pass in front of him. And then he was there, opening her car door and helping her get out. Before she could say a word, he'd taken her into his arms and was holding her tight. All of the loneliness that had consumed her over the past weeks vanished as she leaned against his hard chest, taking the lingering doubts that had tormented her on quiet nights along for the ride.

Being in Mike's arms felt so right. No amount of phone calls or texts could compare to actually being together. She closed her eyes in bliss and breathed him in. After a moment, Mike stepped back.

"We're in the middle of the street."

"Right." She shook her head. "I forgot where we were for a moment."

"You weren't alone," he said with a grin. "Let me get your bag. Is it in the trunk?"

"Yes." She unlocked the trunk, and he took out her suitcase while she grabbed her overnight bag. Corinne had spent a good deal of her life on the road, so she was an expert at packing. Her luggage contained everything she needed for their planned activities. Mike was taking her to dinner tonight. Tomorrow they would go sightseeing. The weather forecast had been for unseasonably warm weather, so he'd promised a walk along Lake Michigan.

Mike took her hand as they crossed the street. When they reached the sidewalk, Corinne stopped and looked around. This was such a pretty block. Although there were brownstones instead of rambling houses, there were mature trees and small, neatly trimmed lawns. Several of the lawns were enclosed by black wrought iron fences. Potted purple mums flanked several doorways. It was all so welcoming, and felt vaguely familiar.

She turned and smiled at Mike. "I like it."

"So do I. I was lucky to find a place that I could afford. My apartment isn't the biggest, but it's close to campus. A lot of my classmates live nearby. And there are a lot of restaurants and coffee shops within walking distance."

"It sounds wonderful."

"It is. You'll see."

It would be great to visit the places where Mike spent his time. That way, she would have a picture in her mind to refer to later as she listened to his stories. More importantly, he would remember the time she was with him whenever he returned to those places.

Mike's apartment was on the top floor of the three-story building. Beautiful stained-glass windows provided light to the wide oak stairway. "It's so quiet."

"Students live in a couple of the buildings on this block, so there's not a whole lot of noise. We're either sleeping or studying. My first-floor neighbor is a law student and the second-floor neighbor is also in medical school. He's in his fourth year, which is good to see."

"Why?"

"Because when it gets hard it's nice to see someone who's been where I am and made it through to the end."

Mike unlocked the door to his apartment and stood aside so she could go in ahead of him. She looked around and smiled. Sunlight streamed through the front windows, illuminating the space. Everything in the neat living room screamed student. Mike had a dark brown leather sofa and matching chair. A small coffee table holding a laptop and a stack of books was situated in the middle of a blue and gray area rug. The aroma of coffee floated on the air.

"You can have my room," Mike said, drawing her attention back to him.

"Thanks."

He led her through a cozy dining room to the bedroom at back of the apartment. His bed was neatly made and took up much of the small room. "You can hang up your clothes in the closet. And I cleaned out a dresser drawer for you."

"Thanks." She looked around. There was a thick book on the nightstand. "Do you study in bed, too?"

He shrugged, looking sheepish. "Sometimes. But not too often. Generally I don't get into bed until it's really late and I'm bleary-eyed and ready to drop. I only get a page or two read before I fall asleep."

"You really are a devoted student. I hope my being here doesn't mess you up." She missed Mike and wanted to be with him, but she didn't want to be the reason his grades suffered. Although she'd been looking forward to this weekend, she wondered if she should have gone straight to Indiana to get ready for the rodeo. Maybe spending the weekend with him was a bad idea.

"No. I think having you here will actually help me do better in class."

"How do you figure that?"

"I'm giving my brain a break."

She laughed. "I hope you didn't mean that the way it sounded."

He shook his head, a grimace on his face. "That didn't come out right at all. What I mean is that I need to take a little time away from studying. Time to recharge. Not a long time, but a weekend. I'm not burned out exactly, but you were right. I need something enjoyable in my life to break up the monotony."

"I can definitely provide you with the fun you need this weekend."

"I'm looking forward to every minute we spend together."

"What should we do first?"

"Have you eaten?"

"Do peanut butter crackers and apple juice count?"

"No. It's almost two and my classes are done for the day. There's this place I want to take you. We can grab some food and then go to the beach after we eat."

"That sounds good. Let me freshen up a bit first."

"Take your time." Mike took two steps toward the door, stopped, turned and looked back. "It really is good to have you here, Corinne. I missed you more than I can say."

Corinne's heart stuttered and her stomach got all fizzy. Before she could respond, Mike had left the room, closing the door behind him. Her heart was singing with joy, and she let it float free as she enjoyed the sensation. Those were the exact words she'd needed to hear. She was still smiling as she unpacked and then freshened up. When she was done, she went in search of Mike.

He was sitting in a leather chair, looking out the window when Corinne stepped into the room. The text-books were nowhere in sight, and she wondered just where he'd hidden them. She'd half expected him to be getting in a bit of last-minute studying while he waited for her, so this was a pleasant surprise. Perhaps he really was serious about making this weekend one of pure fun. She could get with that. They didn't have much time to be together and this was a great start toward living up to the weekend she'd envisioned.

She'd changed into a pair of tight blue jeans and a pretty floral cable-knit sweater and pink boots she'd bought just for this visit. The weather was nice so she would be warm with just her denim jacket. She'd tied her braids back while she'd been traveling but she'd released them and they hung to her waist. She'd put on gold hoop earrings and matching bangles on her right wrist. The bangles clanked as she brushed a braid behind her ear.

Mike glanced up as she entered into the room. He did a double take and then, smiling, he rose and crossed over to her. "Wow. You look absolutely amazing."

"Thanks. I'm in the big city filled with fashionistas. I didn't want to look all country."

Mike took her hands into his. "I like country."

She smiled. "I'll keep that in mind."

The restaurant Mike wanted to show her was less than

a mile away, so they decided to walk. They'd only gone a few blocks when Corinne turned to him. "I haven't been to Chicago before, but I have to tell you, this isn't at all what I expected."

"Do you mean that in a good or bad way?"

"Definitely good. I don't know why I pictured this city as a bunch of concrete and tall, boring buildings. There are so many more trees and autumn flowers than I expected to see."

"There are plenty of skyscrapers. Just not around here."

"There was a lot of traffic, so I thought there would be more people walking around. It isn't as crowded as I expected it to be."

"There are lots of people here. Millions. But they don't all live in the same neighborhood. And they aren't all in the same place at the same time. They're simply going about their lives. But if it's people you want, you're in luck. You're about to see a lot of them now at the restaurant. I have to warn you, Mr. J's is a little bit different from others. But the food is delicious."

"Okay."

"What do you want to eat? Hamburger? Cheeseburger? Fish sandwich? They all come with fries and a drink."

"I want a burger. Don't they have a menu?"

"Yes. Online. I should have let you see it before we left. You need to know what you want before you walk in."

"Oh. Okay. A burger and fries will do."

"There are a few tables, but it's not your typical sit-down restaurant. I've gone to this place a couple of times a month since I started school here last year and I have yet to luck upon a table. Generally I just get my food to go like most other people."

"What kind of restaurant doesn't have enough tables for its customers? I'm confused. And more than a little intrigued."

They crossed the street and joined a line that stretched down the block to a storefront. The people were dressed in everything from suits and ties to jeans, sweaters and gym shoes. Corinne looked around the person in front of her to their destination. The front windows of the building had several illuminated signs advertising Vienna beef hot dogs and charbroiled burgers. A blue sign read Open. The line moved forward, and they did as well. Before long, they were near the open door.

"Do you still want a burger and fries?" Mike asked. When she nodded, he said, "Okay, that's a number one."

They stepped inside the door. A man behind the counter pointed at the woman in front of Corinne. She was wearing a designer suit and carrying a leather briefcase.

"Number four," the woman yelled, startling Corinne, who did her best not to stare.

"Number four," the man called over his shoulder before turning and looking at Corinne.

She glanced at Mike who nudged her shoulder. "Tell him the number."

"Number one," Corinne yelled and then shook her head. She could imagine what her mother would say if she caught her yelling across a restaurant.

The man repeated it and then looked at Mike who hollered out his number.

Mike and Corinne followed the line as it snaked through the tiny space until they reached the cashier. There was only a handful of tables, each of which was occupied. Mike handed over some money. "For her order and mine."

The cashier nodded and accepted the payment. Several apron-clad cooks manned a large grill behind the counter, moving quickly as they efficiently charbroiled burgers and grilled chicken. A young man dropped fresh potatoes into an enormous deep fryer. The aromas were among the best Corinne had ever smelled in her life. When they reached the end of the line, a young man handed them their food and they followed the stream of people out the door.

"That was something," Corinne said with a laugh as she and Mike stood outside on the sidewalk. "People yelling was actually acceptable. I wouldn't have believed it if I hadn't seen it. What happens if you don't know your number?"

"I don't know. I've never seen it happen." He nodded down the street. "There's a park a block away with lots of benches. We can eat there."

"Sounds good to me."

When they reached the park, they found a bench and sat down. Corinne opened her bag and grabbed her burger. She took a big bite and was treated to a delicious, smoky flavor. She closed her eyes and she let out a blissful moan. "Oh. That is so good."

"I told you," Mike said. "I always keep my promise."

As she savored the hot crispy fries, Corinne took in the scenery. The sky was a rich blue with puffy white clouds floating across it. Crows flew in the air, chirping and chasing each other across the vast space. Orange and purple mums surrounded the trunks of trees filled with colorful leaves. If she didn't know she was in the middle of one of the country's biggest cities, she would think she was back home in Bronco. She would never have believed how peaceful the city was if she hadn't been sitting here now.

Her cheeks burned with shame at how closed-minded

she had been. She'd always been so certain what big cities were like—cold and crowded—even though she hadn't spent much time in one. Now she knew that she'd been wrong. Though she had only been here for a few hours, she was already finding it pleasant. She knew that the entire city wouldn't be just like this quiet park. And that was fine. Bronco wasn't one park either. Truth be told, she was looking forward to experiencing Chicago nightlife.

She popped a fry in her mouth. "I don't see how you only eat there a couple times a month. If I lived here, I'd eat there every day."

"Trust me, the temptation is strong. But you can't live on fried foods."

"I suppose your teachers talk a lot about eating well."

"Not as much as you would expect. But I see a lot of sick people and wonder how many of their illnesses could be improved or even prevented by good eating habits. Not saying that everything could be. Diet can't replace medicine or treatment. But I'd probably get tired of it after a while. Too much of a good thing and all that."

"I suppose." She polished off the last of her burger and noticed with no small amount of regret that she only had one fry left. "Do you cook a lot?"

"Not as much as I should. I eat a lot of my meals at the hospital."

"You eat hospital food? By choice?"

"It's not as bad as all that. In fact, some of it is actually decent. And there are a few chain restaurants at the food court. Not that any of it comes close to comparing to Mom's food. Nobody cooks as well as she does."

Corinne nodded in agreement. She'd eaten Mike's mother's food quite often in the past. Jeanne Burris was an excellent cook. "I'll be sure to pass on that message to her."

"Please do. And while you're at it, let her know that I wouldn't be opposed to receiving another care package."

"I'll say it just like that," Corinne said with a laugh.

"I'd appreciate it," Mike said as they tossed their trash into a garbage can. "Are you up for a walk along the lake?"

"Yes. Is it close?"

"About half a mile away. Will you be all right in those boots? If not, we can stop back by my apartment so you can change."

"These will be fine. You may have become citified and wear gym shoes everywhere," she said, pointing at his feet, "but I'm still a country girl. I wear boots most of the time."

"Fair enough."

She took the hand he offered and they began strolling down the street. The neighborhood was an eclectic one to say the least. Nail shops stood beside delis, which were beside office supply stores. They went another block or so and she noticed a change. Basic storefronts were replaced by nice boutiques with gold lettering on the windows and decorative pots beside the doors, then a little bit ahead, she noticed large high-end stores.

Mike held his arms out wide. "We've arrived at Michigan Avenue. The Magnificent Mile. Chicago's premiere shopping district."

The street was crowded with people carrying shopping bags advertising exclusive brands. Yellow cabs darted across traffic to pick up passengers. She might not have pictured parks and tree-lined streets, but she'd pictured the noise and commotion on display here. "Nice. Do you shop here often?"

He grinned at her and pointed to his massive chest. "Medical student here. The money I made on the tour is going to rent and living expenses. Geoff insisted on paying my tuition, for which I'll be eternally grateful, but I still have bills to pay. Besides, I'm not sure I'm ready to drop the kind of money they're asking for a belt."

"Their belts can't compare to the buckles you won competing."

"I agree. I may be living in Chicago, but I'm still a country boy at heart."

She was glad to hear that he still thought of himself that way. "Does that mean you'll be moving back to Bronco after you graduate?"

"I don't know. I haven't thought that far ahead. There's something appealing about working in a city with first-rate hospitals. Northwestern has a superior reputation across the country. Their hospital and associated practices have state-of-the-art equipment for every type of surgery. Their doctors are world-renowned experts in their fields. And I have the opportunity to learn from them. There's no duplicating that."

Her heart plummeted with each word. Mike might not have said it, but she had the sneaking suspicion that he wouldn't be returning to Bronco after graduation. Of course, when he described the advantages Chicago had to offer, she couldn't blame him. There was something to be said about learning from the best. Bronco couldn't compare.

They crossed the busy street and continued to walk toward the shore. Corinne inhaled and caught a whiff of the lake. Anticipation built inside her. They were getting close. Mike stopped and gestured to a massive building that took up nearly the entire block. "That's part of the medical school. Later on I'll show you around inside."

"Your school is this close to the beach? How do you get any work done?"

"It's a lot easier when it's cold outside. The wind is fierce and the last thing I want to do is walk along on frozen sand. But today is nice, and I have the most beautiful companion in the world, so it will be perfect."

She smiled at his compliment. Corinne pointed to a building with an unobstructed view of the beach. "Is that part of the medical school too? I don't think I could concentrate if I had a class there no matter how cold it was."

"No. That's part of the law school. Law students don't need to concentrate as hard as medical students." Mike grinned and Corinne knew he was kidding. At least partly.

"Do you know many law students?"

"I don't know any. Truthfully, I don't know many medical students, either. There are a few that I consider close friends. But others? Not so much. There's not a lot of partying or hanging out happening on a regular basis."

"That sounds a bit lonely. And sad."

He shrugged. "They keep us too busy to feel sad. Or much of anything else for that matter."

"And you think that's healthy?"

He squeezed the bridge of his nose and then sighed. "That's just the way it is. If I want to be a doctor, this is what I have to go through, just like every doctor before me. And honestly, is it any different than being in rodeo? We spent hours practicing in order to be the best in our events. Look at Geoff. He's been in rodeo since middle school. His entire life has been devoted to being the best. And he is. But it took hours of single-minded dedication. Endless hours of practice for years. He had to make sacrifices in other areas of his life in order to accomplish his goals. Same with Jack and Audrey. They live and breathe competition. Heck, competing nearly ruined their relationship. Nothing comes between them and getting the highest score."

"You're right. And it wasn't a criticism. I'm sorry if it sounded like one. I just don't remember you being this… I don't know…"

"Committed?"

"That's not the word I was going to use, but it works. When it came to rodeo, you were more relaxed. You wanted to win, but you weren't *obsessed*."

His lips turned down and he shrugged. She wondered if she'd gone too far. "Fair enough. But rodeo wasn't my calling. It was simply a means to an end. A way to earn money so I could attend medical school while spending time with my brothers. You knew that. I never made it a secret. Medicine is my passion. My reason for being."

"I guess I'm seeing a different side to you."

"Is it good or bad?"

They'd been asking each other that question a lot lately. "I don't know. Neither, I suppose. It just is."

He tugged on her hand and then stepped in front of her, stopping her in her tracks. "I'm still the same man I've always been. You have to know that."

"I hope so."

He turned in profile, the dimple flashing in his cheek. Then he turned his other side to her. Finally he looked at her straight on. "See? No matter what side you look at, I'm still the same Mike. A different career won't change that."

She wasn't so sure. But even if he was different, she had to admit that she was just as attracted to him as she'd always been. Maybe he wasn't as laid-back as she'd once believed, but being driven wasn't a sin. And as it turned out, it wasn't a turnoff either.

There were others enjoying the day and Mike and Corinne nodded at people they passed as they strolled across the sand. They neared the edge of the shore and stood watching as the waves crashed against the rocks. The sun shone on the water, giving it a glassy appearance. If she kept her eyes focused on the lake, she could pretend that she and Mike were alone on a deserted island. As her gaze encompassed the Chicago skyline, she was brought back to reality.

Corinne spotted a shell and picked it up. She studied it for a minute before slipping it into her purse. A souvenir.

"How are things going with you?" Mike asked. "I feel as if all we've done is talk about me. I'm interested in your life too."

"But you know all about my life. It's the same life that you left behind."

"I left *my* rodeo career behind. Not *yours*. You and Remi are still at the top of team roping. That's exciting."

"Only by a hair. And that's because Audrey was on her honeymoon and she and Brynn weren't competing for that time. Now she's back and she and Brynn are gaining on us."

"Ah. The love bug is once more to blame for the near downfall of a Hawkins sister."

Corinne laughed. "Yeah."

"Are you sure you want to take that risk?"

She couldn't imagine a relationship affecting her performance. In her mind, the two were separate. She knew that rodeo wouldn't last forever but she hoped that love would. When the time came to walk away from the circuit, she would do it with no regrets. Her legendary grandmother and mother had performed for decades, but Corinne didn't see that as her future. Until Mike had started medical school, she really hadn't contemplated a future after rodeo. Now she wondered if she should start thinking about her second act.

She'd always done well enough in school, but no subject had piqued her curiosity more than any other. What did that mean? Perhaps rodeo really was it for her. But somehow that didn't sound right either. Although her sisters had made a career out of rodeo, she could easily picture a time when they moved on to the next phase of their lives. Audrey was already married and Brynn was engaged. She would probably be getting married in the near future. No doubt they would be starting families soon. Although they'd been raised on the circuit, she couldn't picture either of her sisters raising their kids that way. Especially since they'd put down roots in Bronco. Corinne had a sneaking suspicion that when one sister left, the others would soon follow, putting an end to this generation of the Hawkins Sisters.

A hand waved in front of her face. She blinked and looked up into Mike's brown eyes. They were filled with a mixture of concern and humor. "Where did you go?"

"What do you mean?" she asked although she knew perfectly well what he was asking. She'd zoned out.

"You seemed so far away all of a sudden."

"I was just thinking."

"About?"

"Oh, this and that. The shore is a wonderful place for daydreaming and letting your mind wander."

"It is. Whenever I get too stressed, I come over here. Even if it's only for a few minutes, when I leave, my mind is always much clearer."

"Perhaps I need to take a little bit of the lake home with me. Do you have a jar?" she joked.

"Not on me, but you can take a picture. Give me your phone and we'll shoot a video together."

Corinne handed over her phone and then posed for a few shots. Then Mike turned on the video and they hammed it up for the camera, keeping the lake behind them. Finally he turned the phone to take pictures of just the water. "There. That should help when you need it."

"It can't hurt. And don't forget I have my shell."

They walked for a few more minutes and then turned back. There was something so nice about being around Mike even if they were simply walking hand in hand without speaking. The wordless communication was something that they had mastered. Not that they didn't talk. It was just that they didn't need words all of the time. Just being around each other was enough. They walked a while longer before heading back to Mike's place.

As they stepped inside his apartment, Corinne's phone rang. She checked the display. *Brynn.* Corinne slapped a hand against her forehead. She'd forgotten to let her sister know that she'd arrived. She knew how protective her oldest sister was. Corinne answered the phone and immediately apologized for the oversight.

"Okay," Brynn said. "I figured you'd forgotten, but I just needed to be sure. Give Mike our love."

"I will," Corinne said and then ended the call.

The rest of the afternoon passed quickly with her and Mike talking quietly. Before long, Corinne was getting ready for a night on the town. Even the cool water of the shower couldn't slow the racing of her heart. After rinsing off her favorite body wash, Corinne stepped onto the tiny rug beside the tub-and-shower combo and looked around. She blinked and looked around again, this time more urgently. She didn't have her clothes. She'd been so preoccupied with thoughts of tonight that she'd forgotten to bring them into the bathroom with her. They were lying neatly on the bed. The only thing she had to wear was a towel.

Mike was in the front room, and she knew that if she called to him, he would bring her clothes to her, no problem. She pictured him scooping up her underwear and paused. That seemed just a bit too intimate for her comfort at this stage of their relationship. Corinne whipped the shower cap from her head, freeing her braids, dried off, and then wrapped the towel around her body. She carefully tucked the end between her breasts, noting with dismay that the fabric only reached her upper thighs. Inhaling deeply, she opened the door and stepped into the hallway. It was possible that she could make it to the bedroom without encountering Mike.

Except Mike was no longer in the front room playing a video game. He was in the dining room, ironing a shirt. The floor creaked and he glanced up. His eyes widened as he stared at her. Time froze, as did she, as his eyes traveled slowly over her body, starting at her painted toes. His eyes paused as they reached her freshly shaven calves, before moving on to take in her thighs. They slowed again briefly at her hips before moving up to her breasts where they hesitated again. By the time his eyes reached hers, her face was flaming, and she was consumed with heat.

Corinne tried to speak, but couldn't think of anything to say. Not that she would be able to form words. She ordered her feet to move, but they seemed to have taken root, gluing themselves to the floor. Sexual tension sizzled in the air, leaving them incapable of movement. Time stalled until Mike's phone beeped, startling them into motion.

He grabbed his phone and turned off the alarm. "Sorry. I'm trying to stay on schedule."

"Okay."

The desire consuming her must have come across as confusion because he began to explain. "I've started using the timer on my phone to keep track of time and how much of it I spend doing each task. You'd be amazed by how much time I used to waste. Every second counts when you're trying to absorb everything the professors are throwing at us."

"That makes sense. You're very disciplined."

He blew out a breath. "My brothers think I'm weird and that I've crossed the line into obsessed, but they don't understand."

"I think they do. Like you said earlier, they're just disciplined in different ways."

He nodded slowly as if absorbing her words.

It was strange to be having this conversation while she was wrapped in a towel, yet here she was. Important conversations didn't always occur at dinner. Sometimes they occurred at the most random times, like with one person ironing and the other fresh out of the shower.

"I should get dressed," she said, pointing to his open bedroom door.

He shook his head as if he was just becoming aware that she was only wearing a towel. She didn't know whether to be flattered that he was so pleased by her comment that he momentarily became unaware of her state of undress or insulted that she was nearly naked in front of him and her body hadn't held his attention. Why choose when she could feel both things simultaneously?

"And I should get into the shower."

Though she longed to sprint into his room and slam the door behind her, she managed to walk sedately. Only when she was in the bedroom with the door closed firmly behind her did she let out a long breath as she sank onto his bed. She didn't know how she managed to not go up in flames earlier, but she'd pulled it off. She just hoped she could maintain that level of control for the rest of the weekend.

Mike grabbed his clothes and stepped into the bathroom. He closed the door and then slumped against it. *Whew.* That was hot. He'd been fantasizing about Corinne for the longest time and seeing her standing there wearing nothing but a towel had exceeded his imagination. Green terry cloth suited her. She was a vision. Sexiness personified. It had taken all of his self-control to keep from grabbing her and showing her just how desperately he'd missed her. How much he longed to have her in his life. But he hadn't. Couldn't. Their relationship hadn't progressed that far yet.

In the beginning, they hadn't put a label on their relationship. They hadn't needed one. Back then they had been getting to know each other. Their schedules had been similar, and they'd crossed paths quite often on the circuit. When they'd been together, they'd had a great time. It was only when he'd gone away to school that they'd felt they needed to put a name to what they had.

It had been easy to say they were friends, because they had been. But had they been more? Had something been developing under the surface while they were unaware? Maybe. Neither of them had been dating. He hadn't wanted to see other women. Being with Corinne had been all that he'd needed. She was fun and easy to be around and she'd more than satisfied his need for female companionship. But this past year had exposed the holes in their relationship.

He shut down that line of thought. This was not the time to try to figure out what was going on between them. He'd tried many times in the past and the only thing he'd come up with was a headache. Besides, they'd answered that question when they'd officially decided to date.

Right now he needed a shower. A cold shower. But when he inhaled a cleansing breath, the familiar scent of Corinne's body wash flooded his nostrils. The aroma was at once sweet and arousing. And it suited Corinne perfectly. The way it blended in with her own natural essence enticed him. He could happily breathe it in all day. Of course, he didn't have all day. He had nineteen minutes to shower and dress if they were going to make their reservations.

He hopped in the shower, washed up, dried off and got dressed with a minute to spare. He'd been tempted to leave his clothes in the dining room and walk out wearing only a towel but thought better of it. His self-control was already in tatters from seeing Corinne half naked. He'd nearly swallowed his tongue when he looked up and saw her.

He'd seen her dressed in everything, from the glittery outfits she and her sisters performed in to tight jeans and boots, so he knew she had a body second to none. But nothing in the past had prepared him for how enticing she'd looked in that towel, or his body's reaction to it. There had been moisture on one of her shoulders, and his hand had ached to wipe it off. But he'd known that if he'd touched her—even innocently—all bets would've been off.

As much as he might want to deny it, his touch wouldn't

have been all that innocent. He liked to believe that he had control over his body, but seeing Corinne standing before him had disabused him of that notion. His body had a mind of its own and it was thinking about how much pleasure he and Corinne could give each other if they allowed themselves that freedom. But he wouldn't. There was too much on the line for both of them. Once their relationship became physical, there would be no taking it slowly as they'd agreed to do.

After checking his appearance and straightening his tie, he stepped into the hallway and strode to the front of the apartment. Corinne was staring out the window at the darkening sky. Her back was to him, so he took a moment to appreciate just how good she looked.

She was a dream in an orange print dress that showcased her fabulous body. Her waist was small and her back straight. Her calves were well shaped and her bottom was wonderfully round and firm. As if sensing his presence, she glanced over her shoulder. Her dark braids, which cascaded over her shoulders, shifted when she moved. When she spotted him, she turned the rest of the way around, giving him a view of the front. She was just as sexy this way, too. Her smile lit up her face and her entire being glowed with the joy that emanated from within. His heart leaped and for a moment all he could do was stare.

"I'm looking forward to dinner," she said as if unaware of the effect she was having on him. "What kind of food will we be eating?"

He cleared his throat and focused on her question. "I made reservations at a Caribbean place not far from here."

"I love Caribbean food."

"I know. That's why I chose this restaurant. When I

knew you were coming, I researched restaurants until I found a few you would like."

Her smile widened. "You did all that for me?"

"Of course. You're worth it."

In an instant, she had crossed the room and wrapped her arms around his shoulders. When she pressed her head against his chest, he inhaled and was treated to a whiff of her sweet perfume. Before he could think, he'd closed his arms around her waist, holding her against him. It felt so good to have her this close to him, even if only for a minute. One moment bled into the next, filling him with longing.

After a while, he eased away. He felt her resistance and smiled. It was gratifying to know that she shared his desire to remain close. But they had a reservation and he wanted to be on time.

Although it had been warm earlier in the day, the evening was chilly, so he grabbed their coats. He dropped his onto a chair and then held out Corinne's for her. She slipped her arms into the sleeves and then fastened the buttons. He put on his coat and then led her out his apartment.

Once they were safely ensconced in his car, he turned on the radio. When the first song began, he smiled at Corinne. "One of the benefits of living in Chicago is the vast number of local radio stations to choose from."

"Are you trying to sell me on the city?"

Was he? Was that why he'd invited her to spend the weekend with him? Was he trying to prove to her that Chicago was as good a place to make a home as Bronco? That she could be happy here? He'd ponder that another time. "I'm just trying to point out some of the things that I enjoy about living here. There's always satellite radio, but there's something special about local stations. And there are a lot of them that play the kind of music I like."

"I agree."

He nodded, satisfied with her answer.

As they drove down the street, they talked about whatever random subjects came to mind. By unspoken agreement, they didn't mention medical school or the rodeo. They'd talked those things to death. Even without broaching those topics, the conversation never lapsed.

When they reached the restaurant and he parked, Corinne made a move to open her door, but he placed a hand on her arm, stopping her. "Let me get the door for you."

She smiled. "Thank you."

Rounding the car, he opened her door and held out his hand. The smile she flashed him made his heart thud in his chest. His night was already made and they hadn't even had appetizers yet.

When they entered the restaurant, the aromas of spices and cooking meat struck his nose and his stomach rumbled.

Corinne looked at him and laughed. "I take it that you're hungry. Again."

"Lunch was hours ago."

"Which means you'll have plenty of room for dinner."

They walked up to a podium where a woman looked up and smiled at them. "Do you have a reservation?"

"We do," Mike replied. "Under Burris."

She looked at her tablet and then nodded. "Right this way."

Mike gestured for Corinne to precede him. He admired the gentle sway of her hips as she wove her way through the maze of tables. When the hostess reached an empty table, she set down two menus. "Enjoy your meal. Someone will be here to take your drink orders soon."

"Thank you," Mike said, walking over and holding Corinne's chair for her before sitting in his own.

"What's good here?" Corinne asked after perusing the menu.

"It's all good."

"Really?"

"Yes. I've only eaten here twice, so I've only had two entrees. But three of my classmates were with me and they each got different meals. They all gave rave reviews on everything."

"What did you have?"

"The first time I had the plantain-encrusted halibut with jalapeño cream sauce. The second I had jalea de mariscos."

"That's my favorite."

"I know. That's why I tried it from three different restaurants. I wanted to find the place with the best food for you. My study group and I had it delivered from the other places, though. This was the winner."

She shot him another one of those devastating smiles and his stomach flipped, this time with a hunger of a different kind.

When the waitress arrived, she took their orders and returned right away with their mojitos. Corinne took a sip and Mike waited for her reaction. When she smiled with pleasure, he knew it was the perfect combination of rum, mint and lime.

"We're off to a good start," she said.

"I told you this place was great."

They continued to talk as they savored every bite of their dinner, making the most of their time together. Before Mike knew it, they'd finished their meals and desserts.

"This has been so much fun," Corinne said with a contented sigh.

"And the night isn't over. Would you like to go for another walk? There's so much that I want to show you. I just wish we had more time."

"I'm loving every minute."

"That's all I want to hear."

As they strolled around the neighborhood, Mike pointed out things he thought Corinne would appreciate. But even as he tried to impress her, he couldn't keep his eyes from straying to her sexy body. With every breath, he inhaled her intoxicating scent. His mind kept replaying the image of her in the towel and sweat beaded on his brow. The weather might be getting colder, but he was growing hotter by the moment.

Chapter Five

Corinne leaned against the back of the sofa and closed her eyes in contentment. Tonight had been all she'd dreamed of and more. Mike had been entertaining and courteous. Attentive and open. All things he'd been before he'd started medical school. Recently she'd begun to wonder if she'd imagined how good they'd been together. How in sync they'd been. If today was anything to go by, they were just as connected as ever.

She glanced over at Mike. He was looking at her, an intense expression on his face. His brown eyes appeared darker. Mysterious. An unexpected yearning sprang up inside her, and she did her best to suppress it. She and Mike hadn't spent any real time together in several months. Their lives had changed, and so had they. Just how much was the question. Until she knew whether they were still a match, she knew she should keep her emotional distance from him. But that knowledge did nothing to stem the desire burning inside her. Because she also knew how much pleasure she could experience in his arms.

She felt a yawn coming on and hurried to cover it. She didn't quite succeed.

"Tired?"

Suddenly she realized that she was. She'd been so excited about this visit that she hadn't slept much in the past couple of days. She'd made an appearance at an exhibition in Kansas yesterday. Then she'd hit the road at zero dark thirty this morning. It had finally caught up with her. "A bit."

"Well then, let's go to bed."

She jerked and he laughed. It was as if he'd read her mind.

"I suppose I could have phrased that better. Let's try that again. I put clean sheets and blankets on the bed, so it's all ready for you."

"Thank you."

He'd been clear when he'd invited her to visit him that he would be sleeping on the couch. She'd appreciated knowing that she was under no pressure to be intimate with him. They hadn't reached that stage in their relationship, and it was comforting to know he intended to keep his word. But then, as he pointed out earlier, he always kept his promises.

They walked to the bedroom and stopped outside the open door. Mike leaned against the jamb, crossed his feet at the ankles and smiled at her. "Well, I guess this is where we say good-night."

She smiled in return even as her heart was pounding hard enough to burst from her chest. "I guess it is."

He brushed a gentle hand against her cheek. "It won't be a proper good-night without a good-night kiss."

She leaned into his touch and looked at him. The expression on his face was intense and her blood began to race through her veins. "I definitely want a proper good-night."

Not breaking eye contact, he leaned down slowly as if giving her time to reconsider. As if she would. She'd been anticipating his kiss all day. When his lips brushed against hers, her eyes fluttered shut and electricity shot from her lips to every part of her body. Of their own volition, her arms slid over his muscular chest and wrapped around his neck.

His tongue licked at the seam of her lips and she opened her mouth to him. His tongue swept inside as he deepened the kiss. Her knees buckled and she tightened her grip on his strong shoulders. His arms wrapped around her, holding her securely against his hard body. The kiss went on and on and she allowed herself to be swept away by the sensations surging through her. She felt him easing away and moaned in protest. She felt his laughter against her lips and sighing, she pulled back too. Slowing things down was the right thing to do. The last thing either of them needed was for their bodies to overrule their good sense.

Breathing hard, she leaned against the door jamb, using it to support her when her wobbly legs didn't seem up to the task. "Wow."

"You took the word right out of my mouth," Mike said, leaning his forehead against hers.

They stood that way for a few seconds as their breathing slowed. When Corinne believed she could stand on her own, she pushed away from the doorway and aimed a thumb over her shoulder. "I should probably get some sleep. Tomorrow will be here before I know it."

"Feel free to sleep in if you want."

"I don't want to. I want to see as much of Chicago as I can." Truth be told, she wanted to spend as much time with Mike as she could. She had rodeo commitments and he needed to study, so she didn't know when they would have time together again.

"Then I'll let you get to bed." Mike stared into her eyes for a few seconds. Then he leaned down and kissed her one more time. The kiss was brief, but it was just as earthshattering as the previous one. "See you in the morning."

"Good night," Corinne said, before stepping into the bedroom. When she was inside, she leaned against the door and closed her eyes. Her breath whooshed out of her. One thought echoed through her mind. *Mike is one great kisser.*

She'd had a few relationships—some more successful and happier than others. But of all the men she'd dated, not one of them had possessed the ability to make her see stars when he'd kissed her. Until Mike. He'd made her feel as if she were riding across the sky on a shooting star. Nothing in her past had led her to believe that she could feel anything this intensely, so her reaction to each of his kisses was a bit startling. She'd enjoyed that kiss so much she wished she could turn back time so she could have the pleasure of kissing him once more. Since she couldn't, she'd have to make do with the memory and anticipation of kissing him again.

Her knees weakened at the thought, and she walked on wobbly legs to the dresser. She grabbed her overnight bag and headed to the bathroom to remove her makeup and brush her teeth. When she was done, she returned to the bedroom and hopped into bed. She closed her eyes and sweet visions of the kiss repeated in her mind.

She was about to have the best dreams ever.

Mike waited until he heard the bedroom door close before he got up from his place on the recliner and headed for the tiny linen closet. He grabbed an extra pillow, sheets and blanket, and then went back to the living room and made a place to sleep on the sofa. Not that he expected to get much sleep knowing that Corinne was lying in his bed.

His body was still sizzling from the fire of the kiss they'd just shared. Even now his lips still tingled. The sexual desire he felt for Corinne far exceeded anything he'd felt for any other woman. He'd been attracted to Corinne from the moment he'd first seen her in Doug's over a year ago. His attraction had grown exponentially since then. He'd known instantly that Corinne was special and he wanted her to be a part of his life. He'd also known that they wouldn't have much time to be together once he started medical school. He hadn't wanted to begin something that he couldn't finish. So no matter how badly he'd wanted to pursue a relationship, he'd kept things friendly.

From the first time that he'd kissed her—*really kissed her*—he'd known that there was no way they could go back to being friends. He'd only been kidding himself if he'd believed that the fire between them could have been denied for much longer. Some things were inevitable and a relationship with Corinne was one of them.

He brushed his teeth and changed into pajama bottoms before lying on the couch. He tossed and turned, trying to get comfortable. Traveling on the rodeo circuit, he'd slept in some pretty uncomfortable places, so the fact that his feet were hanging over the arm of the sofa wasn't an impediment to his sleep. It was knowing that Corinne was lying in his bed, her head on his pillow, lying under his blankets, that kept him awake.

Mike closed his eyes and pictured Corinne as she'd looked at dinner. She'd been so sexy in a dress that caressed her sweet curves the way his hands ached to. And her scent. *Whew.* He didn't know the name of her perfume, but each time he got close to her, he caught a whiff and desire grew stronger inside him. It had taken superior effort to concentrate on their conversation when all he'd wanted to do was breathe her in. Lucky for him Corinne hadn't been aware of his struggle.

Though he knew he was traveling down a dangerous path, he couldn't stop himself from imagining what she was wearing right now. Was she a pajamas girl? He could totally imagine her in a cute pink top and short bottoms with white and red hearts on them. Or, given the fact that it was autumn, he could picture her in plaid pajamas with matching long-sleeved top and bottoms.

Or did she prefer nightgowns? Did she wear frilly, see-through gowns that stopped at the middle of her thighs, or did she wear gowns that resembled men's sports jerseys? She would look so cute in one. Or did she wear shapeless, ankle-length flannel gowns that hid her sexy figure? He shook his head at that ridiculous notion. Corinne didn't dress in an overtly sexual manner, but he didn't think she would wear anything as drab as that. Of course, she was naturally sensual and could make a gunnysack sexy.

He draped an arm over his forehead. Picturing Corinne lying in his bed wasn't doing himself any favors. He would never be able to fall asleep with his imagination running wild like this. But no matter how he tried, he couldn't control his thoughts. So he might as well indulge them.

After a night spent dreaming of holding Corinne in his arms, Mike awoke early. He took a quick shower and then dressed in jeans and a pullover. When he stepped out of the bathroom, Corinne was sitting on the couch. She'd folded the sheets and blankets and stacked everything on the chair. She was wearing blue striped pajamas and her bare toes peeked out of the bottom of the long pants.

She smiled. "Good morning."

"Hey. You didn't need to do that."

"I didn't mind."

"Thank you. The bathroom is free," he said unnecessarily.

"I won't be long."

"Take all the time you need. When you're done, we can go to breakfast. Then we can spend the rest of the day doing what you want. Go to the museums or walk along the Riverwalk. I got us tickets for a play at a local theater for tonight. That leaves plenty of time for us to be spontaneous in between. Of course, if there's something you'd rather do, just let me know."

"That all sounds perfect." She stood and walked in his direction. When she was inches away from him, he moved aside so she could step into the bathroom. The hall was narrow, and she brushed against him as she passed. His skin actually tingled at the casual contact. He needed to get himself under control before he embarrassed himself. More than that, he didn't want Corinne to feel uncomfortable around him.

He downed a glass of cold water, hoping it would cool him from the inside. It wasn't as effective as the cold shower he'd taken that seemed to have worn off, but it was the best he could do under the circumstances.

"I'm ready," Corinne said a while later, coming into the kitchen.

"Great. Get your jacket and let's get this day started."

"Where are we going for breakfast?" Corinne asked as they stepped outside. The sun was shining brightly, but it paled in comparison to her smile. It heated him in a way the sun never could.

"There's this little place a few blocks from here. It's not much to look at, but the food is top notch. And it's reasonably priced."

"It sounds as if you've found another Doug's."

"Nothing will ever be as good as Doug's but it's a close second."

"Well then, let's get going. I'm starved." Corinne grabbed his hand and led him down the stairs.

Although it was early on a Saturday morning, several of Mike's neighbors were already out and about. Mr. and Mrs. Henry, who lived three doors down, were speed-walking down the sidewalk. They nodded as they passed Mike and Corinne. Mr. Gilmore, who lived near the corner, was walking his dog, Max, with a leash in one hand and a covered coffee cup in the other. He called *good morning* as he headed for the dog park. Several people in their twenties wearing backpacks sped down the street on their bikes.

"Your neighbors are really nice," Corinne said, when they'd reached the corner.

"You sound surprised."

She shrugged, looking slightly embarrassed and cuter than she had a right to. "I'm ashamed to admit that a small part of me is. I guess I'm guilty of stereotyping city people. The news is flooded with reports of crime and violence in big cities so I thought people here would be different somehow."

"People are the same everywhere. Good, bad and everything in between. In that respect, Chicago is no different from Bronco or any other place. There are just a few more people here."

"A few?"

"Maybe a couple million. I look at is as a million friends I have yet to meet."

"That sounds exactly like something you would say."

"Not surprising since I'm the one who said it."

She laughed. Although the diner was only a fifteen-minute walk from his apartment, it took twice that long to get there. Corinne was enchanted by the shops they passed and peered in nearly every window to check out their wares. She particularly liked the store selling vintage clothing, so they went inside for a closer look. He didn't get the appeal of old clothes, but she seemed enthralled by a satin-and-lace wedding dress. When she held it up to herself, be briefly imagined her walking down the aisle to him. The thought was at once disturbing and pleasant.

She looked at a few more items before telling him she was ready to go. They passed by other stores, without entering until she came upon an antique store.

"Do we have time to go inside?" she asked.

"Of course." Mike opened the door and held it for her. The minute they stepped inside, Corinne headed for a music box. She twisted the key and music played.

Corinne smiled and then looked at a few more items. But she kept returning to the music box.

"Does this store seem…weird to you?" Mike asked.

"In what way?"

He shrugged. "I don't know. Like maybe it's haunted?"

She laughed. "Be serious."

"I am. Some of these things give me the willies." He pointed to an old doll with weird glass eyes. It seemed to be staring at him.

"Oh my goodness. I bet you believe in the haunted bar stool." She laughed. Doug kept the bar stool behind caution tape at his place because he swore it was haunted and bad luck followed anyone who sat there.

"I don't, but you have to admit that there's something creepy about these dusty old items. They used to belong to people who might be dead."

"And what? Their spirits are attached? Like a poltergeist?"

"When you put it like that, it sounds a bit ridiculous."

"Just a bit?"

He pointed at the music box she'd been staring at for five minutes with longing on her face. "Why don't you get it?"

"Because it's five hundred dollars."

"Wow. That would be a bit of a deterrent."

"Especially for something that might have a ghost attached to it." She gave it one last look, then let him lead her from the store. The diner was on the next block and nothing else attracted Corinne's attention before they reached it.

The place was busy, but they lucked out with a small table by the front window where they could people watch. After they sat, Mike moved the glass vase with the pink carnation to the side so he could have an unobstructed view of Corinne as she studied the menu. He would never get tired of seeing her beautiful face.

A waitress stepped up to the table. They turned their coffee cups up and she poured in the fragrant brew. "Hi. I'm Kelly and I'll be your server. Are you ready to order?"

"Two specials," Mike said.

"I'll be back with these as soon as they're done."

"Thank you," Corinne said.

They sipped their coffee and stared out the window at the passing cars and the pedestrians going about their days. When the waitress returned and set the food in front of them, Corinne looked at her plate and smiled. "Wow. This looks and smells great."

"It tastes even better," Mike assured her.

As they ate, they planned the rest of the day. "So, do you want to go to a museum?"

Corinne looked so cute as she wrinkled her nose. "Not really. That sounds too much like a school field trip to be a lot of fun. Besides, it's a nice day. I'd really like to do something outside."

"The Riverwalk will be fun. We can take one of the boat tours or we can rent bikes and ride the path along the lakefront."

"There's so much to do. I feel like if I say yes to one thing, I'm going to miss out on something else great."

"That's because you are. There's no avoiding it. So you'll have to come back for another visit so we can do the things you miss this time."

The smile she flashed him made his heart stutter. She looked as pleased as he felt by the idea.

"I'll have to check my schedule. Even though Audrey got married, she hasn't wanted to stop competing and

KATHY DOUGLASS 107

the Hawkins Sisters are as busy as ever. Even more so if you want to know the truth."

He smiled to cover the disappointment he had no right to feel. She had a life outside of him. Her goals mattered to her just as much as his mattered to him. If their relationship was going to stand a chance, he was going to have to do more than *accept* that reality. He had to do whatever he could to help her reach her goals. Obviously he couldn't compete for her. But he could support her. Just as she'd come to visit him, he could go to one of her rodeos.

"I'm glad that you're getting more opportunities. You and your sisters deserve them. I know how hard it is for women in rodeo. And I know just how much effort the four of you have put into making the Hawkins Sisters even more well known."

"I am happy about it. And now my cousin is back from Australia and competing over here, so that's good."

He raised his coffee cup in a mock salute. "The Hawkins family is taking over rodeo. You love to see it."

Corinne laughed. "I wouldn't go that far."

"You will. Just wait and see."

When they were finished eating breakfast, Corinne wiped her mouth with her paper napkin. "That was delicious."

"I agree. I would love to just sit here, but time's a-wasting."

"How about we rent those bikes you were talking about? I could use a little exercise after a meal like that."

"Sounds good." He paid the bill, leaving a nice tip for their waitress, and then led Corinne from the restaurant. "We can rent bikes for the day and ride everywhere. And we can check out the Riverwalk, too. Ready?"

"Yes." She grabbed his hand and gave it an enthusiastic squeeze. "I have a feeling this is going to be the best day ever."

With her by his side, Mike had to agree.

Chapter Six

Corinne lifted her head to the sky, letting the warm breeze brush over her face. Although she'd predicted that this would be a great day, it was surpassing her expectations. Riding her bike along Lake Michigan was so much more fun than she'd anticipated. There were lots of other bikers making the most of the day, but they had added to her enjoyment rather than diminishing it. They added an energy that was positively contagious.

Despite the fact that she was in one of the biggest cities in the country, there was an abundance of nature for her to enjoy. She'd also seen some of the city's most popular tourist draws. They'd ridden past the Shedd Aquarium and the Field Museum. Mike had asked if she'd changed her mind about going inside, and she'd shaken her head.

"Having fun?" Mike asked. They were in Millennium Park, standing in front of Cloud Gate, which Mike had informed her was known as The Bean. He pulled out his phone so he could take another selfie of them. When they'd taken a selfie in front of Soldier Field, Mike had announced that he was now a Bears fan.

"Yes. I'm having a great time." She held out her arms, encompassing everything around them. "I like the view of the city, but I wish I could see it from another vantage point."

"Say no more. Your wish is my command."

"How? Don't tell me you know someone who lives in the penthouse of one of these buildings?"

"Not that I know of. But there is the Skydeck at Willis Tower. We can get tickets and you can enjoy the view. And since it's such a clear day, you'll be able to see for miles." He pulled out his phone and after a minute of tapping he looked at her. "We have reservations in forty minutes."

"How long will it take to get there?"

"Depends on how fast you can pedal."

Corinne had been standing beside her bike while she took in the view. At Mike's words, she climbed onto her bike and grinned at him. "Lead on."

Mike nodded and began pedaling. In twenty-five minutes, they had arrived at Willis Tower. They secured their bikes on a rack. Corinne took a moment to stare at Chicago's tallest building before she and Mike took another selfie.

"I should pay for my own ticket," Corinne said, as they entered the building.

"Don't even think about it. I invited you to spend the weekend with me."

"I didn't expect you to pay for everything."

"I'm enjoying the pleasure of your company. If it makes you feel better, consider this weekend one long date."

"Okay." Although she didn't agree with his logic, she didn't want to get into an argument and risk spoiling the moment. She'd always known that Mike was traditional when it came to paying for dates, but she knew that he was a full-time student and wasn't earning money on the circuit any longer.

"Okay."

Mike pulled up the e-tickets on his phone and they waited their turn. When they stepped onto the elevator, Corinne hoped that she wasn't afraid of heights, something she hadn't considered before. They rode to the top of the building and stepped onto the Skydeck. Mike had purchased tickets for the Ledge, a glass box that extended a few feet from the Skydeck so they could really enjoy the moment.

The view of the city from the Skydeck was fantastic.

"Have you been up here before?" she asked Mike.

"No. But it's a popular tourist destination."

Corinne glanced at the Ledge and inhaled deeply while searching for cracks or breaks. She didn't see any. "Are you sure this is going to hold us?"

"I don't see why it wouldn't. People have been coming up here for years. If it wasn't safe, it would have been closed down before now." Mike stepped onto the glass floor and held his hand out to Corinne. "Come on. You'll be fine."

Corinne nodded, crossed her fingers although she didn't know what good that would do if the floor broke, and stepped beside Mike. She looked down and her legs wobbled. She squeezed her eyes shut. "Whoa. We really are up high."

"You said you wanted to see the city from a different perspective. You won't be able to see it at all unless you open your eyes. Come on. If you look straight ahead, you'll be able to see for at least fifty miles."

Mike wrapped his arms around her, pulling her against his chest. Suddenly she felt secure, and she knew he wouldn't let anything bad happen to her. Corinne lifted her head then opened one eye. Not so bad. She heard Mike's laughter and opened the other and then stared through the glass wall. This was the type of view she'd been hoping for. She'd look at it even if it made her knees weak. She could see the tops of houses in the distance. The cars driving over the road looked almost like toys. A few birds flew across the sky, and she smiled as she realized that this truly was a bird's-eye view.

Mike and Corinne took their time, looking at everything. Once she'd become confident that the floor wasn't going to break beneath them and send them plunging to their deaths, she'd been able to relax and enjoy herself. There was something so freeing about this experience. It was not quite like flying, but it felt good. After a while she tugged on Mike's hand.

"Seen enough?" he asked.

"Yes."

"I guess we should go."

When they were on solid ground again, she smiled at him. "Thank you so much. I loved every second of it. I never felt anything like it before. I can't find the words to adequately express myself."

"You don't have to. I was right beside you so I have a pretty good idea how you feel. I'm just glad that you had a good time."

"I did." She wished she knew how to explain to Mike how thrilled she felt. Not just about standing on a glass floor and looking down at the world from thirteen hundred feet. It was the heady feeling that she got from being around Mike and sharing new experiences with him. It was knowing that they would share even more in the future. Although she was standing on terra firma, her knees were almost as shaky as they'd been on the Ledge.

"That makes me happy."

The rest of the day flew by as they rode around the city, seeing as many sights as possible. By the time they arrived at his apartment, she was practically flying on air. She was exhilarated. And exhausted.

They decided to skip the play, so Mike gave the tickets to two of his classmates. Then he ordered a stuffed pizza. When it arrived, they grabbed plates and sat on the living room floor by the coffee table to eat.

Mike watched as Corinne grabbed a piece from the box and set it onto her plate. The cheese stretched several inches before breaking. She took a bite, and her eyes grew wide. "Wow. Chicago pizza is just as good as advertised."

"Don't tell anyone, but I think I'm becoming a foodie."

Corinne laughed. "You say that as if it were a bad thing."

"It's not something I ever expected, but here it is."

As they ate, they relived the events of the day. When they couldn't eat another bite, they leaned against the front of the sofa. Mike reached out and brushed a braid from Corinne's face. Before she could think better of it, she leaned into his hand and pressed a kiss onto his palm. His skin was calloused, a remnant of his rodeo days. He dragged his finger across her bottom lip and butterflies appeared in her stomach. Her eyes immediately flew to his. His normally rich brown eyes appeared darker in their intensity.

Ever so slowly, he moved closer to her, wrapping an arm around her back. The sexual tension arced between them, pulling her undeniably nearer to him. By the time his lips were mere centimeters from hers, her heart was thudding so hard she could practically hear it.

And then his lips brushed hers. His touch was light. Teasing. Seeking. Even so, it was as powerful as dynamite, with enough power to blast through her self-control. Just as quickly as his kiss began, it ended. He leaned his forehead against hers for a moment before backing away.

"When I invited you to stay, I didn't have any expectations of you," he whispered, his warm breath on her lips.

"You told me that already."

"So you aren't feeling pressured?"

She shook her head. "Why would you ask me that?"

"Because I know there are guys who think that if they spend money on a woman, she owes them something in return. I don't think that way."

"I know that. I've always known that about you."

"Just making sure."

She cupped his cheeks and pulled his face back down to hers and murmured against his lips, "Well, now you know for sure."

The kiss went from sweet and gentle to hot and passionate in a flash. He put his arms beneath her knees and she felt herself being lifted and set on his lap. Electricity burst through her body, and she tingled all over. This must be what heaven was like.

Shivers raced down her spine and she leaned in closer to deepen the kiss. She felt the buttons on her blouse being undone one by one, and her heart began to thud in anticipation. Everything around her vanished until it was only her and Mike. He was gently easing her to the floor when his cell phone rang. He froze. It rang twice more, and he began to pull away. Unwilling to let the moment end, Corinne put her hands on his shoulders, holding him in place, and continued to kiss him.

Mike spoke against her lips. "I could do this all night, but I need to answer that."

She sighed and glanced down at herself. Her shirt was unbuttoned so she fastened it while he answered the phone. Corinne didn't want to eavesdrop, so she rose on shaky legs and scooted onto the sofa and began to scroll through her phone's gallery, studying the numerous pictures they'd taken earlier. Mike wasn't saying much but he was listening intently to whoever was speaking. He seemed to have forgotten that she was in the room. That hurt although she knew that he was doing the right thing by paying attention to the conversation.

While he talked, she took a moment to study him. His eyes, which had been dark with desire, were now a study in concentration. The playfulness was gone and he was all business. He rubbed his chin, pulling her attention to his strong jaw. Mike had always been handsome, but he'd grown even more so over the past months. He wasn't the carefree, easygoing man that he'd been before, but he hadn't become a stick-in-the-mud. This weekend had proved that he still knew how to have a good time. But he'd become more than a good time. He was serious about his studies and his dedication to medicine. Truth be told, she liked that side of his personality.

Finally the call ended. Mike stood there a moment, holding the phone in his hand as if replaying the conversation in his head.

"I take it that was good news," she said.

Mike blinked and then looked over at her, as if surprised to see her there. Yep, he'd totally forgotten about her. "You are not going to believe this. That was Dr. Nelson. He's one of my professors and one of the top orthopedic surgeons in the country. I don't know the details of what happened, but he's doing surgery tonight. He's invited me to observe. Isn't that great?"

"Now?" She asked. When they were on the verge of taking their relationship to the next level?

"Yes." Mike still appeared stunned. "I can't believe it. You have no idea what a big deal this is."

"Are you going?"

"Yes." He grabbed his jacket and shoved an arm through the sleeve. He stopped and then looked at her. "That was really rude. You're my guest. I'll call Dr. Nelson back and let him know that I won't be able to come after all."

"Don't do that. This is very important to your career. The fact that he invited you to come means that he thinks highly of you. I don't think he invited the rest of your classmates."

"He didn't. But still, I don't want to just leave you here alone."

She waved a hand, dismissing his concern. "Don't worry about it. I'll be fine. I'll just watch a little TV. Or I'll read. Whatever. I'll be okay on my own for a couple of hours."

"If you're sure," Mike said. He was shoving his other arm into his sleeve and zipping up his jacket as he spoke. His words said one thing, but his actions were saying something else entirely. For all intents and purposes, he was already out the door.

In her heart, Corinne wanted him to stay, but she knew that he would eventually resent her if she messed this up for him. Besides, she didn't want him to miss this opportunity. And if he didn't observe the surgery tonight after he said he would, his professor might think he wasn't reliable, which could negatively affect his chance of ever being asked again.

"Positive." She forced herself to sound jolly though she was anything but. "Hurry up. You don't want to miss anything."

"I won't be late," he said, charging out the door.

Corinne managed to keep her smile pasted on her face until Mike was gone. The moment the door closed behind him, she let her smile fade and she slumped back into the sofa. The night that had held such promise was now circling the toilet, as her father often said.

"You told him to go," she muttered to herself, "so don't start whining now."

Corinne grabbed the remote and turned on the television. After fifteen minutes of searching through the guide—Mike must not watch much TV because he didn't have any of the streaming services—she put down the remote. Nothing was even vaguely interesting. Besides, she didn't want to watch a movie. She wanted to be with Mike.

She grabbed the last piece of pizza from the box, and despite the fact that it was cold and she wasn't very hungry, she picked off a piece of sausage and ate it. Then she gnawed on the crust. Realizing that she was eating out of sheer boredom and not hunger, she dropped the remains of the slice back into the box, gathered up the trash and dumped it all into the garbage. After straightening up the apartment, she checked her watch. Nearly an hour had passed. She wished she would have thought to ask for a spare key so that she could go out, but it hadn't occurred to her. Clearly Mike hadn't thought of it either in his haste to get to the hospital.

She played around on her phone for a while before turning on the television again. Time passed in a blur and one boring program merged into another. She must have nodded off at some point because she found herself waking up, a crook in her neck. No sign of Mike. How long was surgery, anyway? She texted Mike and waited for a response. When none came, she decided to go to bed. She needed to hit the road in the morning to be at the rodeo on time.

Instead of going to sleep, Corinne paced back and forth for another hour, pausing several times to check her phone for a text from Mike. She'd hoped to hear from him, but clearly he wasn't going to get back in touch.

She recalled another time she'd sat around waiting for a man to get back to her. She and Rodney had planned a weekend together. But then a friend of his had come to town, and he'd cancelled their plans and left her alone, waiting for the promised call that had never come. It was almost like déjà vu.

Corinne knew the situations weren't entirely the same, but the effect was no different. Once more, she was relegated to the back burner. Out of sight out of mind. Given proof that she wasn't as important as she'd hoped. Or as Remi had put it, put on the shelf to gather dust.

Her heart ached with fear that history was repeating itself. The man was different, but she was in the same boat. Giving her heart and attention to a man who didn't want it.

She knew that Mike was sacrificing his study time to be with her, but she'd sacrificed to be with him, too. She hadn't wanted him to turn down the opportunity, but she had hoped he would at least respond to her texts.

"You're wasting your time," she muttered to herself. It didn't make sense to wait around and do nothing, so she packed her bags. She'd intended to leave early tomorrow morning, but since she was wide awake now and it didn't look like Mike would be returning any time soon, she might as well leave now.

She scribbled a note, left it on the coffee table, grabbed her bags, stepped out of his apartment, checking to be sure the door locked behind her, and left. After throwing her luggage into the trunk, she got behind the wheel and without taking a second look at Mike's apartment building, she drove away.

Mike did his best to be quiet as he crept inside his apartment. The sun was rising over the horizon, and he supposed that Corinne was still asleep. He was still excited from watching the surgery last night. It had been a rush. Naturally he hadn't been part of the surgical team. He'd actually spent his time in the background watching silently as the doctors worked. But it was as close as he'd ever been. The fact that Dr. Nelson had actually invited him to observe still amazed him. Mike had been working hard and doing his best to impress his professors. Now he was assured that his dedication hadn't gone unnoticed.

He couldn't wait to tell Corinne all about the experience. He didn't know if he was calm enough to tell her how this experience had affected him, but he would do his best. Luckily he and Corinne had developed a unique way of communicating with each other that didn't require words.

The apartment was silent. Too silent. Telling himself he was wrong, he toed out of his shoes and padded to his bedroom. The door was open, and he looked inside.

His heart dropped to the soles of his feet. The bed had been stripped, and the linen was in a laundry basket beside the closet door.

He peered inside the closet. He'd pushed his clothes to one side, making room for Corinne to hang hers. Now only his clothes remained. Corinne had shifted them evenly across the bar, leaving no sign that her clothes had ever been there. It was obvious that she was gone, but he still opened the dresser drawer to see if her clothes were there. They weren't.

"Corinne," he called, hoping against hope that she would reply. Even though he knew she had left, he was disappointed when silence was his only reply. He wandered from room to room before admitting what he'd already known.

Corinne was gone.

But why had she left? They'd had a great time from the moment she'd arrived. Especially last night. Blood pulsed through his veins as he recalled how good kissing her and holding her had felt. If that call from Dr. Nelson hadn't interrupted them, they might even have made love.

Maybe something happened to one of her sisters. He hoped not. He was grabbing his phone to call her when he noticed the piece of paper on the coffee table. Picking it up, he read the note written in Corinne's loopy penmanship.

Mike,
It was good seeing you. I need to get to the rodeo and you're focused on school. Perhaps you were right when you said we should just be friends.
Corinne

He read the message several times, hoping each time that it would make more sense than it had previously. It didn't. After reading it four times, he didn't understand any more than he had initially.

Had he done something wrong? The exhilaration that had carried him home began to dissipate until there was nothing left but loss and confusion. After the surgery, Dr. Nelson had invited him to have coffee in the cafeteria. Mike had jumped at the chance to spend even more time soaking up the surgeon's knowledge. He'd been so overjoyed and on a high from watching the surgery that despite the late hour he wouldn't have been able to sleep. It was good to be able to talk with his professor and ask questions about the procedure. Dr. Nelson had answered Mike's inquiries as well as volunteered information on why he'd made the choices he had. By the time they'd finished drinking their coffee—over an hour later—Mike's head was filled with information, and he was bursting with the possibilities that being a surgeon held.

Now he wondered if he should have skipped the coffee and come straight home. It had been late, and he'd figured Corinne had long been asleep. Now he knew that she'd been awake and waiting for him. Until she'd decided that he wasn't worth the wait.

Just how much damage had he done to their relationship? Clearly a lot if she wanted to end things before they'd started. When they'd only been friends, they hadn't spent every moment together. And he hadn't felt pressured to do so. But things were different now that they were dating. Corinne had expectations—and rightfully so. And he'd let her down.

Now Corinne wanted to go back to being just friends. Clearly she was hurt and angry by how long he'd been gone. Or perhaps she was upset that he'd gone in the first place. But if that was the case, why had she told him to go? He just didn't know.

Maybe he should have followed his first instinct and stayed friends. After all, things had been so easy back then. It had worked for both of them. The minute they'd decided to have a romantic relationship, everything had become harder. Complicated.

Even Corinne had seen the impossibility of their situation, which was why she wanted to be friends now. If he was wise, he'd take the out that she was giving him. So why was his heart aching at the thought? Why did his apartment suddenly feel so lonely and empty without her? It didn't make a lick of sense. But that didn't change things. He missed Corinne.

Despite her note, he knew that they wouldn't be able to go back to only being friends. There was no way to pretend that last night—the good and the bad—hadn't happened. For better or for worse, they'd opened Pandora's box and now had to live with the consequences.

She hadn't written a time on her letter, so he didn't know what time she'd left or how much sleep she'd gotten, if any. Was she still on the road? Was she alert enough to be driving? His head filled with all kinds of disastrous scenarios.

He grabbed his phone and turned it on. Leaving it on during surgery had been prohibited and he'd forgotten to turn it on after surgery had ended. He noticed the missed texts and his heart sank.

Corinne had tried repeatedly to contact him. Each text appeared more worried than the next, and he felt her desperation to hear from him. Her deep hurt when it appeared as if he were ignoring her.

He hit on the icon, dialing Corinne's number. As the

phone rang, he formulated the apology he needed to make. After what he'd done, it needed to be a good one. He'd invited her to spend the weekend so she could be a part of his life. He wanted to show her that there was a place for her there. Instead he'd done the opposite. He'd made her feel as if she came in a distant second behind his education. Worst of all, he'd broken his word to her. He'd promised to spend the entire weekend with her and he hadn't. He hated knowing that he'd made her think less of him.

When the phone went to voice mail, he hung up. Worry gnawed at his stomach as he imagined her car crashed on the side of the road, Corinne injured with nobody there to help her. Even though he knew that his imagination was getting the best of him, he typed out a short text.

Sorry that it took me so long to get home. Even more sorry that I missed you. Please text back to let me know you're okay.

He held his breath for several minutes. Then he received a reply.

I'm fine.

He waited, hoping more would be forthcoming, but after ten minutes and no other message, he realized that was as good as it was going to get. He typed and deleted several messages and then put down his phone.

He forced himself to face the truth. They weren't going to be friends or anything else.

Corinne was really done with him.

He sat on the couch and thought about their weekend

together. How it had felt to be with her, to laugh with her. To kiss her again. And realized that he'd made the biggest mistake of his life.

The question was, was he going to be able to do anything about it?

Chapter Seven

Corinne looked at the clock and then threw her hands into the air in triumph. She had just gotten her career-best score in calf roping. Even better, only Audrey had gotten a better score, which meant Corinne had come in second place. She was grinning from ear to ear as she rode from the arena to the stalls. She slid off her horse's back and gave Princess a pat.

"Great job," Remi said, running up with her other sisters and giving Corinne a big hug.

"Thanks." She was still shaking with excitement.

"You're having your best week," Brynn said. "It's like you're a woman possessed."

Corinne grinned. "I'm just feeling more committed to competition these days. I'm giving my all and then some."

"Does your visit with Mike have anything to do with that new attitude?" Audrey asked, a sly smile on her face. "Those Burris men know how to get a woman motivated."

Corinne thought briefly about Mike and how happy she'd been with him. That was, until he'd set her on the back burner while he went to observe a surgery. Rationally, she knew he'd done that because he wanted to get the most out of his education. It had been a good opportunity for him. But her emotional side felt like she'd come in second place. Unlike coming in behind Audrey, she wasn't thrilled to have placed behind a medical procedure.

This type of circumstance was bound to arise again in the future. She wouldn't like it then either. If it happened too often, eventually she would become resentful and bitter. Unfortunately, she didn't think she and Mike could regain the magic they'd once had. She saw that now. They had too much to lose to try again. She liked Mike too much to start disliking him.

"My performance has nothing to do with Mike. I've just been practicing harder and focusing on improving my skills. I'm not an appendage of Mike Burris if that's what you think." Those last words came out harsher than Corinne had planned.

"Whoa," Audrey said. "Calm down. I was just joking."

Corinne blew out a breath. She hadn't intended to snap at her sisters. "I know. I don't know why I overreacted like that. I should be happy with my score. I *am* happy with my score."

"You're just unhappy with the way things ended with Mike," Remi said gently.

"What went wrong?" Brynn asked. "You were so excited about going to see him."

"Nothing went wrong."

"Tell that to someone who didn't have to let you into her hotel room at the crack of dawn," Remi said. "Not that I minded. It's just that you showed up earlier than expected."

Corinne sighed. "The weekend started off so well. We went to a Caribbean restaurant, did some sightseeing and had a blast. I was so sure that we were going to make the relationship work."

"And then?"

"And then one of his professors called and invited him to observe an operation he was doing. He was out of the apartment so fast you would think his feet were on fire. I waited for hours for him to come back or at least call. I had planned to leave in the morning anyway, so I just left a few hours early. That's all."

"Have you talked to him since?"

"He texted me to see if I was okay and I texted back to let him know that I was."

"That was nearly a week ago," Audrey said.

"Well, we've both been busy," Corinne said. "And I don't want to talk about it any longer."

"And you don't have to," Remi said, wrapping a supportive arm around Corinne's shoulder. "Let's get ready for the award presentation and then hit the road. I'm ready to be back home in Bronco."

"Me, too," Corinne said.

She managed to control her emotions during the closing ceremony, somehow keeping thoughts of Mike at bay. It wasn't going to be easy, but if she and Mike were going to regain their friendship, she was going to have to stop fantasizing about him. She needed to rid herself of all romantic feelings for him. She needed to treat him the same way she treated her other male friends. She was always cordial to them and occasionally she shared a meal with them. But she didn't think about them when they weren't around. She never sat around hoping they would see each other again soon. There had to be a way to fit Mike into the friend zone. Right now, ideas eluded her, but eventually she would figure it out. Wouldn't she?

Once she'd signed the last autograph and posed for the final selfie with a young fan, Corinne changed into her street clothes. She and her sisters had planned to grab a meal before heading home, but Corinne didn't have an appetite. She hadn't had much of one for days. Nor was she in the mood to talk about love and romance, which was all her sisters wanted to discuss these days.

Not that she blamed them. Audrey was a newlywed and Brynn was madly in love. Remi was all romance all the time whether she was seeing someone or not so there was no time when she wasn't talking about love. Most of the time Corinne happily participated in the discussion. After all, she believed in love and living happily ever after with that special someone. But she was so disappointed by the state of her romantic life that even hearing about love was akin to rubbing salt in an open wound. No matter how hard she tried to downplay it, her poor heart was aching. She just wanted to go home where she could lick her wounds in private.

She begged off the late lunch, hugged her sisters goodbye, got into her car and drove away. It was hard to believe that a little over a week ago she'd been excited about seeing Mike. How quickly things had changed. If only she could go back in time and make a different choice and save herself the heartache. But what would she change?

Her decision to go from friends to more? When she'd told Mike that she wanted a romantic relationship, she'd been clearheaded. She'd actually thought that they had

Get Free Books In Just 3 Easy Steps

Are you an avid reader searching for more books?
The **Harlequin Reader Service** might be for you! We'd love to send you up to **4 free books** just for trying it out. Just write **"YES"** on the **Free Books Voucher Card** and we'll send your free books and a gift, altogether worth over $20.

Step 1: Choose your Books

Try **Harlequin® Special Edition** and get 2 books featuring comfort and strength in the support of loved ones and enjoying the journey no matter what life throws your way.

Try **Harlequin® Heartwarming™ Larger-Print** and get 2 books featuring uplifting stories where the bonds of friendship, family and community unite.

Or **TRY BOTH!**

Step 2: Return your completed Free Books Voucher Card

Step 3: Receive your books and continue reading!

Your free books are **completely free**, even the shipping! If you continue with your subscription, you can look forward to curated monthly shipments of brand-new books from your selected series, always at a discount off the cover price! Plus you can cancel any time.

Don't miss out, reply today! Over $20 FREE value.

Free Books Voucher Card

YES! I love reading, please send me more books from the series I'd like to explore and a free gift from each series I select.

More books are just 3 steps away!

Just write in "**YES**" on the dotted line below then select your series and return this Books Voucher today and we'll send your free books & a gift asap!

▶▶ _YES_ ◀◀

Choose your books:

☐ **Harlequin®
Special Edition**
235/335 CTI G297

☐ **Harlequin®
Heartwarming™
Larger-Print**
161/361 CTI G297

☐ **BOTH**
235/335 & 161/361
CTI G29A

FIRST NAME	LAST NAME

ADDRESS

APT.#	CITY

STATE/PROV.	ZIP/POSTAL CODE

EMAIL ☐ Please check this box if you would like to receive newsletters and promotional emails from Harlequin Enterprises ULC and its affiliates. You can unsubscribe anytime.

HSE/HW-1123-OM-123ST

⟠HARLEQUIN® Reader Service —**Here's how it works:**

Accepting your 2 free books and free gift (gift valued at approximately $10.00 retail) places you under no obligation to buy anything. You may keep the books and gift and return the shipping statement marked "cancel." If you do not cancel, approximately one month later we'll send you more books from the series you have chosen, and bill you at our low, subscribers-only discount price. Harlequin® Special Edition books consist of 6 books per month and cost $5.49 each in the U.S. or $6.24 each in Canada, a savings of at least 12% off the cover price. Harlequin® Heartwarming™ Larger-Print books consist of 4 books per month and cost just $6.24 each in the U.S. or $6.74 each in Canada, a savings of at least 19% off the cover price. It's quite a bargain! Shipping and handling is just 50¢ per book in the U.S. and $1.25 per book in Canada*. You may return any shipment at our expense and cancel at any time by contacting customer service — or you may continue to receive monthly shipments at our low, subscribers-only discount price plus shipping and handling.

▲ If offer card is missing write to: Harlequin Reader Service, P.O. Box 1341, Buffalo, NY 14240-8531 or visit www.ReaderService.com ▲

BUSINESS REPLY MAIL
FIRST-CLASS MAIL   PERMIT NO. 717   BUFFALO, NY

POSTAGE WILL BE PAID BY ADDRESSEE

HARLEQUIN READER SERVICE
PO BOX 1341
BUFFALO NY 14240-8571

NO POSTAGE
NECESSARY
IF MAILED
IN THE
UNITED STATES

a chance to make it work. Sure, they were in different places in their lives, but she'd thought they were the same people who'd been so close before. Now she realized the flaw in her thinking.

She and Mike weren't the same people they'd been before. At least Mike wasn't. He wasn't the same easygoing cowboy he'd been, taking life as it came. Now he was an intense medical student, focused on one thing and one thing only. She really hadn't comprehended just what that single-minded dedication entailed until she'd been sitting alone in his apartment. She didn't fault him for pursuing his dream. Nor did she blame herself for waiting so long that night for him to return. She'd had no reason to believe he wouldn't at least call or text her back.

But she would blame herself if she sat around in the future, hoping he'd make time for her. She wasn't a beggar, desperate for the crumbs of his attention. Her parents had raised her to be better than that. So although she really wanted to be with Mike, though she had dreamed for years of finding the right man, she wasn't going to act like a fool. She had her pride and she wasn't going to accept less than she deserved from any man. Even Mike Burris.

That decided, she forced herself to think about other things as she drove down the highway. Like her rodeo performance. She was proud of herself. She just wished Mike had seen it.

"Not going there," she reminded herself sharply. Since her mind was rebelling, she turned on the radio hoping the sounds of music would keep her mind occupied. She found a station playing up-tempo songs and sang along. If she didn't know the words, she made up some. Anything not to think about Mike.

Corinne breathed a sigh of relief when she pulled in front of her house. It was good to be home.

Corinne stepped inside the house and dropped her bags beside the front door. She didn't have the energy to carry them to her room now. Truthfully, she wasn't sure she could make it there herself.

Her phone rang, and her heart skipped a beat as she hoped it was Mike. It wasn't. It was her cousin, Tori.

"Hey," Tori said, after Corinne answered the phone. "How was everything?"

"It depends on which everything you mean. If you're talking about the rodeo, I had some of my best scores."

"And if I'm talking about your weekend with Mike?"

"Then the short answer is that things didn't work out." Corinne tried to keep the sorrow from her voice but failed miserably. There simply was no way to put a happy face on the disastrous way the weekend had ended. Her hopes and dreams had been dashed and lay in tatters at her feet.

"Oh no. Tell me what happened."

Corinne really wanted to lie on bed and cry her misery into her pillow, but what would that solve? Besides, Tori had always been a good listener. She might have good advice. If not, Corinne could throw herself a pity party later. After all, she wasn't going anywhere.

Taking a deep breath, Corinne summarized the weekend, going into great detail about everything so that Tori would have the complete picture. She couldn't help but smile as she described biking through the city and the stunning view of the Chicago skyline. Her knees even felt weak as she recounted how she felt standing on the Ledge and looking down at the world.

"This all sounds great. Well, not standing on a piece of

glass hundreds of feet in the air, but the rest of it sounds fun. What went wrong?"

"Mike left me alone for hours while he observed surgery. He didn't bother to call or text. So I left." Saying it out loud yet again didn't make it sound any better. She still came across as petty and small. She wanted to explain just how hurt she'd felt, how unimportant, but she was unable to make that clear.

"I understand."

"You do?"

"You went all the way to Chicago to spend time with him and he disappointed you."

"Being a doctor is important to him."

"You want to be important to him, too."

Corinne nodded even though her cousin couldn't see her and blinked back unshed tears. "Yes."

"I believe you are important to Mike. But as you said, medicine is important to him, too. Unfortunately, there will be times when he has to choose between the two of you."

"I wish he would have chosen to be with me instead of observing the surgery."

"Maybe he figured this was his only time to see the surgery, but that he has plenty of time to be with you. And since you had already spent hours together, he probably thought you would understand."

"I do understand. And I encouraged him to go. So I shouldn't be upset that he did. I just wish there hadn't been a choice to make. Especially since I ended up on the losing end."

"That's understandable. But remember, the day will come when a great opportunity arises for you and he'll be the one left waiting. The one needing to understand. You won't always get the short end of the stick."

Corinne hadn't considered that. She stiffened her spine, already tired of feeling sorry for herself. She wouldn't be hosting a pity party tonight. "How are things going with you and Bobby?"

"Everything is wonderful. Perfect even. Bobby is the best man that I've ever met in my life," Tori said, her voice filled with joy.

"It's good to see you so happy.

You deserve to be loved."

"So do you. I know that things with Mike aren't going the way you'd hoped they would, but don't give up on him just yet. I have a good feeling about you two."

Corinne mulled over her cousin's words. Tori was an optimist and even more so now that she was in love. Naturally she would believe things would work out. But experience was turning Corinne from a romantic into a realist. Looking at the situation objectively, she didn't believe she and Mike had a chance of making their relationship work in the long term. Her reaction to being left alone showed her that she didn't have the disposition to be a doctor's wife. She wouldn't be happy with broken promises and hastily changed plans. And when Mike became a surgeon, there would be times when his work would have to come first. Corinne wouldn't be happy coming in second repeatedly.

So why did she feel so miserable thinking of living a life without Mike?

"Because you're a glutton for punishment," she muttered to herself.

She ate a quick sandwich and then took a long bath. She was trying to find a way to fill the rest of the evening when her phone rang. She glanced at the screen. *Mike*. Had she somehow conjured him up by talking about him? Although she considered letting the call go to voice mail, she answered. After all, they were friends. And friends didn't ignore each other as she had been doing.

Steadying herself, she answered the call. "Hello."

"Hey, it's Mike. How are you?"

There were at least two ways to answer that question. She could lie and say that she was at the top of the world and living the dream. Or she could confess that she was hurt and confused. Neither way held much appeal, so she decided on a third. "I'm okay."

"Good to hear. How did you do at the rodeo?"

"Great." Were they really going to talk about her scores and ignore the elephant that was currently sitting in the middle of her living room?

"I'm not surprised. I knew you needed to focus in order to do your best, so I didn't call you until I knew you had competed and were at home. But now that you're home, it's the perfect time to clear the air."

She swallowed, and nerves made her sweat. Wasn't she the one who didn't want to ignore the elephant? Now suddenly she was thinking of ways she could arrange the furniture around it. "Okay. But to be honest, I think the air is already clear. We tried to have a relationship and it didn't work. The best thing for us to do is go back to being friends while we still can."

"While we still can? What does that mean?"

She hadn't intended to say that last part. It had simply slipped from between her lips. Now that it was out there, she was glad. It was senseless to beat around the bush. "We don't want to get to the point where the disappointment makes either of us bitter. I really like being your friend and I would like to keep it that way."

"I would like to be friends too. At a minimum. But I thought we agreed to give our relationship a try. That since we'd admitted that our feelings were real, we were going to explore them fully."

"All that is true. But it turns out that I'm really not good at this whole girlfriend thing. I need more attention than you can give me right now."

"Are you really making that decision based on one weekend? And not even a whole weekend? One day? We had a great Friday night and Saturday. And it would have been even better if I hadn't had the chance to observe surgery. Just so you know, this isn't something that happens a lot. In fact, it's the first time that it has happened to me or anyone else that I know. You won't have to worry about me running out on you again."

She frowned. "You're a great student. Probably at the head of your class. I'm sure your other professors are impressed with you, too. Not just by how hard you work or how smart you are, but by your character. I'm sure if there are other opportunities in the future, they'll be offered to you. And I would hate for you to feel you have to turn them down because you think that I might feel neglected."

"Is that how you felt? Neglected? Because it certainly wasn't my intention."

"I know that. I know you would never intentionally make me feel bad."

"But that's what I did."

"Yes. And I don't think that I can deal with it. I don't want to deal with it. I also don't want you to miss out on anything, and I don't want to feel like I've been left on a shelf."

There was silence for a while, and she wondered if she'd offended Mike or if he was simply thinking about what she'd said. She didn't want to hurt him, but she needed to be honest. She'd seen firsthand what happened when someone hid their true feelings from the person they were in a relationship with. She'd done it herself in the past, trying to hang onto a relationship where she'd done all of the giving. It might keep the peace for a while, but eventually resentment grew. You couldn't avoid conversations simply because they were hard.

When she was convinced that he wasn't going to reply, he finally spoke. "This is a conversation that we need to have in person. Semester break is coming up. I'll have a week off school so I'm coming back to Bronco. I know it might seem like I'm putting you on hold again, but trust me, I am not. This conversation is too important to have over the phone. I need to see your face. Is that okay with you?"

The thought of Mike returning to Bronco made her heart leap with hope and anticipation, but she squashed it. What good would having another conversation do? When it was over, their situation would still be the same. She'd still be living in Bronco and traveling on the rodeo circuit, and he would still be a medical student in Chicago. "I don't know, Mike. We gave it a try. Let's walk away while we're still friends."

"Don't give up on us now, Corinne. Unless you're trying to tell me that you only care about me as a friend. If that's true, then I'll accept that and not bug you."

"You know that's not true, Mike. You know how I feel about you."

"Then before you decide to end things, let's talk. Please."

His voice was intense. And he was practically begging, something that she didn't expect Mike to ever do. "Okay, Mike. We'll have that talk when you get to town. But I have to be honest. I don't see how things will change."

"Just keep an open mind. That's all I ask of you."

"I can do that." Because no matter how loud her rational mind objected, her aching heart wouldn't be denied.

Mike ended the call with Corinne and then blew out a relieved breath. For a few tense minutes, he'd been afraid that she wouldn't give him another chance. Their conversation drove home just badly he'd messed up by leaving her alone. Now that he had an opportunity to make it up to her, he was determined to show her just how sorry he was. More than that, he was going to prove to her that she was important to him.

The best way to do that, he figured, was to plan some special dates while he was home. Sure, they were going to talk, but it was just as important to prove to Corinne that he'd go the extra mile so he could rid her of any doubts she still harbored. There was one problem. He wasn't up to date with what was going on in Bronco.

He knew just who to call. His brothers. The four brothers loved each other and were very close friends. He pulled out his phone and began scrolling through his contacts. As they joined the call, he prepared himself for lots of good-natured teasing. He would tolerate it because Corinne was worth it. Besides, he and his brothers always gave each other a hard time. Wasn't that what brothers always did? But at the end of the day, they helped each other and he knew that they wouldn't let him down this time.

"What's up, Doc?" Ross asked, as he always did. And then laughed at his own joke. Again, as he always did.

Mike, Geoff and Jack groaned in unison. Before Mike could launch into the reason for the call, his brothers alternated between bombarding him with questions about school and telling him what he'd been missing on the circuit. After a few minutes, Mike was able to get to the purpose for his call. "I need your help. I'm coming home for a few days and I'm looking for fun things to do with Corinne."

"I don't know what you have in mind, but I suggest you don't leave her alone for hours," Jack said drily.

"You heard about that?" Mike asked.

"Of course I did. Corinne told Audrey who told me. Audrey is not happy with you. Since you aren't around, I had to hear about it. Repeatedly. You had better get your act together. Fast."

"Don't tell me that Audrey is upset with you, too. That would be too ironic." When Jack and Audrey had been dating, Jack had hurt Audrey's feelings and she'd ended things between them. Their breakup had caused friction between Corinne and Mike. It had taken a lot of effort on Mike's part to convince Corinne not to let their siblings' problem ruin their friendship.

"No. But she's very angry with you, so you need to get things straightened out with Corinne fast. Trust me, you don't want to be on Audrey's bad side."

Mike smiled, although his brothers couldn't see it. Audrey was sweet, but she was a firecracker with a strong personality. When it came to his relationship with Corinne, Mike would prefer to have his new sister-in-law on his side. The last thing he wanted was to have Audrey trying to convince Corinne that she could find a man better than him.

"That's why I called. I'm coming home specifically to spend time with Corinne. What will be going on in Bronco? Any concerts? Plays? Special events? I've been too busy with school to keep up with what's going on in town."

"Look at you, wanting to be a tourist," Geoff said, and they all laughed.

"I just want to show Corinne that she's important to me. Part of doing that is planning special dates. We had a great time doing touristy things when she visited Chicago. There's no reason why we can't do the same thing in our hometown."

"True. But explain something to me," Ross said. Although Mike couldn't see his brother's face, he heard the smirk in his voice. "Aren't you the same person who told Corinne that the two of you would be better off as friends? What changed?"

Mike huffed out a breath. He'd known one of them would call him on that. He just hadn't expected it to be Ross. "I realized that I was wrong. I know there are so many things working against us, but I think we'll both be happier in a relationship than we will be alone."

"When did this great knowledge hit you?" Jack asked. "Could it be when Mom told you that Corinne had started dating again?"

Geoff and Ross laughed, and Mike knew he would have to tell them the truth. Not that he'd planned to lie. "Not necessarily. Corinne and I agreed that I might have made a mistake when I said that."

"Might have made a mistake?" Jack guffawed and Mike momentarily wondered if he should have gotten this information some other way. Maybe he should have called his mother instead. But as much as he loved his mother, he didn't want to have a conversation with her about dating Corinne now. Not after he'd disregarded her advice in the first place. Jeanne wouldn't tell him I told you so. But then, she didn't need to say the words out loud for the sentiment to hover in the air.

"Yes. And I'm starting to feel the same way about this conversation. Maybe I should just figure this out on my own."

"Don't get all huffy," Geoff said. As the oldest, he always tried to keep the rest of them in line. Luckily, he seemed to know that Mike had reached his limit.

"Yeah. Nobody expected you to react like this," Ross said. "You're so sensitive all of a sudden."

"I know." Mike had always been so easygoing, totally unbothered by his brothers' ribbing. He was too stressed about possibly losing Corinne to find anything amusing. "It's just that Corinne means a lot to me. I don't think she knows it. So now I need to show her just how important she is to me."

"Got it." Ross cleared his throat. "So when exactly will you be home?"

"In three weeks."

"That's the Bronco Harvest Festival," Jack said without hesitation. "Audrey has been talking about it nonstop for weeks."

"That sounds good. To be honest, I had forgotten all about it," Mike said. "Now, what else?"

"Maybe you could ask Corinne," Ross said. "She might have some ideas."

"No. I want to show her that I've put a lot of thought into it. I just want her to show up and enjoy herself."

"In that case, you should check out the festival website for a list of events. Right off the top of my head, I know there's the hayride, the corn maze... What else?" Geoff's voice faded off.

"Don't forget the chili cook-off, the food truck rally and the pie-palooza," Ross said.

"Somebody's hungry," Jack said.

"You know it," Ross said, laughing. "Unlike you, I don't have a little woman cooking dinner for me."

"You'd better not let Audrey hear you call her that," Jack warned. "Not if you ever want to be invited to dinner again."

"I'm not a total fool," Ross said. "This is just us brothers talking."

"And getting off the subject," Mike pointed out.

"There's an art and jewelry show that weekend too, if I'm not mistaken," Geoff said.

"That sounds good," Mike said.

Ross volunteered a suggestion. "You can always go to the movies or to dinner. That's quaint and predictable, but still fun."

"I don't know," Mike said. "I want this time to be memorable."

"Everything doesn't have to be original to be memorable. It just has to be enjoyable," Geoff said. "It's being together that's important."

"That's true," Mike said slowly. "I guess I forgot for a minute."

"That's because you're in love," Jack teased.

"Let's not go that far." At least not yet. Mike didn't think he was in love, but he wasn't opposed to the idea. And he certainly wasn't going to tell his brothers before he told Corinne. She deserved to be the first one to hear him say the words. That was, once he was sure. Right now, he only knew that he couldn't envision his life without Corinne in it. Didn't want to. He didn't know what it meant for the future, but he was going to follow his heart this time instead of his brain. *Heart over head.* That was going to be his motto from now on.

"Then why are you jumping through all of these hoops?" Ross asked.

"Because I want Corinne to have a good time."

"That's a good enough reason for me," Geoff said. "Let me know if I can help you any other way."

"Will do."

The foursome made plans to see each other when Mike was in town and then ended the call. Mike considered all that he'd heard and began to plan for the week he was going to spend with Corinne.

He was going to sweep her off her feet.

Chapter Eight

Corinne glanced in the mirror and checked her appearance, turning from side to side to make sure she looked good from all angles. She was dressed in jeans that hugged every curve and showed off her backside to its best advantage, and a floral knit blouse that caressed her breasts. She'd taken extra care with her hair and makeup and was wearing a pair of new-to-her earrings that she'd found at a vintage shop last week. They were a bit more expensive than the jewelry she ordinarily bought, but she'd been thinking about her plans with Mike for this week and nothing could have made her leave the store without them. She was determined to look her best this week. After a last glance at her reflection, she declared herself date ready.

Telling herself to calm down, she inhaled deeply, counted to three and then slowly exhaled. She refused to get too excited over today. Or any of the other dates Mike had planned for this week. He'd asked her to clear her schedule so they could be together and she'd allowed him to persuade her to do so. She'd been invited to perform at an exhibition in New Mexico, but she'd declined after she'd spoken with Mike. Though she'd been thrilled, she'd managed to maintain an air of calm reluctance while they'd talked. She didn't want him to know that her dating life had been a dismal failure. She'd tried going out with other men, but her heart just wasn't in it. There had been a couple of first dates. None of the men had interested her enough to give them a second.

Even so, that didn't mean she and Mike belonged together. Still, she would listen to his arguments with an open mind. But she knew a few dates, no matter how enjoyable, didn't form the foundation of a solid relationship. And they certainly couldn't change the past. Even three weeks later, she could still taste the bitterness of being ignored while he did something more interesting than hang out with her.

It was indisputable that he had done the right thing for his education and career. But he'd done the wrong thing for their relationship. The conflict made one thing perfectly clear.

They were incompatible.

He would always have to choose between her and his career. She knew that she wouldn't always end up with the short end of the stick—she wouldn't even be going out with him if she believed that—but she didn't think she would win enough times to be happy. Not only that—Mike shouldn't have to choose. That would only create unnecessary stress for him. There was probably a woman out there for him who wouldn't be bothered by being put in this position.

Corinne's heart squeezed. Just thinking of Mike with another woman was awful. Jealously didn't look any better on her than it did on anyone else and she certainly didn't like the way it felt.

The doorbell rang, rescuing her from further introspection. She'd had these same arguments with herself many times and had yet to come up with an acceptable solution. Maybe there wasn't one and her and Mike's relationship was destined to die. But she couldn't give up hope. Not yet.

"Coming," she called when the bell pealed again. She grabbed her purse and raced down the stairs. She paused a moment to catch her breath and then swung open the front door.

And came face-to-face with Mike. All of the logical reasons they couldn't be together suddenly didn't seem as convincing. All of the loneliness and misery of the past weeks disappeared. Just looking at him made her heart skip a beat and it took supreme control not to melt into a puddle at his feet. Dressed casually in jeans, a plaid shirt, cowboy hat and boots, he looked like the handsome cowboy she remembered. When she realized she was gaping, Corinne snapped her mouth shut and stepped aside so he could enter. "Hi."

He smiled and then pulled her into a tight embrace. "Hi. It's good to see you."

She closed her eyes and inhaled his familiar scent, feeling the thump of his heart beneath her ear. Sighing, she basked in the pleasure. Nothing compared to being in his arms. After a few moments, he eased away. He didn't break contact entirely, but instead placed his hands on her waist and stared into her eyes. His gaze was intense.

"I missed you," she blurted out before immediately clamping her lips closed. She hadn't meant to think that, much less say it out loud. Thinking clearly was hard whenever he was around.

"I missed you, too, Corinne. More than you can imagine. But we're together now. So let's get to it."

"Are we going to talk?"

"Yes. But not now. Right now we're just going to have fun. I hope you don't mind that I set the agenda for the week."

"No. That's fine." Actually it was more than fine. It was great. She was all about spontaneity but knowing that he'd put some thought into their dates made her happy. "What are we going to do?"

"It's the first day of the Bronco Harvest Festival. I thought we could start there."

"That sounds great. I wasn't able to go last year. I heard that it's a lot of fun."

"It is. I haven't been in a while, but my parents used to take me and my brothers every year when we were kids. We entered the scarecrow-making contest, the sack races, and participated in several rodeo events. It was always a blast."

"The Hawkins Sisters are going to participate in the rodeo, of course."

"And I'll be in the front row cheering you on."

"Are you going to compete?"

He shook his head. "I'm retired. But my brothers will represent the Burris family."

She understood why he'd retired—in his place she'd have done the same thing—but she still missed seeing him on the circuit. Competing had been something they'd shared and had brought them close. Nothing in their lives had replaced that.

"Time's a-wasting," he said. "Get your jacket and let's get going."

She grabbed her leather jacket, and he immediately took it from her and then helped her to put it on. When they stepped outside, he waited for her to lock the front door before leading her to his car. The sun was shining brightly, an indication that it was going to be a beautiful fall day.

"I don't think I've ever been to a harvest festival before," she said.

"Really?"

"No. Remember, we grew up on the rodeo circuit and didn't really have a place to call home. Not like you did."

"Well, Bronco is your hometown now."

"Yes." She was pleased to agree. Although she'd never had a problem with life on the road, it had felt good to put down roots and have a place to call home. As her sisters married men who lived here and settled down, the roots would sink even deeper. Mike's roots were here, too, although he didn't seem to feel the need to remain in town. Or maybe he did. "Wouldn't it be cool if you became Bronco's doctor one day? I'm sure you would have a full waiting room."

"If I planned to be a general practitioner, I might give it some thought. But I'm going to be an orthopedic surgeon. Like I told you in Chicago, it's too soon to know where I'll ultimately practice."

"I understand." That wasn't the answer she'd been hoping for, but it was honest.

They rode in silence for the next few minutes. Traffic increased as they neared the Bronco Fairgrounds. When they were stopped at a red light, Mike looked over at her. "Corinne, could we just live in the now? I know there's so much we need to discuss and trust me when I say that we will. And I'm not avoiding your question. I truthfully don't know the answer."

"Since I don't know where I'll be in two years or what I'll be doing, that's fair."

"Thanks." He smiled and gave her hand a gentle squeeze. The simple contact made goose bumps pop up on her skin. That wasn't good. She had no idea how this thing between them would work out by the week's end. If they were going to be friends, she couldn't respond this way to his touch. She needed to be careful or her body would lead her heart down a dangerous path. She had barely managed to pull her heart back from the brink last time and get to a place of relative safety. If her heart ran free again, she wasn't sure she would be able to lasso it a second time.

And then where would she be?

"We're here," Mike said, pulling her out of her musings. And just in time. Corinne didn't want to waste time fretting. She was going to do as he suggested and live in the now. And if, at the end of the week, it was time to say goodbye? Then she would smile and wish him well and mean it.

Mike parked and they got out of the car. Corinne inhaled deeply, filling her lungs with crisp autumn air. The aroma of carnival foods reached her and her mouth began to water.

Mike took her hand in his. "I know it's early, but I need a funnel cake in the worst way."

She laughed and swung their joined hands. "I would rather have a cotton candy. Pink or blue. It doesn't matter, as long as it's gigantic."

"We can get anything we want. After all, we're grown and there's nobody around to stop us."

They made their way to the concession stand, passing food trucks advertising every kind of food imaginable. Corinne made a mental note to come back for a walking taco or corn dog. Ordinarily she did her best to maintain a healthy diet, but this was a special occasion, so the normal rules didn't apply.

She had never been one to count calories or worry about putting on a couple of pounds. She was active and always got a clean bill of health from her doctor. As long as she looked good in her jeans, she was happy, no matter her weight.

Mike and Corinne grabbed their food and continued walking around the fairgrounds. There was something about strolling along without a care in the world that soothed Corinne's soul. She was just finishing her cotton candy when they reached the games. They were lined up in two long rows with a wide walkway in between. Several rowdy kids were clustered in front of the ring toss and other popular games, so Corinne bypassed those and headed for the balloon dart game.

"I think this is a good game to start with," she said.

"Want to see who wins?" Mike asked, handing over cash to the teenager working the booth.

"What are we—Jack and Audrey?" Corinne asked with a laugh.

"No. I just thought it would add to the fun."

"I don't think that's a good idea. The disappointment might put a damper on things and we're supposed to be having fun today."

"I never took you to be the type of person who would get upset over losing a simple game. You seem to be a much better sport than that."

She laughed and poked him in his shoulder. His arm was hard and well-muscled. Impressive. "I was talking about you."

"Oh. Well, you know I can't walk away from that challenge."

"It wasn't a challenge," she denied, laughing. "It was simply a statement of fact. I have perfect twenty-twenty vision. And how hard can it be to throw a dart?"

"My vision is just as good as yours. And I've actually played darts a time or two."

"Okay. You're on. What does the winner get? Besides bragging rights, that is."

"I don't know. I'll have to think about what I want. Can I tell you later?" Mike winked.

Shaking her head, Corinne picked up one of her three darts and stared at the balloons that were fastened to a board against the far wall. Then she took aim and threw the dart. It hit a red balloon and bounced off.

"An inauspicious start," Mike said.

"Using your college boy words?"

"Just trying to impress you."

"Oh, it's going to take more than a big vocabulary to do that."

Mike lifted one corner of his lips in a devastating smile. He leaned against the table and crossed a booted foot over the other. "Just let me know what it takes, and I'll be sure to do it."

"I'll keep that in mind," she replied, wiggling her brows at him. Flirting with Mike was second nature and more fun than she dared to admit. But right now she had to focus on the game. She threw the second dart. It hit a blue balloon, bounced off and landed on the ground.

"That makes two," Mike said.

Corinne glanced at the teen boy manning the game. "Are you sure those balloons are filled with air and not something that won't pop?"

He nodded. "Yes, ma'am. Every game here is legitimate. I wouldn't work here if they were scamming people. Little kids play here after all."

"Clearly you're a man of honor," Mike said.

"Yes, I am," the boy agreed and then turned his attention back to Corinne. "Maybe you should throw the dart a little bit harder."

"Why didn't I think of that?" Corinne muttered to herself.

"Maybe it's because you don't play this game often," the kid offered. Clearly her sarcasm had been lost on him.

Corinne rolled her eyes and threw the last dart. Like the first two, it hit a balloon and bounced off.

"Now watch a pro." Mike picked up the first of his three darts, took aim, and threw it. Corinne didn't know whether it was intentional or not, but his dart hit the red balloon she'd aimed at initially. The balloon immediately popped. Mike shot a glance at her over his shoulder and then picked up the next two darts, throwing them in quick succession. Two more balloons popped.

Turning, Mike leaned his back against the table and flashed her a satisfied smile. "I guess I win."

"Congratulations," the teenager said.

Mike nodded, acknowledging the kid's statement.

Corinne looked at the smug expression on Mike's face. "Double or nothing?"

He shrugged and forked over some more cash to the kid. "I've got nothing but time."

Corinne took the three darts and inspected them.

"What are you doing?"

"Just making sure the darts work. You know, in case you and this young man are in cahoots."

The kid began to sputter indignantly. "I would never cheat anyone."

Corinne raised her hands in surrender. "Just kidding."

"Okay. As long as you were just joking."

"She was," Mike said. "She just doesn't want to acknowledge that she's not good at this."

Corinne glanced from the dart and then back at Mike. "How did you hold them?"

"It's easier to show you than to tell you." He stepped behind her and wrapped his left arm around her waist. The heat from his body scorched her, making it hard for her to focus. He took her right hand into his and adjusted her fingers.

"Like this?" she asked. Her voice sounded breathless even to her own ears.

"Exactly like that," he said, his voice husky. His mouth was near her ear and his breath stirred her hair and longing inside her.

She forced herself to nod. "I think I have it now. But maybe to be on the safe side, you should go first this game."

"Okay." He released her and went back over to the table. Instantly she missed the feel of his body pressed against hers and she longed to call him back over. But she didn't. She couldn't allow herself to be distracted.

He grabbed a dart and threw it. It missed every balloon, hitting the corkboard before falling to the ground. Shaking his head, he tossed the other two. They hit their marks, bursting two balloons.

"My turn," she said. "Now I have to break all three in order to win."

"Don't get ahead of yourself," Mike cautioned. "Concentrate on popping one."

"I think I can do better than that." She picked up the darts and tossed the first one. It burst the balloon with a loud pop. "I did it!"

"Yes, you did. Now aim and do it again." Mike

sounded so pleased you would have thought he'd been the one to burst the balloons.

Aiming, Corinne tossed the next two darts. And popped two balloons. "That's three. I win."

"Wait a minute," Mike said, suspicion drawing out his words. "Did I just get taken?"

She tried to look innocent but had a feeling she didn't quite pull it off. "What makes you ask something like that?"

"Oh, I don't know. The way you went from zero to three balloons in under sixty seconds."

"You make me sound like a car."

"Don't change the subject."

"Maybe you're just a good teacher." She couldn't hold back the giggle.

"I'm not that good."

"Don't sell yourself short."

He grabbed her waist and pulled her into his embrace. "You know how to play this game."

She placed her hands on his chest and looked up at him. "Would you believe it was beginner's luck?"

He shook his head. "Do I look that gullible?"

She gave him a quick once-over. Gullible was the last word she'd use to describe him. Sexy? Tempting? Lust-inspiring? Those words suited him much better. But she wasn't going there. "Well, in that case, yes. I know how to play this game."

Laughing, he picked her up and swung her around. "You really are something."

The world spun and she began to get dizzy. She didn't know if it was a result of being turned in rapid circles or Mike's nearness. Maybe it was a combination of the two. She put her hands on his shoulders and held on for dear life. After a few seconds, he set her on her feet, and she looked up at him. As they stared into each other's eyes, their surroundings vanished. The laughter of children faded; the aromas of the varied carnival food no longer floated on the air. Corinne and Mike were the only two people in the world.

He lowered his head and she rose on her tiptoes, meeting him halfway. Their lips were a breath apart when the teen called out to them. "Hey. Do you guys want your prizes now or do you want to play another game? There are other people waiting in line."

Mike blinked and Corinne jumped back. The spell was broken. Suddenly Corinne was aware of the worker behind the table looking at them, a quizzical expression on his face, and the children shoving each other as they battled to be first in line to play the game.

Mike glanced at Corinne, and she nodded. "I think we're done here."

"Okay. You can choose between blue, green, red and brown teddy bears." He pulled out bears the size of Corinne's hand and placed them on the table. Mike grabbed a brown one and Corinne took a red one.

"Thank you," Corinne said, and she and Mike walked away. They had taken about a dozen steps when they came upon a boy and girl of about seven years old. They were standing in front of a woman whom Corinne presumed was their mother. The children looked positively miserable, which given the candy smears on their mouths and cheeks was surprising.

"I tried, but I couldn't win," the boy said. He kicked at a rock in obvious frustration.

"I couldn't win either," the girl whined. "I wanted a bear so bad."

The woman ran a hand through her hair, and gave an exasperated sigh, clear signs that she'd heard those statements more than once. "I don't know what else to tell you. You did your best, but you didn't win. That happens sometimes."

"But, Mommy, I really wanted a bear," the girl repeated.

Mike nudged Corinne. When she glanced at him, he looked at their teddy bears. She shrugged. "One less thing to keep up with."

Mike stepped up to the woman. "Excuse me, ma'am."

She turned a harried face to him. "Yes?"

"We were wondering if you and your kids could help us out. We won these bears, but we don't want to carry them around all day. And we don't want to lose them. Would it be possible to give your kids our bears? That is, if they want them. You would really be doing us a big favor. We want to be sure they go to a good home."

"We can give them a good home," the little girl said, running over to Corinne. Her hands were outstretched as if it were a done deal.

"You have to ask your mom first," Corinne said. "We're strangers and you shouldn't take gifts from strangers."

"Can we have them, Mommy?" the girl pleaded.

"Please, Mommy," the little boy added. "They don't want the bears and we do."

"You always say we should help others," the little girl pointed out.

The woman smiled at her kids and then turned to Mike and Corinne. "If you're sure."

"We're sure," Corinne said.

"Then okay. Thank you so much."

The little girl squealed and took the red bear from Corinne, closing her eyes as she squeezed the toy against her chest. "I'm going to name you Ariel. That's my best friend's name."

The little boy played it cooler, but only slightly. He hugged the bear but didn't squeal in pleasure or give it a name.

"Thank you again," the mother said, smiling. "You just made their day."

"You're welcome," Corinne replied and then glanced at Mike. She bumped him with her hip. "Aren't you an old softie?"

He laughed. "We don't want that getting out so we'll have to stick to our story."

"Your secret is safe with me. Besides, we'll have more fun if we're unencumbered."

"What do you want to play next?"

She looked around. One game was just as good as the next. She just didn't want to stand in a long line in order to play. "How about Whack-A-Mole?"

"And oldie but goodie."

"And one that doesn't seem to appeal to today's kids."

Mike followed her to the table where the game was set up and placed some money on the table. There were two games side by side, so they were able to play simultaneously. "I'm not going to let you win this time," he said.

"You didn't let me win last time."

"Let's agree to disagree about that."

They picked up their mallets and the worker started the games. In seconds Mike and Corinne were laughing as they tried to hit the little mole that popped in and out of the holes. When the game ended, Mike had whacked the mole one more time than Corinne. He raised his arms in victory, jumping up and down like a heavyweight champion who'd just knocked out his opponent.

"Here's your prize," the teenager said, holding out a tiny stuffed turtle.

Mike shook his head. "How about you keep it and give it to a kid who doesn't win? Would that be okay?"

"Sure."

Mike and Corinne left and looked for another game with a short line. A shooting game fit the bill. After two rounds, it turned out that neither of them was able to knock over the moving ducks.

"It seems cruel to kill them anyway," Corinne said, setting down her BB gun.

"You realize that they're just pieces of metal cut in the shape of ducks and painted yellow. And the quacking is simply a recording," Mike teased.

"Of course I do. But there's a part of me that just can't stand to shoot them."

"Now who's an old softie?"

"*Young* softie."

"Okay. I'll keep that in mind. Even though we're practically the same age."

"*And?*"

"*And* you called me an old softie."

"Point made. I'm getting hungry. Do you want to head over to the food trucks and grab something to eat? My treat."

He gave her a long look before nodding. For a moment she thought he would reject her offer of paying, but when he didn't, she sighed with relief. He'd paid for her cotton candy and all of the games. She wasn't keeping an exact tally in her head, but if they were only going to be friends, she didn't want him to think he needed to pay for everything.

They kidded each other as they wandered over to the concession area. Although Corinne had been doing her best to resist Mike, she was failing spectacularly. It was easy to keep her emotional distance when they were living in two different states. But after only a few hours together, her resolve was crumbling at her feet.

She reminded herself that it was only the first day. Maybe after she'd been around him for a few days, she wouldn't feel this overwhelming pleasure she felt whenever he was near. Perhaps the novelty would wear off. Even as the thought entered her mind, she realized just how ridiculous it was. She wasn't going to get tired of being around Mike or find him unappealing. Ever. If anything, his presence was addictive. The more she was with him, the more she wanted to be with him.

As they neared the food trucks, her senses were assaulted by wonderful aromas of every kind of food. There were trucks serving everything from specialty burgers and corn dogs to smoothies and shakes. Deciding what to eat was going to be a struggle.

"Are we going to the shortest line again?"

She shook her head. "That worked well with games because we weren't looking for the most popular. We wanted the best opportunity to play as many games as we could. But it's the total opposite for food. We want something that appeals to the most people."

"What if you have a different palate? Then we wouldn't want what everyone else does."

"You're not going to give me this, are you?"

"I just never figured you as the type to follow the crowd."

"It's not so much following the crowd as it is wanting to eat what tastes good. Unless you have a preference for food."

"Not really. I could go for some rib tips. Or a walking taco. Actually, all of the food sounds good. I'm just giving you a hard time."

"Just as I suspected. Do you think any of those will have a short line?"

"Nope."

"Then I rest my case."

Although the lines were long, they were moving quickly. In under ten minutes, Mike and Corinne reached the front and gave their orders. Once they'd gotten their food, they headed for the rectangular tables that had been set up near the food trucks. They passed three before they found a table with two empty seats together. They sat across from an older couple who were enjoying barbequed turkey wings, fries and large cups of soda.

The woman smiled at Corinne and Mike. "Those ribs look good, but you don't know what you're missing." She held up the turkey wing.

"It was a tough decision," Corinne admitted.

"But she wanted to go with the longest line," Mike said drily.

The older gentleman chuckled and the rich brown skin around his eyes crinkled. "For your second helping you can always get the turkey. They're second to none."

Corinne laughed. "You read my mind."

"I'm Alexis, and this is my husband, Howard," the older woman said.

"We're Mike and Corinne."

"Are you enjoying yourselves?" Alexis asked.

"We are. We've played lots of games," Mike said.

"You must not be any good. I don't see any prizes," Howard said, and then gestured to the stack of stuffed toys beside his wife and the several plastic necklaces she wore around her neck.

"Pitiful, isn't it?" Corinne asked, with a mischievous grin. "But Mike has other great qualities."

"She's joking," Mike said, elbowing Corinne in the side.

"So you don't have great qualities?" Howard asked, grinning. Clearly he was enjoying teasing Mike.

Mike shook his head, flustered. "I do. She's joking about the games. We won some prizes and gave them to little kids."

"How generous of you," Alexis said.

Corinne nodded. "How often do you come to the festival?"

"We've come every year," Howard said.

"Howard actually proposed to me here." Alexis turned adoring eyes to her husband. He patted her hand and smiled lovingly at her. It was a beautiful sight to see.

"How long have you been married?" Mike asked.

"Three years," Howard answered.

"You're newlyweds?" Corinne said, unable to keep the surprise from her voice.

"Yes," Howard said.

"That's only part of the story," Alexis said. "And it's not even the best part."

"These young people don't want to hear all of the details," Howard protested.

"Oh, yes we do. I love a good story." Corinne wiped her mouth and hands on her napkin and then took a swallow of her drink. She looked directly at Alexis. "Tell me everything. Don't leave out a thing."

"Well, we've known each other since we were five years old," Alexis said.

"We were neighbors," Howard added.

"We lived next door to each other," Alexis continued. "Our parents were best friends. Our moms used to go shopping together and our dads went on fishing trips together. They would take us with them. We were together a lot, so it was natural that we became friends."

"Completely natural," Howard added.

"We never dated. But I had a secret crush on him."

"But she never said a word to me or anyone else." Howard shook his head. "So I kept my crush on her to myself."

"He was the best-looking boy in our class. All the girls liked him. Since I was his friend, they all asked me to set them up with him."

"Did you?" Corinne asked.

"Yes."

"Why?"

"Why not? He gave no indication that he was interested in me as anything other than a friend. Keeping other women out of his life wouldn't change that. Besides, he was my friend and I wanted him to be happy. Even if it wasn't with me."

"That was nice of you."

"Don't be fooled," Howard said. "She wasn't exactly sitting around waiting for me. She dated a lot of guys. I don't think she spent one weekend night at home all through high school. We even double-dated a couple of times. I was secretly in love with her, but I never said a word. I didn't think she was interested. After all, she kept telling me about all the girls who liked me."

"Am I telling the story or are you?" Alexis asked, looking at her husband, a faux frown marring her smooth brown skin. Her eyes twinkled with humor.

"I'm just adding a few details here and there. After all, Corinne said not to leave anything out."

"I did say that," Corinne added, amused by the older couple.

"Anyway," Alexis said, picking up the story without missing a beat, "we finished school and went our separate ways. I moved to the East Coast and Howard stayed here. We each got married in our twenties."

"And both divorced," Howard said.

"And we both divorced," Alexis repeated. "Fast-forward to our thirty-fifth high school reunion. I took one look at Howard and all the old feelings came rushing back. It was as if the years hadn't passed at all."

Howard took over from there, despite Alexis's insistence that she tell the tale on her own. Corinne was impressed by their tag-team storytelling. "We spent the entire reunion talking. And dancing. I knew it would be a mistake to let her get away from me again. We spent the rest of the weekend together."

"Although I liked Philadelphia, I had been thinking of moving back to Bronco for quite a while," Alexis said. "So when Howard invited me to spend the summer with him, I said yes."

Howard smiled. "I managed to convince her that she should spend the fall here, too. When the festival came around, I knew it was the right time to propose. I did and she said yes."

Alexis smiled contentedly. "And we're living happily ever after."

"That's the best story I have ever heard," Corinne said, grinning from ear to ear.

"I only wish that we had gotten together decades earlier," Alexis said.

"So do I," Howard added. "But at least we get to spend the rest of our lives together."

"The best years," Alexis added. "But it's nice to see a young couple like you two. Don't make the same mistake that we did and let time and distance keep you apart."

Corinne wanted to tell the older couple that she and Mike were just friends, but before she could, Alexis spoke again.

"Well, it's been nice talking to you both. We hate to eat and run, but there is a hayride in our future."

"Enjoy the rest of the day." Howard held out his hand to Mike and they shook. Then he winked. "And try to win that young lady a few stuffed animals or beads."

"I'll do my best."

Howard began gathering their paper plates, and Mike stopped him. "I'll take care of your trash."

"Thank you so much," Alexis said. She waved and took Howard's arm and the two of them walked away.

Mike and Corinne dumped the trash and then washed their hands. Mike looked at Corinne. "So, what do you think?"

"About?"

"Alexis and Howard's story."

"I think it was sweet. It's so great that they found each other again after all that time."

"You think that's sweet?"

"Don't you?"

He shook his head. "I think their story was the saddest, most depressing thing I've ever heard in my life."

Chapter Nine

Mike watched as Corinne's happy smile faded into a look of pure puzzlement.

"Sad? Why?" she asked.

Couldn't she see why? "Because they wasted so much time."

Although Corinne might not see parallels between their relationship and the older couple's, he did. Alexis and Howard had been gifted the opportunity to spend their lives together. And they'd blown it. Neither of them had taken the risk to tell the other how they'd felt. Sure, they were together now, but only after they'd squandered thirty-five years they could have spent with each other.

He and Corinne hadn't done that—they had told each other how they felt. He knew that she cared for him just as she knew he cared for her. But while she'd decided that a relationship was too challenging, he was ready to fight for them. He was going to do everything in his power to make up for disappointing her. Although he'd been the one who'd initially said they should just be friends, he realized he'd been wrong. He no longer thought it was best to wait until that elusive perfect time to have a relationship. There was no perfect time. When you found *the one*, you needed to make the necessary concessions and sacrifices to make the relationship work.

Corinne shook her head. "I don't see it that way at all. To me they went out and lived their lives. Fulfilling lives. They each had exciting adventures. And when the time was right, they met up again."

"You're assuming that they couldn't have had those same adventures and fulfilling lives if they had been together. They might have."

She shrugged. "Experiences shape us. Change us into different people. Maybe the people they were at eighteen wouldn't have been able to make a relationship last and they could have ended up hating each other now. You never know."

He started to protest when she raised a hand, stopping him. "You and I see this differently. I don't want to argue over two people who seem perfectly happy with their lives and the choices they made. Do you?"

"When you put it like that, no."

"Good, because I'm having a great time. And I would like for that to continue."

"Me too." He dropped a casual arm over her shoulder and pulled her close to him. He loved the way her body molded against his. The way her scent wafted around him, teasing his senses. "What do you want to do now?"

"I want to ride the Ferris wheel and the merry-go-round."

"Merry-go-round?"

"Yes. That is unless you're worried about motion sickness."

"You can't be serious. I'm a rodeo cowboy."

"*Retired* rodeo cowboy. How long has it been since you've been on the back of a bucking bronc? Or the back of any type of horse for that matter? Let's face it. You're a city slicker now," Corinne said, a teasing grin lighting her face.

He stepped in front of her, stopping her midstride, and put his hands on her waist. "Some things you don't forget how to do. They just come naturally."

"Is that right?" She placed a hand on his chest and leaned closer. His blood began to race. "What kinds of things are those?"

Her voice was a breathy whisper that sent his imagination into overdrive.

"Things only a cowboy knows." He leaned in slowly, inch by inch, until his lips were tantalizingly close to hers. And then he kissed her. He'd intended for the kiss to be brief. But the moment his lips touched hers, that became impossible. He was made to kiss her. And not just friendly little pecks. He needed to give her deep, soul-stirring kisses.

He slid his arms around her waist, intending to deepen the kiss, when he felt her pulling away. Immediately he released her. "I'm sorry. Did I do something wrong?"

"Not at all."

"Then what?"

"Right idea but wrong place and time."

Mike looked around and realized that Corinne was right. They were in the middle of the harvest festival. Although the little kids were too busy running around to pay attention to Mike and Corinne, and their parents were too harried to do more than shoot disapproving looks in their direction, Mike and Corinne had attracted the notice a group of teenagers who'd begun to hoot and holler. Two of them scribbled a number on the back of flyers and held them up, rating Mike's performance. At least he'd gotten tens.

Mike smiled internally as he shook his head. Corinne was right. This wasn't the time or place. "Sorry. I didn't mean to make a spectacle of myself."

"You didn't. I just think that we should let the festival be the main attraction and not us."

"Right. The only time you want to be in the spotlight is when you're winning your events."

She nodded. "So, about the merry-go-round?"

"I think I can handle it."

"If you get scared, you can hold my hand," she said, giggling.

He pretended to shiver and then grabbed her hand. "I'm scared now."

She grinned at him. "After that, I'd like to go on the hayride. That sounds like so much fun."

"Then we will. Come on, let's get this party restarted."

They rode the Ferris wheel and then the merry-go-round. They teased each other mercilessly on each ride and were weak with laughter by the time the rides were finished. They played a few more games and won a few more stuffed animals before deciding to head over to the hayride.

The line for the ride was surprisingly short and the ticket agent said that they would only need to wait ten minutes for the wagon to return.

"I can't believe more people aren't in line," Corinne said, looking around.

"I suppose this isn't as popular with the teens as the

go-karts. And I can't imagine too many parents would want to ride with little kids hopped up on sugar."

"I suppose. But it sounds like it will be a lot of fun."

"I know it will."

The tractor pulling a wagon filled with hay pulled up and a handful of middle-aged people climbed out and wandered away.

"Hop in," the driver said to Mike and Corinne. Mike helped Corinne to get inside and then jumped in behind her. There were no other people around, so the driver told them to get comfortable before going back to his seat on the tractor.

Mike and Corinne settled on one of the bales of hay arranged around the sides of the wagon, sitting close together. He inhaled and got a whiff of Corinne's sweet scent. Her flowery perfume had been tantalizing him for hours, and he allowed himself to indulge for a moment.

"This is fun," Corinne said as the wagon began rolling across the grassy field. The field had small ruts and grooves, and the wagon bumped occasionally, making Corinne knock into Mike's side. "I like the way the earth feels as if it's moving beneath us, but I don't have to worry about being bucked off."

"You aren't afraid of something like that, are you, country girl?"

She poked him in the side, and he laughed. "You know that I'm not afraid of anything."

"If I recall correctly, your knees were knocking together hard when we were standing on the Ledge. They sounded like a drum solo."

"You're exaggerating."

"Are you trying to tell me you weren't scared?"

"I might have experienced a bit of trepidation," she

said grudgingly. "But are you saying that the height didn't bother you?"

"Surprisingly, it didn't. I actually found the entire experience thrilling. I would do it again in a minute."

"I would too. I was nervous at first but once I relaxed, it was fun."

"And you don't have to worry about relaxing here and now."

"Exactly." As if to prove the point, she leaned her head against his shoulder. He heard her sigh as she exhaled and snuggled closer. This was the life.

The sun had set earlier, and the moon was high in the dark, deep blue sky. Brilliant stars were beginning to emerge, making the setting even more romantic. The temperature, which had been so pleasant earlier in the day, had dropped, lending a chill to the air. Corinne shivered, and Mike moved closer to her in an attempt to share his warmth. "Cold?"

"It's not as warm as it was earlier, but I'm not freezing."

There was a stack of blankets on a bale, so Mike grabbed one and covered their legs, tucking it around Corinne's waist. "Better?"

Corinne nodded. "My hero."

"Glad to be of service. When the ride ends, let's grab some warm apple cider. If you want, we can get something to eat."

"I would love to have one of those turkey wings that Alexis and Howard were eating. They smelled delicious."

"Then that's what we'll do. But in the meantime, I think we're supposed to sing."

She raised a curious eyebrow. "We're supposed to sing?"

"Yes."

"I never heard that rule."

"Have you been on a hayride before?"

"Well, no."

"That explains why you don't know the rules. But trust me, it's part of the whole experience."

"If this was a sleigh ride in December, I would agree. Then we would sing Christmas carols. But this is a hayride in the middle of fall. I don't know any songs that would apply. But if you know one, then by all means, let her rip."

He cleared his throat. "Mi-mi-mi."

She laughed.

"Come on," he urged. "You need to warm up your throat. Mi-mi-mi."

"You-you-you."

"Aren't you funny?"

"I'm just warming up my voice. So, what are we going to sing?"

"Do you know 'Home on the Range'?"

She rolled her eyes. "Of course I do. Do you want to sing that?"

Instead of answering, he launched into the first verse. He'd only sung the first line when she chimed in. She had a clear alto voice. It wavered a little as she started, but after a few minutes she was singing with enthusiasm.

When they got to the chorus, she put a hand on his arm. He paused and looked at her. "Don't you know this part?"

"Yes. Everyone does. That's the easy part. But after we sing the chorus, go back to the first verse."

"Why?"

"Just do it."

They sang the chorus and then he started over as

she'd suggested. Instead of joining him, she began singing an entirely different song. He stopped singing and she motioned for him to continue. When they finished the song, he looked at her. "What was that? That was a different song, but somehow it fit with mine."

"In grammar school we had this music teacher who taught us those songs. They're called partner songs."

"I have never heard of that. What's the name of that song?"

"'My Home in Montana.' A fitting song, don't you think?"

He nodded. "Two songs that are independent. Alone they sound good but together they sound even better."

"Yes."

"Just like us."

"How do you figure that?" The confused look on her face was disappointing.

"We each have our own lives and obligations. We aren't physically in the same place all the time, but even though we're doing our own things, we still make beautiful music together."

She groaned.

"I know that sounds a bit cheesy," he admitted, "but you can't deny that it's the truth. No matter how you look at it, you and I are better together than we are apart."

She smiled. "You're pretty clever. And you definitely can think on your feet."

"I'm just trying to make my point whenever and however I can."

"Message received."

"And I have another message I'd like to get across."

"Really? What is it?"

"I'm crazy about you. And since there's nobody around…" He smiled suggestively.

"Message received." She leaned closer and brushed her lips against his.

He'd told himself to go slowly, but that was impossible. Once their lips met, a fire ignited inside him so hot he was surprised flames didn't light up the night. In one quick motion, he swept her off the seat and onto his lap, not breaking contact with her lips for a second.

She opened her mouth and he swept his tongue inside. She tasted as sweet as he remembered. As he deepened the kiss, his arousal grew stronger, chasing all thoughts but one from his mind. *He needed more than just one kiss.*

He felt her pushing against his chest, and he lifted his head. Her eyes were glazed. She began fastening the clothes he didn't remember undoing.

"We're back."

He looked up. They were nearing the gate. Mike shook his head, wishing that they had more time alone. But there were other people in line, so he knew another ride alone wouldn't be happening.

"Yeah." He kept the disappointment from his voice.

"How about we get that cider and those turkey wings?"

That was quite a comedown from a passionate make out session, and definitely not how he'd hoped to spend the rest of the evening. But if he couldn't satisfy one hunger, he may as well address the other. "That sounds like a plan."

Once the tractor stopped, Mike jumped from the wagon and then placed his hands on Corinne's waist and lowered her to the ground. The night might have grown cold, but he was still hot from kissing Corinne. She smiled up at him and the fire turned into an inferno, and a bead of sweat popped out on his forehead.

One thought echoed through his mind as he held

Corinne's soft body against his: they belonged together. If they managed to work through the rough patches, they could have a future. Now he needed to convince her that they could work in harmony just as well as partner songs did.

He knew he couldn't pressure her to feel the same way. He'd never liked when people tried to force their agendas on him. Being the youngest of four brothers, he'd gotten a lot of that. He knew that Corinne would resent him if he tried to steamroll her. He just had to woo her gently and let her come to the conclusion on her own.

"Thank you so much for serenading me," the driver said as he stepped out from behind the wheel and came to stand beside them. "That has to be a first for me."

"You mean singing isn't a tradition in hayrides?" Corinne asked, glancing warily at Mike.

The driver removed his cowboy hat and then swiped his forearm across his forehead. "I've been giving hayrides for close to ten years, and this is the first time that I can recall anyone singing. Of course, I generally do the haunted hayride at Halloween. Lots of screaming on those. Now, sleigh rides, that's a different thing entirely. There's some singing there."

Corinne poked Mike in the chest. "I knew you were making that up. But you were so convincing."

Mike couldn't hold back his laughter. "You have to admit that you had fun."

"I did."

"Then I have accomplished my goal. Besides, we sounded good together."

Corinne and Mike thanked the driver for a nice ride and then stepped aside so that people who were gathering for the next hayride could climb onto the wagon.

The wind blew long and cold as they headed for the food trucks, and they picked up the pace. Once they'd gotten their food, they looked at the side-less tents that now covered the tables and chairs and then back at each other.

Corinne flipped up the collar of her jacket. "I don't know about you, but I think I'll enjoy my food a bit more with walls around me."

"I thought you were made of sturdier stuff than that."

"You've been misled." Corinne stepped in front of Mike, using his body to block the wind. "I'm the least sturdy person you'll ever meet."

"In that case we have two choices. We can eat in the car where we will be warm, our food hot, and with good music playing on the radio. But we'll have limited elbow room. Or we can drive home and reheat the food in the microwave and have plenty of space."

"I vote for the car."

"I was hoping you'd say that. This smells so good I think it would be torture to wait to have to eat it."

They speed-walked to his car. Once they were inside, Mike started the engine and turned on the heat. He held his hand up to the vent and tested the temperature. When it was warm, he turned the blowers up high. "How's that?"

Corinne placed her hands in front of the vents and rubbed them together. "That's wonderful. Thank you."

He nodded and then grabbed his turkey wing and took a bite. It was spicy and juicy and just about the best thing he'd eaten outside of his mother's cooking.

Corinne bit into her wing and then closed her eyes. He wasn't certain, but he thought he heard a slight groan. "This is so good. I should have gotten two."

"Don't be eyeing mine because I'm not sharing."

She laughed. "I suppose it's only fair that you get to enjoy yours, too."

They ate slowly so they could savor every delectable bite. Their conversation flowed freely from one topic to the next. There were very few silences, as if they were attempting to share everything that had happened while they were apart.

When only the well-cleaned bones and empty cups remained, Mike disposed of their trash. Once he was back in the car, he looked at Corinne. She smiled at him and he returned it with a smile of his own.

She was just so beautiful. He could look at her for hours and find something new to marvel over. Her clear brown skin glowed and her dark eyes sparkled. A smile was never far from her luscious lips. No matter how gorgeous her face or how sexy her body, it was her kindness and sweet spirit that was even more appealing. She spread joy to everyone wherever she went.

He didn't want to make her uncomfortable by staring at her too long, so he fastened his seat belt, put the car in gear and drove toward her house.

Corinne closed her eyes in contentment as Mike drove down the quiet street. She couldn't remember the last time she'd had this much fun. That wasn't right. She could pinpoint the exact moment. It was when she'd visited Mike in Chicago. They always had the best time when they were together. But then, having fun had never been their problem. It was the difference in their lives that was the issue.

When she'd agreed to spend the week with Mike, she'd believed that she could keep her emotional distance from him. Though it had been painful to admit, she'd come to believe that Mike had been right the first time. They would be better off as friends. At least for now. If the time was right in the future, then they would find their way back to each other, much like Alexis and Howard had done.

Now, as happiness buzzed through her, she realized she'd only been deceiving herself. The more time she spent with Mike, the stronger her feelings for him became. It wasn't just his physical appearance that drew her, although he was the sexiest man she'd ever seen. With strong shoulders, a sculpted chest, six-pack abs and muscular thighs, he was the perfect specimen of a man. Although he was no longer a professional athlete, his physique hadn't suffered. There was nothing lacking in his face either. It was strong and handsome, with eyes as sensitive and intelligent as he was.

Mike was everything that she'd ever wanted in a man. Except *around*. Sure, he was in town now and he was making a stupendous effort to spend this time with her. But when the week was over, he would go back to his life in Chicago and the status quo would resume.

Despite knowing how it would all play out, she still intended to spend every second with him that she could. That might make her a glutton for punishment—or worse—but she was determined to enjoy the here and now and let the future worry about itself.

Mike turned onto her street and then parked in front of her house.

"Would you like to come in for a nightcap?" The words were out of her mouth before she had a chance to think. It would be rude to call them back, so she sat there, holding her breath, unsure whether she wanted him to say yes or no. Although she planned to enjoy her time with Mike, she didn't want to do anything foolhardy, which could easily happen if they were alone together in a darkened house.

"I'd better not. We have to get up early tomorrow morning, and I don't want you to miss a second of your beauty sleep."

"What are you trying to say?"

The appalled look on his face was more than enough to make Corinne laugh out loud.

"I wasn't trying to say anything," Mike said. "You know I think you're the most gorgeous woman I've ever seen."

"Flattery will get you everywhere."

His eyebrows rose and he flashed her a sly smile. "Is that right?"

"Within reason," she added.

"Ah, *reason*. That horrible word is the enemy of romance."

"I like to have my romance with a splash or two of reason."

"Why? I find that romance is perfect enough on its own."

"And you think that reason detracts from it?"

"Maybe." He shrugged his massive shoulders.

"I don't know what to say to that."

"Then I guess this conversation has come to its natural conclusion."

Corinne shook her head. "I guess you're right."

They sat in the car for a moment longer, content to simply stare at each other. A car horn blew a few doors down, and the enchantment was broken. Corinne blinked and grabbed the handle to open her car door, but Mike placed a hand on her shoulder, stopping her.

"I'll get it for you."

Corinne watched as he circled the car and then

opened her door for her. He extended his hand and she took it. "You're quite the gentleman."

"When you allow me to be."

"I drive myself a lot, so I'm used to opening my own door."

"That's understandable. But I'm here now. I enjoy doing those types of things for you."

He always knew just what to say to make her heart go pitter-patter. She tried to keep herself grounded so her emotions couldn't get the best of her, but it was hard to do when Mike was being this charming. Truth be told, Mike was naturally charming. It was as much a part of him as his brown eyes or deep dimples.

Still holding hands, they walked up her stairs and into the house.

"Thank you for a great time," she said, turning on a lamp.

"I enjoyed myself just as much as you did. The company was outstanding."

Mike rubbed his palms over the front of his thighs and her eyes followed the motion. For a brief moment she thought of how good it would feel if he was caressing her instead. Corinne forced the notion away. That kind of thinking was the complete opposite of what she'd decided was best for her heart. "I suppose we should say good-night."

"If you insist."

"You're the one who said that we needed to get up early for this mystery date," she pointed out.

"So I did."

"And you're not going to give me any clues."

"No. Just be prepared to have the time of your life."

"Clothes?"

"I'm wearing some, but I suppose they can be optional."

She poked him in the chest, telling herself to ignore how good it felt. How solid and warm. "You know what I mean. What should I wear?"

"Oh. Dress warmly. Wear jeans and a sweater. And a coat."

"Okay. Then, good night, Mike."

She stared into his eyes, her heart pumping. They'd kissed before, but she was still filled with anticipation at the idea of kissing him again. Ever so slowly, he lowered his head until their lips met. The kiss was gentle, tentative and extremely powerful. Heat bloomed inside her, shooting from her head to her toes. The fire inside her grew until she was ablaze. She wrapped her arms around his neck and pressed her body against his, molding her curves against his hard muscles. Sighing, she opened her mouth to him, allowing his tongue to sweep inside. As the kiss intensified, he wrapped his arms around her waist, and the fire inside her turned into a raging inferno. She could have kissed him forever, but she knew if she didn't stop herself now, it would be impossible to stop herself later.

Their relationship was far too uncertain to become physical, so she reluctantly ended the kiss and pulled away. Mike took a step back, but he left his hands on her waist as if unwilling to let her go. He leaned his forehead against hers, and they inhaled deeply as they tried to slow their breathing.

Mike lifted his head and blew out his breath. "Wow. I guess I need to get out of here."

She nodded. "That's a good idea. I'll see you tomorrow."

Her knees wobbled as she walked beside him to the

front door. Mike brushed a quick kiss on her lips before stepping outside. Corinne leaned against the doorjamb, watching as he got into his car, letting the cold air cool down her overheated body. She watched until he'd driven out of sight before closing the door. Then she wiped a hand over her brow and leaned against the wall for support.

Her plan to keep Mike at a distance was failing spectacularly. And she wasn't a bit sorry about that.

Chapter Ten

Corinne looked at the plate of food in front of her and rubbed her hands together. She and Mike were having breakfast at the diner. "This looks so good."

"I know." Mike looked at her, his fork suspended in mid-air. "I eat here at least once whenever I'm in town."

"Why? Your mom is such a great cook."

"She is. But she and my dad have gotten into a routine of their own and I don't like to disturb that." He flashed her a mischievous grin. "Besides, I don't have to wash dishes here."

She laughed. "That's a good point."

As they tucked into their pancakes, sausage, grits, biscuits and eggs, Corinne tried to pry more information out of Mike about their upcoming day, but he wouldn't utter a word. One thing about Mike, he knew how to keep a secret. She appreciated that quality when she shared a confidence with him, but by the time they finished their substantial breakfasts, she wished he wasn't so closemouthed.

"Did you get enough to eat?" Mike asked as he ate his last bit of sausage.

"Yes." She couldn't eat another bite.

He left enough money to cover the bill on the table and they stood. He checked his watch. "We have a little while before we need to go so I thought we could check out the art and jewelry exhibition at the convention center."

"Sounds good to me. I'm always on the lookout for one-of-a-kind earrings."

"Wouldn't you prefer two-of-a-kind? You know, one for each ear?"

She laughed. "You know what I meant."

"I do." He smiled and took her hand. "Then let's get this show on the road."

They wandered around the Bronco Convention Center, looking at the most exquisite sculptures Corinne had ever seen. They'd already checked out some amazing paintings and beautiful jewelry.

"We should probably get going," Mike said after a while.

"When are you going to tell me what we're going to do?" She'd enjoyed looking at the artwork, but even as she studied the pieces that intrigued her, in the back of her mind, she'd been thinking about the surprise Mike had in store for her. With each passing moment, her curiosity grew until she was nearly bursting.

"I'm not," he said as they walked toward his car.

"What if I guess?"

"Guess all you want. I don't mind."

"But if I hit on the right thing, will you let me know?"

He shrugged, momentarily distracting her. Even

under a thick sweater and jacket, his muscled torso was still discernible. "I don't know. Maybe. But I don't think you'll guess."

"Then how do you know it's something I'll like?"

"Because you once mentioned that it was something you wanted to try."

"That doesn't narrow it down even a little bit," Corinne admitted. "I've told you a lot of my hopes and dreams."

"And I've done the same with you."

Corinne nodded. She and Mike had been in the early stages of their friendship when she'd realized how easy it was to talk to him. Before she'd known it, she'd been sharing her innermost thoughts with him and listening as he'd shared his with her. He listened without judgment and she'd found herself telling him things she hadn't even shared with her sisters.

He opened the car door for her, holding it until she was settled before he closed it. Then he circled the vehicle and got in beside her. "Get comfortable. We're going to be on the road for a couple of hours."

"Is it waterskiing?" She was joking of course. Not about wanting to go waterskiing. That was something that interested her. But the weather was not at all conducive to that.

"Oh, so close," Mike teased, grinning at her. "But no."

"Close how?"

He paused. Thinking. Finally he answered. "Our outing will involve water."

"What does that mean?"

"That's the only clue you're getting. And I shouldn't have given you that one."

"But it's so vague. It could include anything from swimming to drinking water."

"That's true."

After a moment, she realized that he wasn't going to give her another clue. "Is it rock climbing? We would need to drink water."

"Nope. You need to think outside the box."

"What box?" she asked. As they drove down the highway, she ran through a list of everything she could think of, going from the sublime to the ridiculous. After a while she gave up and turned on the radio, and they sang along to the music.

After about two and a half hours, they reached the Billings exit. Mike got off the highway and drove to the center of the city. He turned a couple of times before parking in a lot next to a plain brick building. There wasn't a sign anywhere, so that was no help. Corinne looked around. Several couples were going inside the building.

"Is this it?"

"Yes."

"What is it?"

"You'll know in a minute." They went through the same door the other couples had used. The halls and floor were marble, an indication of the building's age. They took the elevator to the third floor. When they stepped out, Mike led her down the corridor, still unwilling to give her a clue. A smile played at the corner of his lips. They reached an open door at the end of the hall and stepped inside.

"Welcome," a smiling woman said and then handed them each a white apron with black letters reading *Cooking with Andrea and Phillip.* "Feel free to hang up your coat on one of the hooks and then find your station. We'll be getting started shortly."

"Thank you," Mike said.

Corinne took the apron and then followed Mike to

the hooks and hung up her coat. She glanced at him. "We're taking a gourmet cooking class?"

"You mentioned that you wanted to learn how to cook a French meal, and I found an afternoon couple's class with availability so…" He shrugged. His voice trailed off and suddenly he looked uncertain. "I hope you're still interested."

"Interested?" She stood on her tiptoes and placed a brief kiss on his lips. Hers tingled even after she'd broken contact. "Thank you so much."

"You're welcome."

"What are we making?"

"I don't remember. There's supposed to be a card on the table along with the ingredients we'll need."

There were stations spread out across the room with a larger one in the center. Each station was equipped with a sink, counter space and a cooktop. Mike and Corinne introduced themselves to their classmates, and then found the station with their name cards. Corinne danced a happy jig in excitement. "This is going to be so much fun."

The class was being team-taught by a husband and wife. They introduced themselves as Andrea and Phillip, owners of a popular restaurant and cooking store. Two books the couple had authored would be available for purchase at the conclusion of class.

"We started this class because we love cooking and have so much fun in the kitchen together." Phillip wiggled his eyebrows suggestively, making the class laugh.

Andrea shook her head. "Pay no attention to my husband. He's not nearly as funny as he believes. But to be fair, we do have a lot of fun in the kitchen. We like to create new dishes as well as put our own spin on old favorites. We also started this class because customers wanted to learn how to make many of the dishes we serve at our restaurant. Today we're going to cook one of our most requested selections—a delectable three-course dinner. We're going to teach you the classic way of roasting chicken and making French sauces. We'll also make frisée salad with bacon lardons and mustard vinaigrette. Then we'll bid adieu to our exciting evening by creating sumptuous profiteroles with vanilla pastry cream and chocolate sauce. Sounds yummy, doesn't it?"

Corinne nodded. Actually it sounded challenging, but she was up for it.

"This is going to be so good," Mike said.

"Let's get started."

They washed their hands—the water in Mike's hint—and dried them on towels embroidered with the name of the chefs' restaurant. As they reviewed the recipe card, Phillip brought out the chickens, giving one to each of the couples. Then he returned to his station and began to discuss the chicken, describing it as if nobody had ever seen or cooked one before. But as he went into detail, Corinne realized she had plenty to learn.

After they used kitchen twine to truss the bird then put it into the oven, they moved on to the tarragon sauce. Andrea and Phillip demonstrated their technique first and then circulated, giving individual pointers to the students as they whipped up their own.

There was a lot of laughter and conversation as they worked, and after making mistakes and receiving gentle correction, the couples had a completed meal in front of them. There was a smattering of applause by the students, and Andrea and Phillip dipped their heads, acknowledging the appreciation.

Corinne shook her head as she looked at the food. "I can't believe we actually cooked this."

"I know," Mike said, grinning. "It is a lot more work than I thought it would be, and a lot more complicated, but taking it step-by-step made it easier."

"And having the necessary ingredients in the proper amount helped, too."

Andrea and Phillip passed out platters and after placing the food onto the serving dishes, the students followed them to the attached dining room. Eleven tables elegantly set for two with white table linens and expensive china were spread around the room.

Mike held Corinne's chair and then sat across from her. She placed her napkin on her lap and then looked out the window. The sun was setting and the darkening sky was streaked with orange and red. The outline of the mountains was visible in the distance. The magnificent view coupled with the flowers and candle centerpieces created the most perfect setting Corinne could imagine.

They served themselves salad and then Mike held up the carving knife and fork. "Would you like to do the honors?"

"If you don't mind." She took the knife and then began slicing it in the manner that Andrea had instructed. The breast was so tender that the knife slid straight through it. Once she had sliced several juicy pieces, she placed half on Mike's plate and then took the rest for herself.

They each sampled their food and then smiled with pleasure.

"It tastes delicious," Mike said.

"I know. Like food we would order at a restaurant."

As they ate, they talked about how much fun they had cooking, laughing as they recalled every detail. After they'd eaten their fill, they wrapped up the leftovers and placed them into the insulated bags Phillip had distributed. They thanked Andrea and Phillip for a wonderful time, then wished their classmates a good night before heading back to the car. When they were sitting inside, Corinne let out a sigh.

"Tired?" Mike asked.

"Not at all. I was just thinking. This is the best date that I've ever been on." She'd mentioned wanting to learn how to improve her cooking skills last summer. It had been a passing statement in a larger conversation, and she hadn't thought Mike had noticed. He had. And he'd remembered. More than that, he'd made it possible. How was she supposed to resist someone as thoughtful as that?

"How do you feel about making a pit stop on the way home?" Mike asked, breaking into her thoughts.

"I would love to. Any place in particular?"

"Yes."

"Is that a secret, too?"

"Not at all. I thought we could stop somewhere in ranch country and stargaze."

How romantic. "Sounds good to me."

After about forty-five minutes, Mike pulled onto a narrow rode and turned off the car. They got out and he grabbed a blanket from the trunk. After spreading the blanket on the cool grass, they lay back, their hands behind their heads, and looked at the sky.

"I missed this," Mike said.

"Missed what?"

"A sky full of stars."

"Don't they have stars in Chicago?"

"They do, but they don't look like this. There are so many lights in the city that most of the stars aren't visible."

She leaned up on one elbow and looked down at him. "I'm surprised to hear you say that."

"Why?"

"Because you seem to love that city so much. It's odd to hear you say something that is less than complimentary."

"I do love Chicago, but that doesn't mean I can't be objective about it. It's a scientific fact. Stars and lights don't mix."

Corinne wished she could be objective, too, but that feat was just beyond her ability. She had enjoyed her time in Chicago, and if she didn't have the illogical belief that the city was turning Mike's affection away from her, she would be more open-minded.

"But that's not all that I miss," Mike said. His voice was low and husky, sending shivers down her spine.

"What else do you miss?" Suddenly it was impossible to speak above a whisper.

"You, Corinne. I miss you."

Though Mike's voice was soft, it rang with unmistakable sincerity. Corinne's heart skipped a beat before beginning to thud. The blood pulsed in her veins. She went from a sense of serenity to burning with desire in the space of a breath. Ignoring the voice ordering her to keep calm and not lose focus on her plan, she leaned over and kissed him. The second their lips touched, she was swept away by longing. He wrapped his arms around her, pulling her down beside him, and deepened the kiss. Time stood still as their tongues tangled and danced.

Gradually she became aware that Mike was easing away from her and she instinctively pressed her body against his, maintaining the contact. She felt his smile against her lips as he extended the kiss. His breathing was just as labored as hers, which was incredibly satisfying. It was apparent that he was equally as affected as she'd been.

Finally, he cupped her cheek and pulled away. Though the yearning in his eyes was unmistakable, he said, "We need to slow things down. If you keep kissing me like that, I…" His voice trailed away.

He didn't need to explain. "I know." But it was hard to think logically when she was this close to him. Although they were no longer kissing, her body still hummed with unfulfilled desire. As if sensing her conflict, Mike skimmed his fingertips across her cheek and ran them over her bottom lip, leaving fire in their wake. Then, sensing she was close to losing the battle raging inside her, he removed his hand.

"I suppose we need to get going," he said. "You have to practice tomorrow. I don't want to cause you to compete at less than your best."

"I would never hear the end of it from my sisters."

He smiled. "Neither would I."

He stood slowly and then held out a hand, helping her get to her feet. Unable to stop herself, she leaned against him and inhaled deeply, filling her lungs with his familiar scent.

A cold wind blew, howling through the trees and shocking her into motion. Mike grabbed the blanket and draped it over her shoulders to keep her warm. They jogged to the car and hopped inside. Once they were on their way, she leaned back and closed her eyes as contentment swept through her.

Mike got a text notification moments before he stepped into his parents' living room. Pulling out his phone, he read it twice, not quite believing what it said.

"What's with the look on your face?" his dad asked.

Mike glanced at the screen again to be sure he hadn't imagined the words. They were still there. "I just got a text from a reporter who's making a documentary about rodeo competitors who take on additional careers. He wants me to be a part of it. He knows I'm in town, and so is he, so he wants to meet tomorrow."

"That's good, isn't it?"

"Yes."

"Then why don't you look happier?" Benjamin asked as he took a seat on the sofa.

"I don't know why he wants to interview me."

"Perhaps because you fit the bill. You're a rodeo rider and you're taking on a new career."

"That's just it. I don't fit the description. I've retired from the rodeo."

"He knows better than you the direction he wants to take. It's his documentary after all. Maybe he wants to let people know that there's life *after* rodeo. That there are a broad range of career opportunities available for cowboys. Though to be honest, I'm not sure most people would consider becoming a surgeon one of them."

"That's true," Mike said slowly, glancing down at his phone again. "I hadn't thought of it that way."

"How were you thinking of it?"

He looked up at his father and hoped his emotions weren't obvious in his eyes. "As a roundabout way to get closer to Geoff, Jack and Ross. They're the real stars in the family."

He shouldn't have doubted Benjamin's insight. "I didn't think your rodeo career mattered that much to you. I always thought it was a means to an end."

"That's true. But even so, I wanted to live up to the Burris reputation. I didn't want to do anything to bring shame on the family name."

"You didn't. I hope you know that."

"I do. But it's good to have confirmation." Benjamin Burris was a straight shooter and the most honorable man that Mike knew. If his father was proud of him, that was all Mike needed.

"How was your date?" Jeanne asked, coming into the room carrying a large bowl of popcorn.

"It was great." He'd planned to say something more neutral so that his mother wouldn't get overly excited, but the truth burst from his lips.

"I take it Corinne enjoyed the couple's cooking class."

"She did. You were right. Doing it together was fun for both of us and much better than signing her up for a class that she could take on her own." After pumping his brothers for date suggestions, he'd broken down and conferred with his mother.

Jeanne smiled. Mike knew she wouldn't say *I told you so*. But then, it wasn't necessary. One day he would learn not to doubt his mother when it came to affairs of the heart.

"So, what's on the agenda tomorrow?" Jeanne asked.

"She's getting ready for the rodeo, so we won't be seeing each other. I'll miss her but I know that her career is just as important to her as mine is to me. I respect that."

"That's because we raised you right," Jeanne said. She patted his cheek and then sat down. "We're about to watch a movie. You're welcome to join us if you want."

Mike shook his head. His mother loved romantic comedies, something Mike had yet to develop a taste for. He knew his father wasn't a fan, but Benjamin managed to sit through movie after endless movie because it made Jeanne happy.

"Thanks, but no. I don't want to intrude on your private time. Besides, I need to get ready for the interview tomorrow."

Mike bade his parents good-night and then headed for his old bedroom. He'd missed his parents and was glad for the opportunity to spend time with them. When he'd been traveling on the rodeo circuit, he had come home whenever he'd had the chance. He'd enjoyed connecting with his brothers, who'd often been competing in different rodeos. They'd spent countless days laughing and teasing each other as they caught up with their lives. The highlight of those visits had been continuing their years-long Ping-Pong tournament with their father, the undefeated champion.

But being home felt different this time. It was as if he were trying to regain a feeling and time that was gone. Trying to reclaim the past. Perhaps the interview would be helpful to him, too. Maybe it would remind him that rodeo was no longer a part of his life. Sure, he still loved it and would support his brothers and friends, but that was the extent of it.

He was looking ahead to his future now. Somehow he had to convince Corinne that she could be a part of it.

Chapter Eleven

"Relax. This won't hurt a bit. I promise," Steven Jones, the interviewer, said.

Mike heard the humor in Steven's voice and forced his shoulders to relax. He didn't know why he was so nervous. It wasn't as if he hadn't been interviewed numerous times before. But those had been with local reporters after rodeos. And his brothers had been with him on those occasions. Since Mike hadn't been the main focus, he'd managed to fade into the background. This time he was in the spotlight alone.

Not only that, the other interviews had been about his performance in various events. This interview would be about him.

Mike inhaled and then blew out the breath in an attempt to slow his heart rate. "Sorry. I don't know why I'm so tense. I've done plenty of interviews."

"So, this isn't your first rodeo?"

Mike grimaced at the bad pun.

"Sorry. You have no idea how long I've wanted to say that to someone."

"I'm glad I could be of service," Mike said with a wry smile.

"I thought the familiar location would help put you at ease."

They were meeting in a small conference room in the Bronco Convention Center. Mike was about to say that the familiarity did help when there was a knock on the open door and a woman stepped inside. She walked rapidly across the room and held out her hand for Mike to shake, which he did.

"Hi. I'm Kandy. Spelled with a *K*. I'll be doing your makeup." There was a large canvas bag slung over her shoulder. She slipped off the strap, set the bag onto the table beside Mike's chair with a loud clunk and began to rummage through it.

"My what? Why do I need makeup?" Mike looked from Kandy to Steven and then back. "I don't wear makeup."

"It's just a little bit for the camera," Kandy said. She glanced briefly at him before turning her attention back to the bag. "To make you look natural."

Makeup to make him look natural? "I already look natural. So let's not and say we did."

Kandy shook her head and pulled a big brush and a large pallet from her bag. Then she pulled out a barber's cape and draped it over his chest and shoulders. "You big strong types are all the same. Scared of a little color. Trust me, when I'm done, you'll look the best you've ever looked. And completely natural. Not even your mother will be able to tell that you're wearing makeup. Now, hold still. I'm on a tight schedule here. I've got a lot of cowboys waiting."

Mike glanced at Steven, who gave a slight nod. Resigned, Mike sighed as Kandy with a *K* went to work on his face. The brushes felt odd against his skin and he hoped like heck he didn't end up looking like a rodeo clown. After about ten minutes he wanted to call an end to the proceedings. Surely he didn't need that much makeup.

"Finished," Kandy said. She whipped a mirror from her enormous bag and handed it to him. Mike sucked in a steadying breath before looking at his reflection. If he didn't like what he saw, he was going to wash his face. There was no way he would memorialize himself looking ridiculous. He looked into the mirror.

"Well?" Kandy asked, amusement in her voice.

"I look like myself."

"Who did you think you were going to look like? Don't tell me. Bozo the Clown."

Mike chuckled. "Well, yes. But in my defense, you seemed to be putting on a lot of paint. I didn't know what to expect."

"I was blending. That's important. You're going to look great on film."

With that, Kandy sprayed something onto her brushes before shoving them and the makeup into the bag, took the mirror from Mike and added that too, and then hurried away, presumably to her next appointment.

"Ready?" Steven asked.

"As much as I'll ever be."

Steven gestured to the cameraman who'd come into the room while Mike had been getting made up. "Mike, this is Trevor, the best cameraman I know. He'll get some great shots of you. Trevor, this is Mike Burris, rodeo rider turned medical student."

Mike and Trevor exchanged nods. At Steven's signal, Trevor began filming.

"I'm Steven Jones, and I'm here with Mike Burris, youngest of the renowned Burris brothers, some of this generation's most famous rodeo stars. We're going to discuss rodeo riders who have taken jobs outside of rodeo."

Mike nodded.

"As I understand it, you've left rodeo, at least temporarily, to pursue a career in medicine. Tell me, what prompted that? I can't think of two fields that are farther apart than medicine and rodeo."

Mike laughed. "Any rodeo rider will disagree with you there. We have medical professionals at every event, although we hope to never need their services. Rodeo is great family entertainment, but it comes with risks. I can't think of one performer who isn't relieved to know that a doctor is backstage just in case he or she is needed."

"I get your point. But being a cowboy and a doctor are two very different careers."

"Absolutely."

"Why did you leave the rodeo behind and go to medical school?"

Mike felt himself relaxing as he answered. This was an easy question. "Medical school was always the plan. I've just reached the place in my life where I'm able to make the dream a reality."

"Why medical school?"

"The easy answer is that I've always liked the sciences and had a natural ability to learn them. So medical school was the best fit for me. But it's more than that. I've seen people that I love suffer from illnesses that can be cured, but who lack the resources to access quality medical care. People that I've gotten to know on the circuit who've been injured and not get the treatment that they need. Treatment that every person deserves. That's a problem. I know I can't help everyone, but I can be a part of the solution."

"Even though you were a short-timer, did you form any close relationships?"

Mike immediately thought of Corinne. No one was as close to his heart as she was. "Absolutely. I made many lifetime friends and met many people that I respect. I might not still be active in rodeo, but rodeo is now and always will be in my heart. I'll always care about rodeo and everyone involved in it."

They talked a few more minutes about the rigors of medical school and how rodeo prepared him for the amount of studying and dedication it took to be successful. At the end of their interview, they stood and shook hands.

"Thank you so much for your time. I wish you the best with your studies," Steven said.

"Thank you for including me in your documentary. To be honest, I was never a huge star like my brothers, so I'm surprised you contacted me."

Steven grinned. "Actually, your brother Geoff heard about my documentary and suggested that I reach out to you."

"Oh." Mike should have suspected something like this. Geoff was one of the most famous athletes in the world. Although he didn't rub his fame in other people's faces, he clearly wasn't opposed to using his influence to help his brothers. "I'm sorry…"

"Don't apologize. I wouldn't have agreed if I didn't think you had something worth saying. And you did. You've added a rich dimension to the documentary that no one else could."

"In that case, I'm glad my brother mentioned me."

"I'll email you a copy of your interview in the next day or so. I'm going to ask you not to share it with the press."

"Of course," Mike replied. He nodded to Trevor, and then headed down to the arena where the rodeo would be held tomorrow. The air carried odors of dirt, livestock and leather. The familiar smells brought back fond memories. It wasn't as if he didn't miss rodeo. He did. Being this close to it made him miss it even more. He knew that quitting had been the right decision. Even so, there were times when he ached to test his roping and riding skills against the best in the world. But he couldn't have it both ways.

The arena was filling up with competitors, and he stopped to talk to a few friends before going on his way.

Mike had just stepped outside when he heard someone calling his name. He smiled as his brothers approached. Although he had been home for a couple of days, his brothers had been competing out of town, and this was the first he'd seen them.

"Hey, baby brother," Geoff said, giving him a big hug.

"Welcome home," Jack said, patting his back.

"It's good to be home."

"What are you doing here? Thinking about participating this weekend?" Ross asked.

"Nah, he has too much rust on him for that," Jack said, laughing.

Mike pointed at Jack and smiled. "What he said."

"Then what are you doing here?" Jack asked. "Oh, you wanted to spend time with us."

"Always. But that's not why I'm here. I just finished doing an interview for a documentary about rodeo riders with outside jobs."

"Oh. You're going to be on TV," Jack said.

"Our baby brother is going to be famous. I suppose I should get a selfie with you now while I can get close to you," Ross joked. He pulled out his phone and then stepped beside Mike, putting his arm around Mike's shoulder.

"We want to get in, too," Jack said as he and Geoff stepped beside them. Ross handed the phone to Jack, who was on the outside. Jack snapped a few photos and then handed the phone back to Ross. "Text me a copy of those."

"Sure." Ross looked at his sleeve and then rubbed his palm across the fabric. He gave Mike an odd look. "Are you wearing makeup?"

Mike frowned and rubbed his face. "I knew I forgot something. This woman put makeup on me for the interview. She said it would look natural on the camera."

"You look better than you've ever looked," Ross said, smirking.

"That's exactly what Kandy said. I just hope I look natural."

"Stop wiping your face. You look fine," Geoff said.

"Yeah, you're almost as good-looking as me," Jack said.

Mike laughed and his brothers shoved Jack's shoulder. "Seriously, it's good to see all of you."

"How are things going with Corinne?" Geoff asked.

"So far, so good. We've spent a lot of time together. I think I'm convincing her that we belong together."

"So, Mom was right," Ross said. "Does this mean I need to rent a tuxedo again?"

"Don't get ahead of me. I'm just trying to make this week perfect. I don't want to lose my chance to be with her."

"So, fear is motivating this change of heart?" Geoff

asked. There was disappointment in his voice. "Are you afraid that Corinne will get tired of being alone, meet someone else while you're in Chicago and decide that she wants to be with him? Because that's no reason to be with her."

Was that what was behind his change of heart? Fear? "No. Maybe. I don't know. I care about Corinne."

"If you're supposed to be together, then no matter the problems you have, you'll be together," Jack said.

"And he should know," Ross said. "He did just about everything wrong with Audrey—including losing her—and somehow they ended up married."

Jack nodded in agreement.

"So, are you saying that I'm supposed to stop seeing her? Because that's not what I want at all. And neither does she."

"Good, because that's not what I'm saying," Ross replied. "We think that you should do what makes you and Corinne happy. We're your brothers and we want you to be happy."

Mike looked at his brothers. He'd always known that they'd had his back, but it was good to have confirmation. "Thanks. I know you guys have a lot to do to get ready for the rodeo tomorrow, so I'll get out of your way. I'll see you later."

His brothers gave him one last hug and then went inside. As Mike stood outside, he felt a little nostalgic for the past. He didn't like being on the outside and looking in. But then, life was filled with choices. And he'd made his.

Corinne brushed her horse and then looked down at her clothing, making sure her outfit was still pristine. She was wearing her favorite outfit, a red satin shirt with white fringe, white pants, and red boots. And, of course, her red cowgirl hat. She'd even braided a red ribbon into Princess's tail. She stepped outside the stall. She and Remi would be competing in the team roping event in a few minutes. Then Corinne would compete in barrel racing. Ordinarily she wouldn't be nervous—she'd been participating in rodeo for most of her life—but today she was jittery. Perhaps it was because she had spent so much time with Mike that she hadn't practiced as much as she should have.

And that made her angry with herself. She knew there were women who sacrificed their careers in order to help their man advance in his, and she never wanted to be one of them. She wanted to stand beside her man, not behind him. Yet somehow, she had fallen into that trap this week. True, she'd devoted a day to practice, but if Mike hadn't been here, she would have practiced several days. Instead of working on her craft in preparation for her hometown rodeo, she'd spent endless hours with Mike, walking around town, going to dinner, and just being together. Now she was worried that she wasn't at her best and that she would let down Remi in their team competitions.

"What are you frowning about?" Remi asked as she approached. The Hawkins Sisters always competed in matching outfits, so Remi was dressed identically to Corinne. Red was a great color on all of them, although Remi looked especially nice in it.

"Nothing." Remi gave her a look of disbelief, so Corinne continued. "I was just thinking about how I spent my time this week."

Remi smiled. "Lots of dates with Mike. I don't know why that would make you frown."

"I should have been practicing."

"You can practice any day. This was the only time that you and Mike could be together. To me, that's a no-brainer."

"That's because you're a hopeless romantic. You live in a world where a happy ending is lurking around every corner."

"For others. I'm not so sure there's a special someone for me." Remi's smile had faded.

Corinne immediately shoved aside her feelings—she'd examined them enough times to make herself nauseous—and put her arm around Remi's shoulders. "Of course there's someone just for you."

"I'm having a heck of a time finding him. All the men I meet turn out to be jerks."

"That's because you're so wonderful that every man wants to be with you. Even the jerks. That's why you need to weed them out before you finally meet your Prince Charming. Trust me, he's out there looking for you. No doubt he's just as frustrated as you about how long it's taking to find you."

"You're only saying that because you and your Mr. Wonderful have found each other. Or should I say Dr. Wonderful?"

"I'm not sure we're meant to be together. At least not now. That's what these past few days have been about. Finding out."

"I can't believe you actually have doubts. You've been happier this week than I've ever seen you. The only difference between now and every other week is Mike."

"I *have* been happy. That's the problem."

Remi looked puzzled. "Because you don't want to be happy?"

"No. Of course I want to be happy. But I don't want

to put my own dreams on hold in order to experience temporary happiness. That will only make me resentful and sad later."

"That's true."

"I know how committed Mike is to medical school. And he should be. He absolutely loves it. I would never want to do anything to stop him from pursuing his goals."

"What are you saying?"

Corinne shook her head. "I don't know. I love being with him. If things were different, it would be so easy to make a relationship work. But I want to pursue my goals, too. Maybe we met too soon. Or maybe we should have been content with just being friends. I just don't know."

"If you don't know, then I surely don't. But I have a feeling it's going to be clear very soon."

"If you say so."

"I do." Remi looked up at the schedule posted on the wall. "It's almost our turn so we need to get moving."

Corinne and Remi mounted their horses and then trotted out to the starting line. The bell rang, signaling the start. Remi was the header, and she took off on Butterfly, her horse. When she passed the line, Corinne kicked Princess and they went flying down the alley. Remi roped the calf around the neck and then swung it around so Corinne could rope its hind legs. Corinne swung her rope and instantly lassoed the calf. Her eyes flew to the clock. Eight seconds. That wasn't their best score, but it was good enough to put them atop the leader board. But since there were two other teams after them, including Audrey and Remi, there was no guarantee they would win the event.

"Way to go," Audrey said when Corinne and Remi returned backstage.

"Thanks. I hope the time will stand up."

"That's a good time. You should be proud of it."

Corinne nodded and mentally crossed her fingers. If they could beat Audrey and Brynn, then maybe Corinne wouldn't feel as bad about not practicing more. Remi was laughing with one of the other competitors so clearly she was happy with their time.

Corinne watched as the next team competed. The heeler didn't rope the calf, so their score wouldn't beat hers and Remi's. Corinne wished her sisters good luck and then watched as they rode out into the ring.

Audrey and Brynn were like a well-oiled machine. The years of practice and competition were evident as they worked in tandem. The roar of the crowd when they finished was all that Corinne needed to know that her sisters had beaten her time. It was only a matter of by how much.

Corinne checked the official clock. Brynn and Audrey had beaten her and Remi's score by over a second. Despite being disappointed in herself, she was happy for her sisters and she ran over to congratulate them.

"That was great," Remi was saying as she held the reins of Brynn's horse so she could dismount.

"It really was," Corinne repeated. "And coupled with your earlier scores, you guys are in first place."

"And you came in second," Audrey said. "Congratulations."

"Thanks," Corinne said. There was a time when she would have been delighted to finish right behind Brynn and Audrey. And a part of her still was. Audrey was easily one of the best rodeo riders on the circuit. She was head and shoulders above all of the women and could best many of the men. There was no shame in losing to her in any event. Even so, Corinne was beginning to question her own dedication. Sure, she'd always practiced hard and had done what she'd thought was her best. But had it been? Had she pushed her limits? Challenged herself to improve each day? Maybe she needed to develop the single-mindedness that Audrey had. The focus that Mike was showing in his studies.

She knew that natural talent played a role in success and that she didn't have the same aptitude that Audrey did. Corinne was naturally easygoing and winning had never motivated her in the same way that it animated Audrey. Audrey seemed to fear losing more than she enjoyed winning.

There was no time like the present. She had one more event today. Barrel racing wasn't her best event, but perhaps that was because she hadn't tried as hard as she should. That stopped now. She was going to put her all into today's ride. She was going to ride faster, cut the corners closer, and get the best score of her life.

She watched as other riders competed, keeping track of their scores. There were some good ones. Corinne's palms began to sweat, so she wiped them on her pants as she whispered words of affirmation to herself. She was a good cowgirl. She was fast, steady and smart. A third-generation rodeo rider. Rodeo was in her blood.

And then it was her turn. She glanced over at her sisters who smiled and nodded. She kicked Princess into action. As she sped through the alley, she urged her horse to go faster than usual.

Corinne raced toward the first of the three barrels arranged in a triangle. Princess circled it with ease and dashed for the second. Corinne's internal clock informed her that she was still behind Audrey's time.

She lowered herself over the horse and urged Princess to go even faster. They circled the second barrel and then raced toward the third. Corinne's mind was turbulent as she rode faster toward the barrel. The roar of the crowd egged her on and she went even faster still.

At the last second, she glanced into the stands and caught a glimpse of Mike. That brief distraction was all it took to break her concentration. She crashed into the barrel. The reins were ripped from her hands, and she felt herself hurtling through the air. Terror gripped her as she realized she had no control over her body. She landed on the ground with a hard thud. The wind was knocked from her lungs, and she gasped for air. Princess neighed and raised her front hooves into the air before galloping away.

A hush came over the arena as Corinne struggled to catch her breath. She tried to move and a sharp pain in her arm stopped her, and she yelped in misery.

"Be still," she heard a voice say as hands traveled over her body. *Mike.* She recognized his voice and turned her head to look at him. "Stop moving."

"I'm fine," Corinne said, but she held still. "I just hurt my arm."

"Did you hit your head?" Mike asked. Although his question was clinical, she heard the concern in his voice.

"No. I just landed really hard."

Mike must have been satisfied with what his examination revealed because he helped Corinne into a sitting position. She turned slowly and for the first time noticed the others around her. Her sisters.

"What in the world made you ride like that?" Remi said, stooping and brushing a hand over Corinne's hair. A few clumps of dirt fell onto Corinne's lap.

"I've never seen you be so reckless," Brynn said.

"I'd expect that sort of behavior from Audrey, but never from you."

"Hey, I'm right here," Audrey said. Corinne's hat had flown from her head and Audrey dusted it off and then held it out to her. "You scared me half to death."

"Sorry. I was just trying to do my best."

"Riding like a maniac is not the way to do it," Audrey said firmly.

"Is Princess okay?"

"She's fine," Remi answered. "A little nervous but she'll be okay."

"Let me through."

Corinne turned her head as the rodeo doctor pushed his way through her family. At some point Mike's brothers must have entered the ring because they had joined the small but slowly growing crowd. Everyone stepped aside at the doctor's command, making room for him. He looked at Mike, who looked right back at him, not moving from Corinne's side.

Sighing, the doctor shone a light into Corinne's eyes. "Do you know what happened?"

"She was thrown from her horse," Brynn said.

The doctor frowned and shook his head at Brynn. "I was asking *her*."

"I was racing around the barrel, trying to get a good score. One minute I was on Princess's back, the next I was soaring through the air. It turns out that I can't fly."

"Oh, you've got the flying part down. It's the landing that gave you trouble."

Corinne huffed out a laugh at the doctor's remark and then sucked in a breath. Nothing was broken, but the adrenaline rush was gone and she felt the pain in her arm. "I think I'll leave the whole process to the birds."

"That's an excellent idea."

"Can I get up now?"

"Not yet." He poked and prodded her, checking her head and ears. He listened to her heart and did a few more tests, including manipulating her arm. Once he was satisfied, he nodded. "Everything looks okay now, but I suggest that you get a more thorough checkup. And needless to say, don't even think about competing until you do."

"That was my last event."

Now that she'd been cleared, Corinne breathed a sigh of relief. Mike immediately helped her stand, keeping an arm around her waist. The audience applauded as Mike led her from the ring. He walked slowly and carefully, and it took several minutes for them to get backstage. Her sisters and Tori swarmed her, asking a million questions at once.

Corinne held up a hand, and amazingly they all stopped talking. That was something that never happened, so they must really be worried. "I'm fine. I just need to sit down."

Before the words were out of her mouth, Jack was there with a chair that he'd gotten from somewhere. He slid it behind her and she gingerly lowered herself onto the seat.

"Thank you."

"You're welcome, little sister."

Corinne couldn't help but smile. He'd begun to refer to her that way immediately after he and Audrey got married. She liked having a big brother-in-law.

Her sisters and cousin hovered for a moment, watching her every move as if she were the first person to get thrown from a horse. "I'm fine. Really. Just a little battered. Go on."

"If you're sure," Remi said.

"I am."

She must have been convincing because they slowly drifted away and returned to the arena.

The truth was, she wasn't fine. Far from it. She was embarrassed. And her ego was more than a little bit bruised. She wasn't as good as she thought she was. Clearly she needed to practice longer and harder if she was going to live up to her potential.

"How are you really?" Mike asked. He stooped in front of her and took her hands into his. His eyes were gentle.

"I feel foolish."

"Even the best athletes fall at one time or another, so there is no reason for you to feel that way."

"That's not why."

"Then why?"

"For not doing everything in my power to be the best that I can. I have to put everything else aside and give my career my undivided attention. That's the only way that I can maximize my abilities."

"You have a good work-life balance."

"I thought that too, but looking at my scores, I know that I can do better. I need to do better."

"Will that make you happy? Or is this something you think you have to do."

She shook her head and winced. "I have a bit of a headache, so I'm having a hard time following you."

"How about I drive you home? Then, if you're up to it, we can talk."

"I drove. I don't want to leave my car here."

"Give me a minute. I'll take care of getting it back to your house. Okay?"

"Okay. Thanks." One less thing for her to worry about.

Mike was gone and back in under two minutes.

Corinne stood and he was by her side immediately to help her walk. He'd parked near the entrance and within minutes they were on the way to her house. He turned the heat on high and she glanced at him.

"It's probably inevitable, but I think the heat will help you keep from getting stiff."

"Thanks. I'll take a nice hot bath when I get home."

"Also a good idea. And a heating pad might help, too."

Mike was quiet and Corinne wondered what was on his mind. She waited until they were inside her house before saying anything. "I know this isn't the way you pictured our evening going."

"It's not. And not because we aren't on our way to dinner at DJ's Deluxe, celebrating your scores. It's because you're in pain. My heart stopped when you went flying through the air. I was so afraid that you were going to land even harder than you did." He inhaled and then whispered, "You could have been killed."

Corinne heard the fear in Mike's trembling voice, and she was filled with regret. She'd taken an unnecessary risk without thinking about how people who cared about her would feel if she'd been hurt.

"I'm sorry. I didn't mean to scare you."

"I know that. To be honest, I'm worried every time you compete. I know it doesn't make sense, but there it is. I was never scared when I competed. And I wasn't scared for you before." He ran a hand over his chin and shook his head. "But that's my problem. I'll have to deal with it."

"Today was scary," she admitted. "But getting thrown was a onetime thing. Once I practice more, I'll be able to get better. And faster. I just need more focus."

"You mentioned that before."

"Yes." Clearly he didn't understand what she was saying: That she needed to take a step back from their relationship. This was not the time to try to maintain a romance. She knew she should make her position clear, but her arm hurt. The rest of her body was starting to ache, too. She didn't feel up to having a serious conversation now.

He opened his mouth as if he was going to continue the conversation. Before he could say anything, his phone pinged, stopping him. Thank goodness.

He read his text and then looked at her, a smile lighting his face. "Remember the interview for the documentary I did? Steven, the interviewer, just emailed me a link to my part."

"That's great. Can we watch it?"

He nodded. "If you feel up to it."

"I do."

They sat on the sofa and he opened his email on the laptop that was sitting on the coffee table, and then set her computer on his lap. She leaned in close so she could view the screen. His wrapped his arm around her shoulder and then moved closer. "Can you see?"

She nodded. Mike clicked a button and then he appeared on her computer. He gave a little chuckle and then stopped the video. She looked over at him. "What's wrong?"

"I don't know. It feels a bit strange to look at myself. I thought I could do it. I've watched Geoff's and Jack's interviews with no problem. Now though..." Mike shrugged, and his shoulders moved beneath her head. "Do you mind looking at it without me?"

"No." She understood. She'd watched plenty of interviews of herself with her sisters. Being one of four had put her at ease. Besides, Audrey had always been the star and most of the questions had been directed to her. Corinne had been more window dressing than anything else, which had suited her just fine.

"I'll make that tea you wanted."

"Thanks." She settled the computer on her lap and then waited until he had left the room before pushing Play. The first thing she noticed was just how photogenic Mike was. He looked so good in his blue shirt and black jeans. Although he wasn't wearing his cowboy hat or boots, it was clear from his erect posture and muscular torso that he was a rodeo star.

The view widened to show a man sitting on a stool across from him. After introducing Mike to the viewing audience, he began to ask questions. Mike listened and answered each inquiry thoughtfully and Corinne was impressed.

"The differences between rodeo and medicine are obvious but are there any similarities?" the interviewer asked.

"Believe it or not, there are," Mike replied. "In both careers, there is a time clock. Those precious seconds that make a difference in the outcome. In rodeo, it's staying on the back of a bucking bronc or bull for eight seconds. In medicine, time is often of the essence when it comes to diagnosis and treatment. Especially in a trauma. A few seconds can make a big difference between a positive outcome or a negative result. Both jobs straddle the line between life and death.

"There's a rush with rodeo. Racing the clock. Besting your competitors and the rankest bulls and broncs. Improving on your previous scores. Those things are undeniably thrilling. But the rush that comes from medicine far exceeds anything that I ever felt in rodeo. It's very gratifying to be part of the team that possesses the ability and the knowledge to help people heal. Nothing in my life has ever felt that good. The high that I got from competing pales in comparison."

Corinne's heart stopped as the full import of Mike's words hit her. The realization that he'd been right about ending their relationship all along crashed over her. What had she been thinking? A romance was not only jeopardizing her health and career, but his studies, too. There was no way they could maintain a long-distance relationship, not with the pressures of her life in the rodeo and his studies.

Maybe if they'd met each other at a different time, their relationship would stand a chance. But she didn't believe it could work in the present.

They needed to end things. Today. *Now.*

Chapter Twelve

Mike grabbed the whistling teakettle from the stove and then poured the piping hot water into a mug. He waited until the tea bag had steeped completely before stirring in two teaspoons of honey and a little lemon juice. Just the way Corinne liked it.

He drummed his fingers against his thigh as he waited for the interview to be over. He heard his and Steven's voices, but the volume was low enough to keep him from making out the words. Thank goodness. When he could no longer hear their conversation, he grabbed the mug of tea and went back into the living room. Corinne had turned off the laptop and set it on the coffee table. Her hands were folded in her lap, and she appeared to be deep in thought. Mike wasn't sure if that was good or bad.

He'd given honest answers to the questions. People would watch the documentary to gain insight into rodeo performers and to learn about him and the path he'd chosen. He would be doing a disservice to them and to Steven if he gave pat answers. Now he wondered if he had been too revealing. Maybe his answers had stunned Corinne.

Or he could be reading too much into her posture. She'd just been thrown from a horse. Her body had to be aching. That thought propelled him into the room. He was wasting time thinking of himself while Corinne needed her soothing tea.

"What did you think?" Mike asked. Corinne reached for her mug and he handed it to her. "Be careful. It's still a little hot."

"Thank you." She blew on the tea before taking a tentative sip. She smiled. "You used honey instead of sugar like I prefer. You even added the splash of lemon juice."

"Did you think I would forget?"

"You only saw me make tea once before."

They'd gone horseback riding over winter break last December. It had been a cold, dry day and Corinne had developed a sore throat. She'd told him that she sweetened her tea with honey and always put lemon juice in her tea even when she didn't have a sore throat. She just liked the taste. "And I remember the way you prefer it. I remember everything about you."

She took another sip and then looked at him. Her eyes were turbulent. Troubled. That didn't bode well at all. "You asked what I thought about your interview."

He nodded, unsure if he still wanted to know. He didn't think he had said anything wrong, but maybe he had. The last thing he wanted to do was offend her or any other rodeo riders. He respected them all immensely. He was in the middle of saying that when Corinne stopped him.

"I know all of that, Mike," she said, putting a hand

on his arm. "I thought the interview was wonderful. Illuminating. You expressed yourself so well. I think that viewers will learn a lot about rodeo and about you."

"I hope so. I want the interview to be informative."

She nodded, and a look of sorrow crossed her face. "Watching your interview made me realize that you were right about us all along."

His heart plummeted. He had a feeling where this was going but needed to be sure. "About?"

"We should just be friends. If my accident proves anything, it's how fleeting life is. How fragile the human body is. How much we need to chase after our dreams while we can. I got lucky this time. But I could really hurt myself if I lose focus a second time. And you need to be free to concentrate on your studies without the distraction of a relationship."

"You got that from the interview? If you did, Steven must have edited my answers in a way to make them fit an agenda."

"You should watch it, but not because he took anything you said out of context. It's clear how much your future in medicine means to you. And it's equally clear that you're going to be a wonderful doctor. You're going to do so much good in the world. Help so many people. I don't want to get in the way of that." She sighed and then looked directly at him. Her eyes were clear. "I'm letting you go for real this time."

He shook his head, unable to believe what he was hearing. Taking the mug from her, he set it on the table, sat beside her and took her hands into his. Her hands were small and delicate, yet he knew they were strong. Powerful. Capable of cradling his heart. And of crushing it. "It's interesting how two people can have such different reactions to the same event. You took your accident and to a lesser extent the interview as a sign that we should end our relationship."

She nodded.

"Your accident had the opposite effect on me. When I saw you get thrown from the horse and go flying through the air..." He swallowed around the lump in his throat. "You landed so hard, I nearly died of fear, Corinne. I was so afraid that you were badly hurt. Or worse. In that moment, everything became clear to me. You are my world. Nothing else matters. I can't imagine a life without you in it. I don't want to lose you. I can't lose you. Not now. Not ever."

"I just don't see a way to make it work. I need time and attention. I need to know I'm the most important thing in your life. And given the importance of your studies, that's just plain selfish on my part. And I don't want to be selfish.

"But I also need to be realistic. If we keep going on this way, we'll only end up disappointed and angry. That is the last thing I want. I always want to have good feelings for you."

He realized she hadn't understood what he'd said. He ignored the disappointment at their failure to communicate. He needed to make his position clear. "I don't think you understand just how much you mean to me. You can't because I only just realized it myself. You mean more to me than medicine. Yes, I want to be a doctor, but I want you more. You're my endgame. When I think about the future, you're by my side. And we're surrounded by kids who look exactly like you."

"What are you saying?"

Corinne's voice was a mere whisper, making it impossible for Mike to decipher the emotion behind it. Was she thrilled as he hoped, or stunned or horrified as he dreaded? Had he read her wrong? He'd thought that she was as invested in their relationship as he was. But he needed to be honest with himself. He had been running hot and cold for weeks—months even—so he couldn't blame her for being wary. It was time for him to put his cards on the table.

"I love you, Corinne." There was probably a more flowery way to express himself, but making a simple statement was the best he could do. When she only sat there, her palms pressed against her chest, he repeated himself, suffusing his words with everything he felt in his soul. "I love you."

Still, she just looked at him. The silence was unbearable, and he wondered if he'd jumped the gun. "I'm sorry. Forget I said anything. You were just in an accident. You don't need this now. The last thing I want to do is put pressure on you."

"I don't feel pressured," Corinne said, slowly.

"Then what do you feel?" The not knowing was killing him.

She smiled and her face lit up. The churning inside his stomach slowed. "I'm happy. Happy that you love me."

"Then..." He didn't want to push her, but he needed to hear her say the words.

"I love you, too. Mike, I've loved you for forever." Her smile faltered as she continued. "It's because I love you that I think we need to step apart. I don't want to be in your way. I love you enough to put you first. And by doing that, I'll be putting myself first, too. It's a win-win."

Although she'd been looking into his eyes when she said she loved him, she was looking down by the time she'd finished speaking. Very gently, he lifted her chin so that their eyes met. "I don't think you believe what you're saying. I know I don't. We need to be honest. Please, tell me what you really feel and what you really want."

"I love you, but I don't want to end up heartbroken. I don't see how a relationship can work."

"Do you want it to work?"

"More than anything. But I don't want to lose myself in the process. I don't want to sacrifice the career that I've worked for. I don't want to make unreasonable demands on you and force you to make choices you don't want to make. Choices you shouldn't have to make. I want to be fair to both of us."

"Let me worry about myself. Just think about what you want and need."

"That sounds selfish," Corinne said softly.

"It isn't." His voice was equally as soft.

"What if what we want isn't compatible?"

"What if it is?" Mike countered.

"I'm serious."

"So am I."

"What if we have insurmountable problems?"

He took her hands into his and gave them a gentle squeeze. "Nothing is insurmountable. We just have to talk. As long as we keep the lines of communication open, we'll come up with a solution that works for both of us. My parents have been married for a long time. They don't always agree, but they make it work. Sometimes my father sacrifices, sometimes my mother does."

"Who gives more?"

"I don't think they're keeping score."

"My parents are separated."

"I'm sorry about that. But I don't understand what that has to do with us."

She sighed. "I think that their relationship failure

changes the odds of our success. You saw a working relationship all of your life. I didn't. My parents didn't hang in there and fight to make their marriage work. I'm scared that I'll walk away if it gets too hard. I'm afraid that I won't know how to make it work between us."

"You can't make it work. Only *we* can. We each have to do our parts. The only real question here is this: Are you willing to try?"

Was she? Corinne had already admitted that she was in love with Mike. Although she hadn't had any successful relationships, she knew that it was possible to have one. Jack and Audrey might be newlyweds, but Corinne had seen them together often enough to know that they had what it took to go the distance. The same was true of Brynn and Garrett. And Tori and Bobby. Corinne wanted to believe that she and Mike could make it work, but she wasn't sure. Their circumstances were different. But she wanted to be with Mike. She loved him. If she was going to give her all to advance in her career, could she give any less to her relationship?

Throwing caution to the wind and ignoring her lingering doubts, she blurted out, "I'm willing to try. I want to try."

"Then let's do it. Let's try."

"Saying that is the easy part. How are we going to make it work?"

"We're going to have to keep in touch."

Her heart sank. "We've already tried that. It didn't work. Having the same plan will get us the same result."

"I'm not sure we tried our best. We may have started out strong, but that didn't last. Our lives are busy, but we can set aside time each night to talk about our days."

"Communication is key," she agreed.

"And we'll find time to be together. I'll take long weekends when I can. And on school breaks, I'll travel to wherever you are. I'll follow you around all summer. I won't be competing in rodeo, so we won't have to wait until we're actually in the same town to spend time together. I'll make sure you know you're just as important as my studies, Corinne. You're not an afterthought. You were never an afterthought."

It was just like Mike to address her biggest fear. His willingness to adjust his schedule went a long way to assuring her that she did matter to him. "That sounds like a plan. And I'll do the same. I'll coordinate my schedule to work with yours. It is a two-way street after all."

His expression changed. The stress that had been there before vanished. Now he was looking at her with intense longing. Her heart began to thud in her chest and her blood began racing. No matter how many times they'd kissed, her body still tingled with anticipation. Time stretched as he lowered his face to hers. When their lips brushed, electricity shot from their lips throughout her body, and she trembled. Closing her eyes, she gave herself over to her emotions. She sighed and snuggled closer. The warmth from his body enveloped her and she shivered.

His tongue swept inside and bliss filled her as her tongue danced and tangled with his. Never before had she felt the earth move just from a kiss, but she felt it now. Sparks ran through her body, so intense she was sure they'd burst into fireworks.

She turned to get closer to him and pain shot through her arm. She gasped and tensed.

Immediately, Mike pulled away. "I am such an idiot. I lost control and forgot that you were in pain."

"You weren't the only one who got carried away. And until the moment I turned in the wrong direction, I was feeling no pain. Quite the opposite. I've never felt so good."

"Same." He pressed a kiss against her lips and then leaned his forehead against hers. "You need to take a hot bath. I know the doctor said everything was fine and you said that you didn't hit your head, but I'm reluctant to leave you alone just in case. Why don't you take your bath and I'll wait down here for you. At least until Remi gets home."

"She should be home soon."

"I'm not in a hurry."

"If she gets back before I'm out of the tub, you won't leave without telling me, will you?"

"Of course not."

"I won't be long."

"Take as much time as you need."

Corinne nodded but she knew she wouldn't be long. Now that she and Mike had what she hoped was a workable plan, she wanted to be with him as much as possible.

She contented herself with a short bath, dressed in pink loungewear and then went back downstairs. Mike was sitting on the sofa watching television. When he heard her enter the room, he jumped up. His eyes lit up and he smiled. "That was quick."

"I decided a short bath was good enough for now."

He helped her to the sofa even though she was perfectly capable of walking there herself. Once she was sitting, he grabbed a throw from the arm of the couch and covered her with it.

"I could get used to being spoiled like this."

"Good, because that's my plan." He caressed her cheek with his fingertips. His fingers were warm and gentle, comforting and arousing at the same time.

She leaned into his chest and snuggled against him. The bath had helped with her soreness but being in Mike's arms worked wonders. "I don't think I'll move."

He laughed and his chest rumbled beneath her ear. They sat there together, letting the time stretch between them. She heard footsteps on the stairs and then the front door burst open. Remi flew inside with Brynn, Audrey and Tori close on her heels. They rushed over to her, nearly shoving Mike aside. The room filled up as Mike's brothers and Bobby Stone entered behind the women.

"Sorry to interrupt," Jack said, not looking at all sorry in Corinne's estimation. "Mike asked Audrey and me to drop off your car, Corinne. I don't know what all these other people are doing here."

"One of those 'other people' lives here," Remi said.

"You got me there," Jack said, grinning. "I meant the *other* other people."

"We would have been here earlier," Audrey said, "but there were autographs to sign and pictures to take. And of course interviews. Then Brynn thought it would be a good idea to pick up food for you. We all agreed, so we stopped by DJ's Deluxe and got something to go."

"On a busy Saturday night? How did you pull that off?" Corinne asked.

"Have you forgotten who our brother is?" Ross asked. "Geoff asked for a favor and they were more than willing to accommodate him."

"Thank you," Corinne said. "I am kind of hungry."

"We have tons of food," Brynn said. "We'll set it up in the dining room."

"I appreciate it."

"No thank-you is needed. We're sisters."

"And brothers," Geoff said.

"And cousins," Tori added.

"And a cousin's fiancé," Bobby said with a grin.

"This is getting out of hand," Corinne said, laughing. "But now that we've started, is there anyone here whose category hasn't been mentioned?"

"Yes," a woman's voice said. "I believe nobody said 'boyfriend's parents.' Or whatever it is the two of you are calling yourselves these days."

Corinne looked up as Mike's mother and father entered the room.

"The door was standing wide open," Mike's father said. "Don't worry. I closed it."

"Thank you," Corinne said.

"How are you doing?" Jeanne asked. She gave Mike a look and he slowly rose, letting her take his spot beside Corinne. Jeanne took one of Corinne's hands into hers.

"I'm doing much better. Mike made me some tea."

Jeanne beamed with pride. "His father and I raised him right."

"You certainly did." Corinne glanced up at Mike and held her free hand out to him. "Which is why we have decided to give our relationship another chance."

"Really?" Jeanne asked, looking positively pleased.

The others had been chatting to each other. With Corinne's statement, the room grew perfectly silent and everyone turned to look at Corinne and Mike. She felt all of the curious eyes on her, but she didn't feel uncomfortable with the attention. After all, this was her family. "Yes."

Mike took over from there. "We know that there are a lot of things working against us, but we also know that love makes anything possible."

"I hope you aren't trying to convince us," Brynn said.

"We've always known that the two of you belonged together."

"But—but you said…" Corinne sputtered.

Brynn shrugged. "We were just playing devil's advocate. You've always done the opposite of what you were told."

Corinne smiled. She should have known.

"We were just waiting for the two of you to catch up," Audrey said.

"Well, we have," Corinne said confidently.

"How will you make things work?" Ross asked.

"The best way we know how," Mike replied. "It will take some sacrifice, but anything worth having is worth working for."

"Hear, hear," Jack said. He grabbed a stack of plastic cups and began passing them out. Audrey was at his side, filling the cups with soda. When everyone had been served, Jack lifted his in a toast. "Here's to a long and happy relationship."

Everyone cheered and then took a swallow of their drinks.

Jeanne rose and Mike sat back down beside Corinne.

"I hope you're okay with me telling everyone about us," Corinne said to him.

"Are you kidding? Good news is meant to be shared. I was just hoping for more alone time with you."

Corinne nodded. "Me too. But I don't see that happening tonight. And you have to leave in the morning."

"True. But if we play our cards right, we'll have the rest of our lives to spend together. And I promise you, I'll do my best to make you happy and know that you're loved."

"And I promise the same."

"Then we don't have to worry. Our relationship is going to last forever."

She lifted her cup. "I'll drink to that. To forever."

Mike raised his cup. "To forever."

* * * * *

Look for the next title in the
Montana Mavericks: Lassoing Love continuity

The Maverick's Holiday Delivery
by Christy Jeffries
On sale November 2023, wherever Harlequin
books and ebooks are sold.

And don't miss

The Maverick's Surprise Son
by New York Times *bestselling*
author Christine Rimmer

A Maverick Reborn
by Melissa Senate

A Maverick for Her Mom
by USA TODAY *bestselling*
author Stella Bagwell

Available now!

Chapter One

Ian Steele leaned back in his full grain leather chair, the one he'd just dropped three grand on, and looked out at the sparkling waters of San Francisco Bay. The light in his office this time of day was soft, golden. The sun filtered in through the blinds in warm rays, making the dust particles in the air look like stars. He'd always liked San Francisco this time of year. It was almost Christmas, but it didn't necessarily feel *Christmassy*, which suited him just fine. He could almost look out the window at the sailboats bouncing over the swells and mistake it for summertime.

There was a soft knock on his door, but he didn't take his eyes off the view below. "Come in," he said evenly.

"Ian, there's a call for you on line one."

At the sound of Jill's voice, he swiveled around to see her standing with her hands clasped in front of her stomach. She always looked apologetic these days, like she didn't want to upset him. He could be an ass, but she was the consummate professional, which was why he'd hired her in the first place.

He smiled, trying his best to put her at ease. But truth be told, he'd probably have a better shot at swimming across the bay without being eaten by a shark. She had the distinct look of someone standing on broken glass.

"Who is it?" he asked.

"Stella Clarke. Says she's from Christmas Bay." She frowned. "Where's that?"

Ian stiffened. It had been years since he'd thought of that place. Maybe even longer since he'd heard anyone mention Christmas Bay. He'd cut that part of his life out as neatly as a surgeon. He was too busy now, too successful to spend much time dwelling on things like his childhood, which quite frankly didn't deserve a single minute of reflection.

"Tiny little town on the Oregon Coast." He rubbed his jaw. "What the hell does she want, anyway?"

His assistant's eyebrows rose at this. Clearly, she was taken aback. Ian was usually smooth as scotch. Unruffled by much of anything.

Clearing his throat, he leaned back in his brand-new chair. He had the ridiculous urge to loosen his tie, but resisted out of sheer willpower. "Did she say? What she wants?"

"She has a favor to ask. She said she knows you're busy but that it won't take much time."

Typical Stella. Exactly how he remembered her. He could see her standing in the living room on the day he'd arrived at the foster home, when his heart had been the heaviest, and his anger the sharpest. Wild, dark hair. Deep blue eyes. Even at fourteen years old, she'd been a force to be reckoned with. Even with all she'd probably endured. Just like him. Just like all of them. She'd been whip-smart, direct, always trying to negotiate something for her benefit.

But he couldn't exactly talk. Now he made a living out of negotiating things for his own benefit. A very nice living, as a matter of fact. As one of the Bay Area's top real estate developers, he'd been snatching up prime property for years, building on it and then selling it for loads of cash. He had people standing in line to do his bidding. The question was, what was this favor she was talking about? And how much time would it actually take?

He looked at his Apple Watch, the cool metal band glinting in the sunlight. Almost noon. He had a meeting across town at two thirty, and he hadn't eaten yet. He could have Jill take her number, and he could call her back. Or not. But for some damn reason, he was curious about what she wanted. And whether he'd admit it or not, he was itching to hear her voice again. A voice that would now be seasoned by age, but would no doubt still be as soft as velvet. He hadn't talked to her since he'd graduated from Portland State. They'd run into each other at a swanky restaurant in the city where she'd been a server. They'd awkwardly met for coffee after the place closed, and it hadn't gone well. At all.

"Thanks, Jill," he said. "I'll take it. Have a good lunch."

She smoothed her hands down the front of her cream-colored pencil skirt. "Do you want me to bring you something back?"

He smiled again. "No. Thank you, though. Why don't you take an extra half hour? Get some time outside if you can. You've been working hard this morning, and the weather's nice. Enjoy it."

"Are you sure?"

"Positive. Go."

She reached for the door and pulled it closed behind her.

He looked down at the blinking button on the sleek black phone and felt his heart beat in time with it.

Picking it up, he stabbed the button with his index finger.

"Ian Steele," he said in a clipped tone.

"Ian? It's Stella Clarke. From Christmas Bay..."

He let out an even breath he hadn't realized he'd been holding. He'd been right. Her voice was still soft as velvet.

"Stella."

He waited, imagining what she might look like on the other end of the line. Wondering if that voice matched the rest of her. If she was that different than she'd been ten years ago. Because back then, the last time he'd seen her, she'd been very beautiful, and very pissed.

At least, she'd been pissed with him.

There was a long pause, and she cleared her throat. "How have you been?" she asked.

She was obviously trying to be polite, but he didn't give a crap about that right about now. He had things to do, and opening a window into the past was definitely not one of them.

"What do you want, Stella?"

"Well, it's nice to talk to you, too."

"I know you didn't call for a trip down memory lane."

"I took a chance that you might care about what's happening here," she said evenly. "Even if it's just a little."

"Why would I care about Christmas Bay?" He had no idea if that sounded convincing or not. Because he thought there might be an edge to his voice that said he did care, just the tiniest bit. Even if it was just being curious as to why she was calling after all this time. Curiosity he could live with. Caring, he couldn't. At least not about that Podunk little town.

"Because you have memories here, Ian."

He shook his head. *Unbelievable.* Of course she'd assume his memories at France's house were good ones. Worth keeping, if only in the corner of his mind.

The thing was though, she was actually right. Not that he'd ever admit it. There were some good memories. Of course there were. Of Stella, whom he'd always gravitated towards, despite her sometimes-prickly ways. She was a survivor, and he'd admired that. She was a leader and a nurturer, and he'd admired that, too. He'd seen in her things he wished he'd seen in himself growing up. Things he'd had to teach himself as he'd gotten older, or at least fake.

And there were other memories that weren't so terrible. Memories of Frances. Of his aunt. And snippets of things, soft things, that he'd practically let slip away over the years, because they'd been intermingled with the bad stuff, and tarnished by time.

He gripped the phone tighter, until he felt it grow slick with perspiration. Those decent memories were the only reason he hadn't hung up on her by now. Those, and his ever-present curiosity.

"What do you want, Stella?" he repeated.

And this time, the question was sincere.

"I can't believe I just did that," Stella muttered under her breath.

Sinking down in her favorite chair in the sunroom, she looked over at Frances, who was wearing another one of her bedazzled Christmas sweaters. Her fat black-and-white cat was curled up on her lap, purring like someone with a snoring problem.

"Uh-oh," Frances said, stroking Beauregard's head. "What?"

Stella worried her bottom lip with her teeth, and gazed out the window to the Pacific Ocean. It was misty today. Cold. But still stunningly beautiful—the ocean a deep, churning blue gray below the dramatic cliffs where the house hovered. One of the loveliest houses in Christmas Bay. But of course, she was biased.

She'd moved in when she was a preteen and brand new to the foster system. At the time, she'd thought Frances's two-hundred-year-old Victorian was the only good thing about her unbelievably crappy situation. After all, it was rumored to be haunted, and how cool was that? But she'd also been a girl at the time, and incredibly naive. She had no way of knowing that Frances herself would end up being the best thing about her situation. Frances and the girls who became not only her foster sisters, but her sisters of the heart. Getting to live in the house had been a bonus.

Now, as the thought of selling it crept back in, along with the thought of Frances's Alzheimer's diagnosis, which had changed things dramatically over the last few years, Stella felt a lump rise in her throat.

Swallowing it back down again, she forced a smile. This was going to be hard enough on her foster mother without her falling apart. Selling was the right thing to do. They just had to find the right buyer, that was all. Frances's only caveat was that a family needed to live here. A family who would love it as much as her own family had. As much as all of her foster kids had over the years.

"I asked someone for a favor," she said. "And now I'm wishing I hadn't."

"Why?"

She took a deep breath. "Since *Coastal Monthly* is doing that Christmas article on the house, I thought it would be a great time to kill two birds with one stone. Drum up some interest from potential buyers, and get the locals to stop telling that old ghost story."

Frances leaned forward, eliciting a grunt from Beauregard. "What do you mean? How in the world would you do that?"

It had been a long time. Almost fifteen years. Frances might have Alzheimer's, but her long-term memory was just fine. Stella wasn't sure how she'd react to this next piece of information. Maybe she'd be okay with it. But maybe not.

She braced herself, hoping for the former. "I called Ian Steele..."

Her foster mother's blue eyes widened. She sat there for minute, and Stella could hear the grandfather clock in the living room ticking off the seconds.

"Wow," Frances finally muttered. "Just...wow."

"I know."

"How did you find him?"

"I googled him and he came right up. He's this big shot real estate developer in San Francisco."

Frances sucked in a breath. "You don't think he'd want to buy the house, do you?"

"No way. He hates Christmas Bay, remember?" Still, Stella couldn't shake the fact that he'd seemed to perk up when she said the property was for sale. He'd asked several specific questions, the real estate kind, until her guard had shot up, leaving her uneasy.

"It's been a long time, honey. People change."

She shook her head. "Not Ian."

"Then why call him?"

"Because I thought if he gave the magazine a quick interview over the phone, it could help when the house goes on the market. You want a legitimate buyer, not some ghost hunters who will turn it into a tourist trap. You know people around here still talk about that silly story, and he's the only one who can put it to rest."

Frances looked skeptical. "But would he want to?"

"I'd hope so after what he put you through while he was here. Including making up that story in the first place and spreading it around. It's been years. I'd assumed he'd matured enough to at least feel a little bad about it"

Frances was quiet at that. She'd always defended Ian when he'd been defiant. He'd had this innate charm that seemed to sway most of the adults around him, but Stella had been able to see right through him. Maybe because she'd come from a similar background. Abuse, neglect. Nobody was going to pull the wool over her eyes, not even a boy as cute as Ian.

Suddenly looking wistful, maybe even a little regretful, Frances gazed out the window. The mist was beginning to burn off, and the sun was trying its best to poke through the steely clouds overhead. Even in the winter, Frances's yard was beautiful. Emerald green, and surrounded by golden Scotch broom that stretched all the way to the edge of the cliffs of Cape Longing. As a girl, Stella thought it looked like something out of *Wuthering Heights*. As a woman, she understood how special the property really was. And how valuable.

She truly hadn't believed Ian would be interested in the house, or she wouldn't have called him. It wasn't the kind of real estate he seemed to be making so much money on in the city, at least according to the internet. He and his business partner bought properties and built apartment buildings and housing developments on them, and the Cape Longing land was smaller than what they were probably used to. But after talking to him, even for just those few painful minutes, Stella knew he was more calculating than she'd given him credit for. If he smelled a good deal, even if it was in Christmas Bay, he might just follow his nose. Which was the *last* thing Frances needed.

"So, what did he say?" her foster mother asked. "Will he do the interview?"

"He wouldn't say. I never should've called him. I could just kick myself."

"At least you got to talk to him again."

Stella bit her tongue. *Yeah, at least.*

"Did he say how he was?" Frances asked hopefully. She was so sweet. And it made Stella indignant for her all over again. She'd loved and cared for Ian like he was her own, seeing something special in him, even under all the surliness and anger. She'd told him that often, but it didn't matter. He'd made his time with her miserable, and had ended up running away. He'd disappeared for days, worrying Frances sick, and ultimately breaking her heart when he was sent to live with a great-aunt instead.

Stella had a hunch it was *because* of the love Frances had shown him, not in spite of it. If Ian sensed anyone getting close, he ran. He was a runner. She'd be willing to bet he'd run all these years, and had ended up in San Francisco, still the same old Ian. Just older. And maybe a little more jaded, if that was possible.

Stella liked to think that despite their similar background, one that had helped her understand him better than most people might, she'd turned out softer, more approachable. And she credited Frances for that. Maybe if Ian had stayed put, he might've had his rough edges smoothed out some, too.

She smiled at her foster mother, determined not to say what she was thinking. Determined to show some grace, at least for the time being. "We didn't get that far," she said. "I guess he had a meeting or something."

Frances nodded. "So, he's done well for himself?"

If his website was any indication, he was doing more than well.

"He seems to be."

"I wish things had turned out differently," Frances said. "I wish I could've reached him."

"It wasn't because you didn't try, Frances. We all did."

"But maybe if we'd tried harder…"

Frowning, Stella leaned forward and put a hand over Frances's. Her foster mother smelled good this morning. Like perfume and sugar cookies. She was in her early sixties, and was a beautiful, vital woman. Nobody would ever guess that she struggled with her memory as much as she did. So much so that her three foster daughters had moved back home to help her navigate this next chapter of her life.

In the corner of the sunroom, one of the house's two Christmas trees glittered. The decorations were ocean themed, of course. The blue lights glowed through the room like a lighthouse beacon. Christmas cards from previous foster children, now long grown, were strung around one of the double-paned windows. The old Victorian came alive over the holidays, and its warmth and coziness was one of the reasons Stella loved it so much. She knew it would be heartbreaking to sell it. Frances was right to want a family living here. Somehow, it softened the blow.

"You were the best thing to happen to us," Stella said quietly. "I'm just sorry he couldn't see that."

Frances smiled, but it looked like she was far away. Lost in her memories.

Stella scratched Beauregard behind his ears, before leaning back again with a sigh. Lost in some of hers.

Ian shifted the Porsche into second. This was the first time he'd driven it in the mountains, and not surprisingly, it hugged the hairpin turns like a dream. If he was in the mood, he'd be driving faster. After all, why own a German-engineered sports car if you weren't going to break the speed limit every now and then? But he wasn't in the mood. And getting to Christmas Bay any faster wasn't exactly tempting.

Gritting his teeth, he glanced out the window to the ocean on his left. Then at the GPS to his right. He'd be there in less than half an hour. Plenty of time to wonder about this decision. Yeah, the Cape Longing property might be the deal of a lifetime (*if* he could convince Frances to sell to him), but was it worth stepping foot back inside the little town he'd left so long ago? He wasn't so sure.

Which brought him back to Frances again. And to Stella. Ian could smooth talk anyone. Anyone having second thoughts, or experiencing cold feet, was putty in his hands after about five minutes. Less, over drinks. But true to form, Stella had been immune to everything he'd thrown at her over the phone. The conversation had turned stilted in *less* than five minutes, which he wasn't used to.

Thinking about it now, he bristled. She'd always been

different than the rest of the kids he'd known in the system. Foster kids were usually wise, but she was wiser.
They were tough, but she was tougher. They had walls,
but Stella had barricades. He'd never been able to scale
them, and then he'd just stopped trying. He didn't need
anyone, anyway. Not Frances O'Hara, not Kyla or Marley, and sure as hell not Stella. So, he'd done anything
and everything in his power to test them. He'd stolen,
lied, smoked, drank. You name it, he'd done it. And
for the cherry on the crapcake, he'd come up with that
dumbass story about the ghost, knowing what a headache it would be for Frances. Knowing how it would get
around and eventually stick in a town that was known
for every kind of story sticking. Especially the bad kind.

But now, he had a chance to rectify it. That's what
Stella had said. *Rectify.* Like he owed them something
by talking to *Coastal Monthly* for their fluffy Christmas piece. *It's not like it matters,* he'd said evenly. *These
days, a story like that only helps sell houses.*

And that's when she'd told him that Frances wanted
a family living there. Someone who would love it as
much as she did.

When he'd hung up, he'd gotten an idea. Why *not* do
the interview?

He'd tracked down the lady writing the article, and
she'd practically begged him to come up to Christmas
Bay so she could take pictures. And if he got a good
look at the property in person, through the eyes of a
real estate developer, well, then... What could it hurt?
Other than shocking the hell out of Stella, who'd asked
him to talk to the magazine but definitely would *not*
expect him to do it in person. No way would she have
wanted to open up that can of worms. She'd suspect a
deeper motivation, and she'd be right.

In the beginning, money had been the driving force. Of course it had. But as he made his way up Highway 101, his Porsche winding along the cliffs overlooking the ocean, he had to admit there was another reason he was doing this. For once, it had nothing to do with money and everything to do with wanting to see Stella again. Just so she could see what he'd become. Just so he could flaunt it in her pretty face.

He downshifted again and glanced over at the water. It sparkled nearly as far as the eye could see. It was deep blue today, turquoise where the waves met the beach. The evergreens only added to the incredible palate of colors, standing tall and noble against the bluebird sky.

It had been so long since Ian had been up this way that he'd almost forgotten how beautiful it was. Easy, because the Bay Area was beautiful, too. But in a different way. There were so many people down there that sometimes it was hard to look past all the buildings and cars to see the nature beyond. On the Oregon Coast, the people were sparse. So sparse that it wasn't unusual to go to the beach and not see anyone at all. The weather had something to do with that—it was usually cold. But the scenery? The scenery was some of the most spectacular in the world, and Ian had been a lot of places.

Swallowing hard, he passed a sign on his right. Christmas Bay, Ten Miles. Ten miles, and he'd be back in the town where he'd been the most miserable, the loneliest and most confused of his entire life. But also, where he'd caught a glimpse of what love could look like if he'd only let it in. But he hadn't let it in. In the end, he hadn't known how. And he'd been too pissed at the world to try, anyway.

There was absolutely no other reason, other than

maybe a little spite, that he wanted to come back here again. No reason at all.

That's what he kept telling himself as the trees opened up, and Christmas Bay finally came into view.

Stella opened up the front door to see a woman in trendy glasses standing on the stoop. She looked the part of a journalist. Her hair was in a messy bun, and she had a camera bag slung over one shoulder. It was a beautiful day, perfect for pictures, but it was cold, and she was dressed appropriately for a December day on the Oregon Coast—rain boots and a thick cardigan.

When she saw Stella, she smiled wide. But her gaze immediately settled on the entryway behind her. It was obvious she couldn't wait to get a look inside.

"Hi, there," she said, holding out a hand. "Gwen Todd. And you must be Stella?"

Stella shook it. "I'm so glad the weather cooperated."

"Oh, I know. I thought it was going to pour. We got lucky."

"Please come in," Stella said. "Frances has some coffee brewing."

Gwen stepped past her and into the foyer. Before Stella could turn around, she heard the other woman gasp. She couldn't blame her. The house was incredible. Three stories of stunning Victorian charm. Gleaming hardwood floors, antique lamps that cast a warm, yellow glow throughout. A winding staircase that you immediately wanted to climb, just to see what treasures waited at the top. A widow's walk on the third floor that looked out over the cliffs, where Ian said he'd seen a ghost all those years ago. A coastal cliché that the entire town had latched on to, but that her family would finally shake free of today. At least, Stella hoped they would. It was just an article—it wasn't going to go viral or anything. But for the locals, for someone most likely to buy this house and live happily in it, it would be a start.

Gwen Todd ran her hand along the staircase's glossy banister. "Oh, it's just lovely. I've always wanted to see inside."

Stella had heard that more times than she could count. From certain places in town, you could see the house, perched high above Cape Longing, its distinctive yellow paint peeking like the sun through the gaps in the trees. It had been built when Christmas Bay was just a tiny logging settlement, and Frances's grandparents had had to get their supplies by boat, because the mountain roads were impassible by wagon in the winter and spring. As the town had grown, the house had become a fixture, near and far. It even had its own display in the local maritime museum—the fuzzy, black-and-white pictures taking people back to a time when the West was still fairly wild.

And Gwen Todd was clearly a fan. Shaking her head, she looked around, enthralled.

Stella smiled. She understood how Gwen felt, because that was exactly how she'd felt as a girl, walking through the doors of this place for the first time. In absolute wonder and awe. For a kid who'd gone from surviving on ramen noodles in a broken-down trailer on the outskirts of town, to this? It had been almost too good to be true. For the first six months of her new life with Frances, Stella had expected someone to come and take her away at any moment. Or worse, for her mother to get her back. She'd had nightmares about being deposited back into that cruelty and filth. Into that never-ending cycle of neglect and abuse. It wasn't until after the first full year that she'd begun to trust her good fortune. That she'd been able to start opening her heart again. Cautiously, and just a little at a time.

Now, standing here, those days seemed so far away, they were just as fuzzy as the pictures in the museum down the road. But other times, they were clear as a bell, and those were the days that tended to hit her the hardest. When the pain and memories were too sharp to take a full breath. Thank God for Frances. Otherwise, there was no telling where she would've ended up. Or *how* she would've ended up. She hadn't spoken to her biological parents in years. She simply had nothing to say to them.

Gwen looked at her watch, just as Frances walked in holding out a reindeer mug full of steaming coffee. This time of year, Frances served all her drinks in Christmas mugs. She was proud of her collection.

"Oh, thanks so much," Gwen said. "This will help wake me up before Mr. Steele gets here."

Stella froze. Frances froze, too.

"I'm sorry," Stella managed. "What?"

"Mr. Steele. He's supposed to be here at eleven, but I think he might be running late…"

Stella stared at Frances, who sank down in a chair by the staircase. She looked pale.

"Oh…" Gwen set her coffee cup down. "Oh, no. I thought I mentioned that he'd be coming?"

"I don't think so," Stella said. There was no way she'd mentioned that. Stella would've remembered.

"There were so many calls back and forth, I must've totally spaced it. I'm so sorry. Will it be a problem?"

Gwen looked genuinely concerned, but if she'd known exactly how Ian had left things all those years ago, Stella knew she'd be downright horrified. He hadn't stepped foot inside this house since he'd left with his social worker at sixteen. Frances had been crying. She'd stood at the window watching them pull out of the driveway with tears streaming down her face. She'd felt like she'd failed him. Which was ridiculous, but that's how she'd felt, which made Stella furious with him all over again.

She forced a smile to ease Gwen's mind. And maybe her own, too. There was always the chance he'd show up and apologize to Frances for how he'd treated her back then. Or that he'd acknowledge that what he'd said at that coffee date years ago had been horribly untrue— suggesting their sweet and loving foster mother had only taken them in for the money. A disgusting comment that had brought up every single insecurity that Stella had ever had about finding a genuine home. But she doubted he'd do either of those things. She also doubted that he was coming back to Christmas Bay simply to do this interview and help Frances sell her house. No way. He had other motives in mind. Probably like getting a good look at her property, since, like an idiot, Stella had practically waved it in his face.

"It's okay," she said. "We just haven't seen him in a long time. He was one of Frances's foster kids, and he left…suddenly."

Gwen frowned, glancing at Frances, and then back at Stella again. "Are you sure? I feel terrible about this. I wouldn't want it to be awkward for you."

Too late.

Frances shook her head. "No, honey. Don't worry. He's come all this way to do the interview, so that says a lot. Maybe this is a blessing in disguise."

As if on cue, there was the roar of a car coming up the drive. All three of them moved over to the bay window and looked out, like they were waiting for Santa

Claus or something. Stella crossed her arms over her chest, annoyed by her own curiosity. She didn't care that she'd be seeing Ian again. She couldn't stand him and his giant ego. And she managed to believe that. Mostly.

Outside, a beautiful silver sports car pulled into view, mud from the long dirt driveway spattered on its glossy paint job. Stella's heart beat heavily inside her chest as she saw the silhouette of a man through the tinted windows. Short black hair, straight nose and strong jaw. Sunglasses that concealed eyes that she remembered all too well. Blue, like Caribbean water. But not nearly as warm.

Letting out a low breath, she watched as the door opened, and he stepped out. Tall, broad shouldered and dressed impeccably in crisp, white-collared shirt and khaki slacks. Like the car, the clothes looked expensive. Tailored to his lean body in a way that she'd really only seen in magazines. So, this was how Ian had turned out. Probably with an even bigger ego than she'd remembered.

Frances looked over at her. "I can't believe how handsome he is. He looks so different."

There were differences. But there were also similarities, and those were what made Stella's chest tighten as she watched him swipe his dark sunglasses off and walk toward the front door with that same old confidence. That same old arrogance that had driven her bananas as a kid. That had driven them *all* bananas.

But there was no doubt he'd grown into that confidence. As a woman, she could imagine feeling safe and secure in his presence. And at that, she recoiled. Nothing about Ian Steele should make her feel safe. He was a piranha, only here for a meal. She'd bet her life on it.

Beside them, Gwen cleared her throat and touched

her hair. Probably taken with his looks—something that made Stella want to snap her fingers in front of her face. *Snap out of it, Gwen!*

Instead, she walked over to the front door and opened it with her features perfectly schooled.

He stood with his hands in his pockets, gazing down at her like she was some acquaintance he was meeting for lunch. Instead of a girl he'd shared a home with, a family with, for two tumultuous years.

He smiled, and his straight white teeth flashed against his tanned skin. Two long dimples cut into each cheek. *Good God, he's grown into a good-looking man.* The kind of man who stopped traffic. Or at least a heart or two.

Stella stood there, stoic. Reminding herself that it didn't matter how he looked. It only mattered that he gave this interview and went on his merry way again. Got back in his sports car and got the heck out of Christmas Bay.

"Stella," he said, that Caribbean gaze sweeping her entire body. He didn't bother trying to hide it. "It's been a long time."

She stiffened. If he was trying to unnerve her, it wasn't going to work. He might be trying to brush those two years underneath the rug, but she sure wasn't going to. He'd made their lives miserable, and had left a lasting scar on Frances's heart. Something she refused to minimize or forgive. And that slippery smile said he wasn't the least bit sorry about what he'd said over that fateful coffee date. Whether he'd meant it or not, he'd definitely wanted to wound her, probably since she'd stayed and found happiness in Christmas Bay, and he hadn't. No, he wasn't sorry. Not by a longshot.

"Ian," she said. "Exactly the same, I see."

His smile only widened at that. "Now, how can you say that? It's been years."

"Oh, I can tell." She glanced over her shoulder into the living room. Frances and Gwen were talking in low tones, obviously waiting for her to bring him inside. She looked back at him and narrowed her eyes. "I know exactly why you're here."

"I don't know what you're talking about."

"Cut the crap, Ian. Frances wouldn't sell to you if you were the last man on earth."

Rubbing the back of his neck, he seemed to contemplate that. "Oh, you mean because the house is coming up on the market, and I'm a real estate developer, you just assumed I'm here to schmooze…"

"I *know* you're here to schmooze," she whisper-yelled. "But it's not going to work. You're not going to just waltz in here after all this time and get what you want. Life doesn't work that way."

"Oh, I beg to differ. It does, in fact, work that way." He leaned back in his expensive Italian loafers and looked down his nose at her. "Are you going to invite me in, or are we going to stand here and argue all day? I mean, don't get me wrong, the sexual tension is nice, but there's a time and place for it."

She felt the blood rush to her cheeks. "Give me a break."

He smiled again, his eyes twinkling. She wanted to murder him. But that wouldn't be good for the sale of the house, either, so she stepped stiffly aside as he walked past, trying not to breathe in his subtle, musky cologne that smelled like money.

When Frances saw him, she took a noticeable breath. Then she stepped forward and pulled him into a hug. He was so tall, she had to stand on her tiptoes to do it.

But he bent down obligingly, even though Stella could tell his body was unyielding. Ian had always had trouble with giving and receiving affection.

Stella couldn't bring herself to feel sorry for him. He'd had plenty of opportunities to be loved. Frances had tried, but he'd only pushed her away. It was what it was.

Still, she couldn't help but notice how his jaw was clenched, the muscles bunching and relaxing methodically. How his gaze was fixed on the wall behind Frances, stony and cold. Like he just wanted to retreat. And before she could help it, there was a flutter of compassion for him after all. Because she could remember feeling the same way a long time ago.

After a second, he pulled away and looked down at her with a careful smile on his face. Not the almost playful one he'd given Stella a minute before. This one was more structured. Like he'd been practicing it a while. Like fifteen years, maybe.

"Hi, Frances," he said. "It's good to see you."

Stella could see that she was having a hard time with a reply. Her eyes were definitely misty. Poor Frances. She'd just wanted the kids who'd passed through her doors to leave happy. She'd wanted to give them a home, whether it was for a few months, or the rest of their childhoods. The fact that she hadn't been able to give Ian any of those things still bothered her. Probably because, despite that carefully crafted smile, his pain was clearly visible. It had been brought right to the surface by this visit. Stella had to wonder if he'd been prepared for that when he'd hatched this asinine plan.

"Ian," Frances said. "You grew up."

"Probably all those vitamins you made me take."

"Well, they worked. Just look at you."

Gwen stepped forward and fluttered her lashes. She actually fluttered her lashes. Stella wanted to groan.

"Oh, I'm sorry," Frances said. "Gwen, this is Ian Steele. Ian, this is Gwen Todd, from *Coastal Monthly.*"

Ian took her hand, appearing just short of kissing it. Gwen didn't seem to mind. In fact, her cheeks flushed pink.

"Gwen, it's a pleasure."

"Thank you so much for making the drive up," she said. "I know it's a long one, but I'm so glad you did."

Stella eyed him, waiting for him to admit to wanting to take a look at the house, even in passing. Otherwise, why not do the interview over the phone? But he didn't. He just smiled down at Gwen innocently. *Who me? I just want to help with the article, that's all...*

Frances took all this in with interest. If she was worried about Ian's true intentions, she didn't let on. She just seemed happy to see him again. Which, in Stella's opinion, he didn't deserve. But that was Frances for you. Kind to the core.

Clapping her hands together, Gwen smiled. "Are we ready? I thought maybe we could start with some pictures of the upstairs, Frances. Maybe the widow's walk?"

"Sounds good to me."

"Me too," Ian said.

Stella stepped forward, narrowly missing Ian's toe. All of a sudden, Frances's spacious living room seemed as big as a postage stamp. She stepped back again, putting some distance between them, but not before catching his smirk. Of course he was enjoying this. Of course he was.

"The widow's walk is where Ian said he saw the ghost," Stella said tightly. "Are you sure you want to put that in the article, Frances? Maybe we shouldn't focus on that part?"

Frances frowned. "That's true…"

"Well, that's no problem," Gwen said, fishing her camera out of the bag. "We'll just start with a few by the Christmas tree, and then we can go outside to the garden. The sun is coming out. The light should be perfect."

Stella smiled, relieved. As long as things went smoothly, this article might actually end up painting the house in the light it deserved, which was what she'd hoped for in the beginning. And maybe she was just being paranoid as far as Ian was concerned. Maybe after he got a look at the place, he'd dismiss it like he probably dismissed so many other things in his life. After all, this was Christmas Bay, and what she'd told Frances was true. He hated Christmas Bay.

He stepped up to the bay window and looked out toward the ocean. The muscles in his jaw were bunching again, his blue eyes narrowing in the sunlight.

"My God, I'd almost forgotten that view," he said under his breath. Almost too softly for anyone else to hear.

But Stella heard. And even though it had been years since she'd seen Ian Steele, or that look in his eyes, she recognized it immediately.

This was something he wanted. And he intended to get it.

Chapter Two

Ian walked behind Stella, having trouble keeping his eyes off her amazing rear end. She'd been slightly over-weight as a kid, always refusing to get into a swimsuit at the city pool. She'd worn a T-shirt and shorts instead, which he'd thought was dumb. She'd looked just fine, but the girls he knew had a way of obsessing over things like that. If it wasn't their weight, it was their skin. Or their hair. Or a myriad of other things. Even the pret-tiest ones, who had absolutely nothing to worry about, worried anyway. Stella had been that way.

But he could see those days were long gone. She was no longer the girl in the oversize clothes. She was a con-fident, stunningly beautiful woman, who was looking over her shoulder at him like she wanted to stick a knife between his ribs.

"Be careful," she said. "The railing is wobbly."

They were climbing the stairs to the widow's walk after all. Frances had changed her mind, and thought it would be a fitting end to the article to have a picture of Ian standing there, looking out over the ocean. A grown man, coming back to the place where he'd spent so much time as a boy. A place that, as a confused, overwhelmed kid, he'd once said was haunted, but that he now realized was only a sweet old house that didn't deserve a dark reputation. The whole thing was a little too cute for his taste, but that's what people around here liked. Stella was absolutely right, thinking this article would help sell the house. That is, if he didn't get his hands on it first.

He smiled up at her, running his hand along the railing. "I remember."

She didn't smile back. Just turned around and kept climbing, her lovely backside only inches from his face. Good Lord, he really was a jackass. But he couldn't help it. She had a gorgeous body, and his gaze was drawn to it like it was magnetized. It wasn't like he wasn't used to gorgeous bodies, either. The women he usually dated were high maintenance, and keeping themselves up was part of their lifestyle. But Stella's body was soft, curvaceous. Something he could imagine running his hands over, exploring, undressing. Her skin would probably be just as velvety as her voice, and at the thought, his throat felt uncomfortably tight.

Taking the last few steps up the narrow, winding staircase, he stepped out behind her on the widow's walk. Frances and Gwen were already standing near the iron railing, looking out over the ocean. He stared at it, too, and for a few seconds, all thoughts of Stella's body were forgotten in favor of the house's property value.

He fished his sunglasses out of his front pocket and put them on. The yard below was spacious and pretty. A peeling white picket fence that was covered in climbing vines and rose bushes enveloped it like a hug. In the summer, the whole space was alive with colorful, fragrant blooms that made the garden look like something out of a fairy tale. In the winter, it was more subdued, but still a beautiful, luscious green.

Beyond the yard was the ever-present Scotch broom that butted right up to the edge of the cliffs that dropped into the sea. Cape Longing was one of the most dramatic stretches along the Oregon Coast, and finding land here that was prime for development was rare. Ian's wheels were turning so fast, he could barely think straight. *Condos.* He could picture a small row of expensive condos or townhouses. Simple, midcentury modern style, with lots of glass and metal. Balconies that overlooked the sea. Perfect for reading, or having a glass of wine, or entertaining in the evenings. Bachelor pads, or a couple's paradise... They could go in any direction, appeal to anyone. And with a setting like this, he could sell them for more than he'd even dreamed.

He looked up to see Frances smiling over at him.

"I hope you have some good memories of being up here," she said. "I know this used to be your favorite part of the house."

He smiled back, determined not to let that get to him. Determined not to tumble back into the past, to those lonely nights when he'd sat up here, looking out at the ocean reflecting the full moon above. Feeling scared and alone, and then ashamed for feeling so scared and alone. He guessed that's where that stupid ghost story of his had come from. Underneath everything, it had been a cry for help, a bid for attention. And now he was going to debunk it very publicly, in this article. If he owed Frances anything, that was it. And then they'd be even as far as he was concerned. She wasn't going to look at him with those doe eyes, and make him feel guilty for seeing a good business opportunity here. She just wasn't.

"I wasn't always easy to live with," he said, "but I do have some good memories of this place."

He was in the beginning stages of buttering her up, but maybe that was a bridge too far. It's not that it wasn't true—he did have good memories. Not that he'd ever admitted that…until now. But he could feel Stella watching him from a few feet away, her gaze like a laser beam boring into his head.

"Oh, really?" she muttered.

He turned to her. She knew exactly what he was thinking. He didn't know how, but she did. Not that it mattered. Frances was the only one who mattered here. It wasn't Stella who would be choosing a buyer, it was Frances.

"Really," he said.

"I'm glad to hear that," Frances said. "So glad."

Gwen was fiddling with her camera, looking like she was trying to get the lighting right. "So, this was where you said you saw the ghost?" she asked, holding the camera up and peering through the lens.

"This was the spot," he said. "Only, you know by now I didn't really see anything."

Gwen lowered the camera again. "So, why did you do it? Why did you make up that story?"

"Because I had a problem with the truth back then. Troubled kid, going off the rails—you know the drill."

Gwen nodded. Behind her, Frances frowned, her expression sad.

Back then, Ian hadn't believed her when she'd said she cared about him. He hadn't believed anyone when they'd told him anything. His mother had lied over and over and over again. About her relationships, about Ian's future with her. About everything. So, he'd learned to lie, too. And he'd learned to use lies to get exactly what he wanted.

Stella kept watching him. Maybe waiting for him to apologize. What the hell—he needed to stay on Frances's good side, anyway.

He let his gaze settle on the older woman with the kind eyes. He'd resented her so much back then. She'd been just another adult forcing him into a mold that he'd never wanted or asked for. *Troubled kid, going off the rails...* But he could never quite lump her into the same category as his parents and everyone else who'd let him down over the years. She was different then. She was different now.

"I'm sorry, Frances," he said. He had been bitter about his time in foster care, and she'd been a convenient target. She'd remained one for a long time, even after he'd left Christmas Bay. But she hadn't deserved his behavior. Today, he found he could say the words, but he still couldn't forgive her in his heart. Even though that was ridiculous, of course—none of it had been her fault. But he still couldn't get past her role in all of it. He'd been taken away from the only home he'd ever known and placed with a complete stranger, and the anger had nearly eaten him alive.

But he could at least say the words. And the words were all he needed right now.

She smiled, clearly moved. *Goal achieved.*

"Honey, you have nothing to be sorry for. It's all behind us now."

It wasn't behind them. Not by a long shot, since he was acutely aware that he was still lying for his own benefit. In this case, that benefit was her house. But he'd said he was sorry, and she seemed to accept it, and in that way, they could move forward. He could pile on the charm, convince her to sell, make a ton of money and leave Christmas Bay in his rearview mirror. This time for good.

"Frances," Gwen said, "why don't you move over to the railing next to Ian, and I can get a picture of you both."

"Oh, that's a good idea. Stella, why don't you get in here with us?"

Stella shook her head. "No, that's okay. This one can be just you two."

"Are you sure?"

"Positive."

Ian watched her as Frances walked over, leaning into his side for the picture. She watched him back, her blue eyes chilly. Her long dark hair moved in the ocean breeze. It was wild around her face, wavy, but not quite curly. Her skin was pale, delicate. Almost translucent, and there was a spattering of freckles across her nose. She was so pretty that he could almost forget how he'd never been able to stand her.

But even as he thought it, even as Gwen told them to smile and say cheese, he couldn't believe that same old line he'd always repeated to himself. He hated Frances. He hated Stella. He hated Marley and Kyla, and all the other foster kids who'd come in and out of the house during his time there. But the truth, which Ian still had trouble with, was more complicated than that. More layered. He hadn't really hated them. The truth was, he'd *wanted* to hate them, and there was a difference.

"Perfect," Gwen said, lowering the camera again. "I think that's about it. I've got everything I need. I'll call you if the gaps need filling in, but I think this is going to be a great Christmas article."

Frances touched Gwen's elbow. "Let me walk you out."

And just like that, Ian found himself alone with Stella. Just the two of them, facing each other on the widow's walk, the salty breeze blowing through their hair. He caught her scent, something clean, flowery. Something that made his groin tighten.

"We might as well not beat around the bush," he said evenly. "I'm going to be honest with you."

"Well, that's a first."

"I'm interested in this property, you're right. I think it's a great development opportunity."

Her lovely eyes flashed. "I knew it. I knew that's why you came."

"I came because I owed it to Frances. And I was curious about the house, too."

"You're so full of it, Ian. You were *only* curious about the house."

She was going to think what she was going to think. There was nothing he could do about it, and he didn't care, anyway.

He leaned casually against the railing and smiled down at her. Something he remembered had always driven her crazy. "Now that I've seen it," he said, "I'm going to talk to Frances about making an offer."

"Forget it. She'll never sell to you."

"Says who?"

"Says me."

"Last I checked, you don't own it."

She glared up at him. "No, but she'll listen to me. She'll listen to Marley and Kyla. And all we'll have to do is remind her that she wants a family here."

"She may have some romantic notion of selling to a family, but in reality, money talks. And I think she'll sell for the right price."

"You're insufferable," she bit out. She was furious now. Her cheeks were pink, her full lips pursed. Before he could help it, he wondered what she'd be like in bed.

All that passion and energy directed right at him. But that wasn't a fantasy that had a chance of coming true any time soon. By the looks of it, she'd rather run him over with her car first.

"Don't assume Frances would just sell to the highest bidder," she continued. "She doesn't need the money. Despite what you've always thought."

She was obviously talking about that idiotic comment he'd made about Frances's motives that night at the coffee shop in Portland. Something he'd said out of bitterness. It had been a rotten thing to say, not to mention categorically untrue. Stella hadn't given him a chance to take it back, though. She'd gotten up and slammed out before he could utter another word. Fast-forward almost ten years, and now here they were.

"I didn't mean that," he said huskily. "What I said back then."

She crossed her arms over her chest.

"And I know she doesn't need the money *now*," he continued. "But what about later? On the phone, you said she's got Alzheimer's. That's why she can't handle the house anymore. Retirement homes are expensive. Care facilities are even more expensive. This would give her a nest egg for her future. She's smart—she's got to know she'll need one."

Stella gaped at him. "Oh, you are disgusting. You're even lower than I thought you'd be when you showed up here, and believe me, that's pretty low."

"How is it low? The way I see it, I'd be helping her out."

"You *would* see it that way." She shook her head, her dark hair blowing in front of her face. She tucked it behind her ears again and took a deep breath. "She wants a family here, and that's the only thing that's going to sway her. Believe me, you don't stand a chance."

He put his hands in his pockets. "Hmm."

"What?"

"I'm just saying, if she wants a family living here, I might fit the bill there, too."

She laughed. "What? Come on."

"I don't have a family. Yet. But eventually I might, and it'd be great to have the house checked off the list." She was right. He *was* low.

Stella watched him suspiciously. "You just said this place is a great development opportunity. You expect me to believe you'd actually live here?"

"I might. For a while."

"Baloney. You're just saying that to get what you want."

"Believe me, don't believe me. Doesn't matter to me, Stella. What matters to me is what Frances believes. And by the way, this whole archrival thing we've got going on? It's only making me want the house more."

"Oh, really."

"Really."

"You'd buy a house out of spite?"

"No, I'd buy a house to make money. I'd sell it out of spite."

She glared up at him. She was fuming. But if she thought she was going to stand in his way, she was wrong. Nobody stood in his way. At least not people who didn't want to get bulldozed.

After a second, she looked away. She stared out at the ocean that was sparkling underneath the midday sun. He couldn't be sure, but he thought her chin might be trembling a little. And if it was, that would be a surprise. A crack in her otherwise impenetrable armor.

"Hey," he said.

She didn't look at him. Just continued staring at the water.

He took a breath, not sure what to say. Taken off guard by her sudden show of emotion. Ian could take a lot of things, and did on a daily basis. But the sight of a woman crying had always unnerved him. Talk about an Achilles' heel. He remembered walking in on Stella crying once when they were kids. She'd been trying to be quiet, so as not to call attention to herself. She'd looked up at him, her cheeks wet with tears, and the expression on her face had nearly broken his heart. He remembered very clearly wanting to cross the room to hug her, to comfort her. To take some of her pain away, just a little.

"You can tell me to go to hell," he said now. "But I'll give you some advice, Stella. Sometimes there's such a thing as caring too much."

At that she looked back at him. And he'd been right. There were tears in her eyes. He had to stop himself before he reached for her, because really, she was a stranger to him. He didn't know her anymore, and he didn't care to know her. He was only here for a business deal.

"She's eventually going to forget all the memories she has of this place," she said. "The only thing that comforts her is the thought of someone making new memories here. For me, as far as Frances is concerned, there is no such thing as caring too much."

He grit his teeth. *There's no such thing...* He wondered how it was that they'd ended up so differently. Her caring too much, and him not caring at all. They were two stars at the opposite ends of the universe. And she still shone just as brightly as she had when she was fourteen. Maybe he was jealous of that. Deep down. Maybe he wanted to love just as fiercely as Stella Clarke did.

She lifted her chin. "So, yes, Ian. You can take your money, and your offer, and you can go to hell."

And she walked out.

* * *

"Here's your room key, sir." The woman smiled up at him, wrinkles exploding from the corners of her brown eyes. Her Christmas tree earrings sparkled, coming in a close second to her sweater. She looked like Mrs. Claus.

"Thank you," he said.

"There's a vending machine right down the breezeway, and if you want to rent a movie, we have a pretty good selection of DVDs, but the front desk closes at nine."

He took the key card and tucked it in his back pocket, preoccupied with the events of that afternoon. Frances owned a candy shop on Main Street, and she and Stella had gone back to work right after their meeting with Gwen. That had left him zero time to approach her about the house, so he'd made the incredibly annoying decision to stay in Christmas Bay overnight.

He'd called and asked if he could meet Frances for coffee before heading home tomorrow, and she'd seemed genuinely happy about that. He'd make his move then. Her defenses were already down because of this cheesy article. If he could frame the sale in a way that would tug on her heartstrings, it would be easier than he'd thought.

Pushing down the slightest feeling of guilt, he grabbed a razor, comb and toothbrush from a rack beside the counter and paid quickly, not wanting to encourage any more small talk with the Jingle Bell Inn front desk lady. He'd already had to endure enough nosy questions— what brought him to town, where had he bought a car that fancy, etcetera, etcetera. All topped off with a story about someone who'd stayed here not long ago who drove a Ferrari. The kind Tom Selleck had in *Magnum P.I.* He'd smiled and nodded politely. But inside, he was dying. This was exactly the kind of interaction he never had to deal with in the city. In the city, people couldn't care less why you were staying overnight. They just took your credit card and told you where the best seafood places were.

Gathering his things, he told the lady to have a good evening and walked out the door. The sun was just beginning its fiery descent toward the ocean. The sky was a brilliant swirl of pinks and purples, and the salty breeze felt good on his skin. He breathed in the smell of the water, of the beach, letting the air saturate his lungs. Letting it bring him back, just a little, to the last time he was here.

He'd left Christmas Bay the second he'd graduated from high school—right after he'd turned eighteen and was done with the foster system for good. His mother had made some weak overtures about him coming to live with her again, and letting her "help" him with college. He hadn't been able to tell her off fast enough. This, after an entire childhood of not caring whether he was coming or going, or that he'd basically served as a punching bag for her ever-revolving door of boyfriends.

He slid the key card into the lock, watching the light blink green, then opened the door and walked into the small room with his stomach in a knot. He really couldn't believe he was back here after all this time. He'd never planned on it. His mother had passed away a few years ago, and the only relative still living here was a great-aunt who was in a retirement home across town. He'd gone to live with her after he'd run away from Frances's house. She'd tried to make a connection with him, and had been the only one in his family who ever acted like they cared at all. But he'd kept her at an arm's length, anyway, protecting himself the best way he knew how. The thought of coming back to visit her had never crossed his mind. He'd left. And that meant leaving her, and everything else, behind, too.

Opening the sliding glass door, he stepped onto the balcony with the beginnings of a headache throbbing at his temples. The guilt he'd felt earlier had settled in his gut like a small stone. If he had any chance of convincing Frances to sell to him, he needed to bury that guilt, along with any strange pull he was feeling toward Stella. These people were simply part of his past. They had no place in his future. And if they registered in his present at all, it was only because they were a means to an end.

It wasn't in Ian's nature to let fruit like this slip through his fingers once he realized how ripe it was for the picking. And no matter what kind of bleeding-heart reasons Frances had for wanting to sell her house to a family, he knew he'd been absolutely right about her needing the most money she could get out of it. What kind of local family would be able to come up with the cash to outbid him? What he was doing would only end up helping her, not hurting her.

Sinking down in one of the plastic deck chairs, he watched the waves pound the beach. In the distance, a woman was being dragged along by her golden retriever, the dog barking joyously at the water. Up ahead, two boys in hoodies were playing football in the sand. Other than that, the beach was empty. So unlike San Francisco, where the amount of people on a sunny winter day could make you feel like you couldn't catch your breath. Which, normally, he didn't mind. The hustle was what he liked about California. The opportunities, the possibilities. But the deep breathing you could do up here was undeniable.

He leaned back in the chair and pulled out his phone to do some quick calculations. How much the house might be worth on the market, how much the land alone might be worth and what kind of builders might be interested. Ian had instantly seen a few luxury condos perched on that cliff in his mind's eye. But honestly, it would be a great place for a high end spa, too. Maybe even a small, quaint hotel... He'd been worried the house would be on the National Register of Historic Places, but miraculously, it wasn't. Probably because it had always been a private residence and nobody famous had stayed there. Or maybe Frances's family had never gotten around to listing it. He knew there was an indepth nomination process. Either way, his initial worry that he'd run into red tape was null and void.

Looking out over the water, he rubbed his chin. The golden retriever was in the surf now, its owner standing with her hands on her hips, looking resigned. She'd lost the battle. Despite his headache, Ian smiled. It was a Norman Rockwell kind of moment. But then again, Christmas Bay was a Norman Rockwell kind of town. Scratch that. It was for some people. For people like him, he remembered how dead-end and limiting it really was. Yeah, Frances would definitely be thanking him after this. Even if he did have to stretch the truth initially, she'd thank him in the end.

He'd bet on it.

"Frances, I'm not sure you realize who you're dealing with here, that's all."

Stella leaned against the counter next to the cash register, watching her foster mother go from window to window with a bottle of Windex and a wad of paper towels. She was just about done, and the glass was crystal clear. It wouldn't last, though. When you worked in a candy shop, you got used to fingerprints everywhere. Even some nose prints thrown in for good measure.

Frances didn't turn around. Just kept spraying and wiping, spraying and wiping. "I know you're worried, honey. But we're only going to have coffee. I'll just see what he has to say."

"I *know* what he's going to say."

"I keep telling you, people change."

"Yeah, sometimes they get worse."

"You still think he's selfish."

"Does the Pope wear a funny hat?"

Frances laughed. "Well. That would be a yes."

"I'm just saying, we spent an hour with the guy, and that was plenty. He's only here to make money. He doesn't care about the house."

Frances did turn around at that. "What kind of person would I be, what kind of foster mother, if I didn't at least hear him out? If I didn't give him a chance to prove himself?"

Stella sighed.

"You're just going to have to trust me on this one, Stella. I know my memory is going, but it's not gone yet, and I need to give him a chance."

Frowning, Stella chewed the inside of her cheek. Damn him. Frances was already being swayed by that big-city charm. By those blue eyes, and that calculating smile. He probably knew exactly how Frances felt about him, and was going to use that to his fullest advantage. But at the end of the day, this was Frances's house, Frances's decision. All Stella could do was try to advise and be there for support.

"I do want you to come, though," Frances said, walking over and setting the Windex on the counter. "Would you do that for me?"

Stella's chest tightened. She hadn't been prepared to

see him again so soon. Or maybe ever. The thought of looking up into that smug face made her want to chug a glass of wine.

She licked her lips, which suddenly felt dry. "What about the shop?"

"We'll close it. It's just for a little while."

Well, there goes that excuse.

She forced a smile. "Then of course I'll come."

"But you have to promise not to kill him."

"I can't promise that."

Frances reached out and took her hand, suddenly looking serious. Almost desperate in a way, and Stella knew she was asking for reassurance. And comfort.

"I can't explain it," Frances said, "but I just want him to leave on good terms this time. Things with Ian have bothered me for years. This is a way to fix it, even if it's just to smooth it over. I need that. Can you understand?"

She could. She knew the sale of the house was the beginning of smoothing a lot of things over for Frances. She was settling her affairs, mending broken fences, looking back on mistakes she felt she'd made. And no matter how much Stella mistrusted Ian, she had to respect how Frances felt about him. Her foster children were her children. No matter how long they ended up staying with her. And having one of her children out there in the world, alone, unanchored, was too much for her to take, without at least having coffee with him and hearing him out, apparently.

Stella squeezed her hand. Frances had beautiful hands. Soft, and perfectly manicured, her nails usually painted some kind of fuchsia or cotton candy pink. Today, they were Christmas themed, green with little red polka dots.

"I can understand that, Frances," she said. "And I won't kill him. I promise."

Chapter Three

Ian sat in the sunroom of the old Victorian, with Stella sitting directly across from him. Frances had gone into the kitchen to get the coffee and pastries, insisting that "you kids sit and chat" for a minute.

So far there hadn't been any chatting. Just the chilly gaze of a woman who looked even more beautiful today than she had yesterday, if that was possible. She wore a gray Portland Trail Blazers hoodie and had her dark hair pulled into a high ponytail. Her face was freshly scrubbed, her cheeks pink and dewy. She still looked like she wanted to push him in front of a bus, though. Which was fine. Whatever.

He smiled at her and leaned back in the wicker chair. Everything in this room was wicker. Even the coffee table. It felt like he'd been teleported back to 1985.

"I wasn't expecting you to show up today," he said. "You seem like you'd rather be doing something else. Like getting a root canal, maybe."

Her lips twitched at that. But if he thought the teasing would get her to relax, he was sadly mistaken.

"That would be preferable, yes."

"Then why are you here?"

"Frances asked me to come, and I couldn't say no."

"Even though you wanted to."

"Exactly. But I promised I'd behave, so this is me behaving."

"Good to know. I'd hate to see you misbehaving."

A tubby black-and-white cat sauntered in with a hoarse meow, and blinked up at him through yellow eyes. Then it proceeded to wind itself around his ankles.

Ian stared down at it. He hated cats. He was allergic. In fact, he thought he could feel the beginnings of a tickle in his nose.

"Beauregard," Stella said. "No."

The cat looked over at her, unconcerned. Then he turned around and rammed his little head into Ian's shin.

"Beauregard." She leaned down and snapped her fingers at him, but he ignored her completely. Ian had to work not to laugh. He didn't like cats, but he did appreciate them. They did what the hell they wanted, when the hell they wanted to do it. If they came to you, it was because you had something to offer. If they left, it was because something else was more appealing at that moment. As a human, he could relate.

He reached up and rubbed his nose. Definitely a tickle.

"Oh, I see you've met Beauregard," Frances said, appearing in the doorway with a tray. "Just nudge him with your foot if he's being a pest."

Ian nudged him, but the cat only seemed encouraged by the contact. He immediately came back for more.

"Oh, dear," Frances said, setting the tray down on the coffee table. "I think you've made a friend."

Ian looked down at him dubiously.

Sitting beside Stella, Frances handed over his coffee. "Black, like you said."

"Thank you."

"Honey," she said, handing Stella a cup. "Here you go."

"Thanks, Frances."

"That's homemade blackberry jam for the scones. Kyla and Marley made it last summer." She smiled over at Ian. "They came back to Christmas Bay, too. They're busy with their own families, but we see each other nearly every day, don't we Stella?"

Stella took a sip of her coffee, eyeing him over the rim of the mug. A Christmas tree, draped in blue lights, twinkled next to her. The ocean outside the windows was gray and misty today. The perfect backdrop to the house on the cliff. It all felt like a movie set, and he was about to deliver his lines. The ones he'd rehearsed last night. The ones Frances wouldn't be able to resist.

He took a sip of his coffee, too, and burned his tongue. Wincing, he set it on the coffee table.

"Frances," he said evenly. "I want to talk to you about your house."

Clasping her hands in her lap, she waited. She'd obviously known this was coming. Stella sat beside her with a tight expression on her face. But whatever warning she'd given Frances, it obviously hadn't been enough to dissuade her from meeting with him today.

Sensing an opening, he leaned forward and put his elbows on his knees. "I'd like you to consider selling it to me."

She nodded slowly. "Is that the reason you came up here? To make an offer on the house?"

"I could've made an offer from San Francisco," he said, pushing down that annoying sliver of guilt that kept pricking at his subconscious. It was absolutely true. He could've made an offer from California, but he'd come up to do the interview, and he'd done it. He'd also come up for the house, but again, she didn't have to know that. Right now he needed to work the seller. He'd done it a thousand times before. Frances was no different.

"I wanted to do the interview for you. But when I saw this place again…" He clasped his hands and looked around. "Well, I really couldn't resist."

"It's a beautiful house," Frances said. "And you have to know what it means to me."

"I do."

"I was raised here. And my parents and grandparents, too. And then all of you kids…"

He clenched his jaw. *You kids…* He still couldn't believe she thought of him as more than just a shithead teenager who'd slept here for a couple of years.

Pushing that down, he smiled. "I know. The emotional value far exceeds the monetary value. But I have to be honest, Frances. That's a lot, too."

"I don't care about the money."

He didn't believe that. Everyone cared about the money.

He licked his lips. Stella watched him steadily, saying *I told you so* with that cool gaze of hers.

Taking a page from the cat's playbook—who right that minute had his sizeable girth spread out on Ian's foot—he ignored Stella and doubled down on Frances. If he wasn't careful, he'd lose control of the room, and he never lost control of the room.

"I know you don't," he said softly. Shaking his head.

Milking the moment. "I know you want someone living here who will love it just like you do."

Her kind eyes, which had been slightly guarded a minute ago, warmed at that. He could hardly believe it was going to be this simple. But he went on, not wanting to lose any ground, and not trusting Stella to interrupt when he was just getting to the good stuff.

"I'm not married yet," he said. "But of course, I'd like to be someday." For such a whopping lie, it rolled off his tongue fairly easily. He just had to keep reminding himself that it could be true. Technically. Anything was possible.

"And I'd love this house just as much as you do, Frances," he finished. That part was downright true. He'd love the massive payday it would bring, and that was practically the same thing.

Stella sat there stiff as a board. It was obvious she was trying to keep her mouth shut, but was having a hard time of it. He was sure he could handle her and whatever she threw at him, but it would be nice if he could get in a few more minutes with Frances before she started winding up.

"I'd love to believe that," Frances said.

Stella cleared her throat.

He ignored that, too.

"So, you're saying if you bought the house," Frances said, "you'd want to live here."

"That's what I'm saying."

"But you haven't been back to Christmas Bay since you left after high school, right?"

"You hate Christmas Bay," Stella said flatly. "Why would you live in a town that you hate?"

He held up a hand. "Now, I never said I hate it." That was also true. He hadn't said it. He'd been thinking it.

"Oh, come on, Ian."

"I have complicated memories of Christmas Bay," he said. "But now that I see it as an adult, it's obviously a great place to raise a family."

Stella made a huffing sound. But Frances's interest seemed piqued.

"Honestly," she said. "I love the idea of someone I know buying the house, over complete strangers..."

He smiled.

"And you really think you'd want to settle down here? It's awfully fast. Or have you been thinking of settling down for a while?"

Stella had been taking a sip of her coffee, but she coughed at that.

"Sorry," she croaked. "Went down the wrong pipe."

Ian narrowed his eyes at her before looking back at Frances. "Oh, you know. For a while now." If he was keeping track, that would go in the whopper column. But it couldn't be helped. She'd painted him into a corner.

"How convenient," Stella muttered under her breath.

"Now, Ian," Frances said. "I'm going to tell you the truth. If you made an offer, I think I'd consider it before I'd consider anything else. But I just can't get past what a change this would be for you, coming from the city. What about your job?"

"Oh, I could work remotely for a while. And I'm used to traveling. That wouldn't be a problem."

"But would you be able to acclimate back into small-town life?"

Ian resisted the urge to shift in his seat. He needed to appear convincing, and squirming around like a fibbing third grader wasn't going to get him anywhere.

"It would be an adjustment," he said. "But I've been wanting to make a change for a while, so..."

Frances nodded thoughtfully. He almost had her, he could feel it. But then again, he'd been expecting it. Ian did this for a living, and he was good at it. Really good. By this afternoon, he'd be on the phone with his office, getting the ball rolling. This should be an easy sale, barring anything popping up with the inspection. But that really didn't matter, either. It was the property he was after, not the house, and he'd pay whatever he had to for it.

He leaned back in his chair, the wicker squeaking obnoxiously under his weight. He felt confident, in control. The guilt that had been plaguing him earlier was tucked away in the farthest corners of his mind, ignored. It was all going to work out exactly how he'd hoped. He'd get a kick-ass piece of land, and Frances, whether she realized it or not, would be better off. Taken care of financially. Sure, she'd hate him in the end, but that was inevitable. He could live with it. He'd lived with a lot worse.

Stella continued to stare at him, her eyes cold. Under different circumstances, he probably would've asked her out by now. Taken her to the nicest restaurant he could find, and impressed her by ordering the most expensive bottle of wine. If she'd been a stranger, he would've done his damnedest to get her into bed afterward, too. He'd push that dark mane of hair off to the side, and move his lips along her jaw, down her throat. He'd work to get her to look at him the way so many other women did. He might even turn himself inside out for that.

But it was only a fantasy. Because she wasn't a stranger. She'd never liked him before, and she sure as hell didn't like him now. Again, he reminded himself that he didn't care.

Still, as he stared back at her, he knew that deep down, where that sliver of guilt lay, he did care. Just a little. Just enough to swallow hard now, his tongue suddenly feeling thick and dry in his mouth.

Frances took a sip of her coffee. Then another, as the clock ticked from the other room. The cat continued purring on his foot, and he thought his eyes felt itchy now. Or maybe that was just his imagination.

"I know you want the house, Ian," she finally said, setting the coffee cup down again. "And I want you to have the house."

His heart beat evenly inside his chest.

"On one condition…"

He raised his brows. Stella raised hers, too, and looked over at her foster mother. Even the cat, probably sensing the sudden stiffness in Ian's body, shifted and yawned.

"If you're serious about this," she continued, "if you're serious about living in Christmas Bay again, I want you to stay for a few weeks. Until Christmas Eve."

He stared at her. Stella stared at her, too.

"If you can work remotely," she said, "that shouldn't be a problem. You can get reacquainted with the town, with the people. Stella can show you around and introduce you. Then, you can truly decide if you want to put down some roots here. And if that's how you feel in your heart, I'll be able to tell. I'll be able to see it written all over your face."

Ian felt his mouth go slack. The house—his great investment opportunity, a deal so sure, he'd been writing up the papers in his head—was so quiet you could hear a pin drop. Outside the windows, there was the muted sound of the ocean, the waves slamming against the cliffs of Cape Longing. He felt his pulse tapping steadily in his neck as he let her words, her surprisingly genius condition, settle like a weight in his stomach.

Well, son of a bitch.

He hadn't been expecting *that*.

Stella couldn't stop gaping at Frances. She knew she was doing it. She must've looked like a sea bass, but she couldn't help it. The shock was all-consuming.

Across the room, Ian was apparently just as shocked. He didn't look like a sea bass—unfortunately he was too handsome for that. But he did look like Frances had dropped a sizeable bomb right in his lap.

He seemed at a loss for words. Stella couldn't blame him. She was in the same boat.

"I'm sorry," she managed after a minute. "What?"

Frances folded her hands in her lap, her Christmas sweater sparkling in the morning light. This one had a sequined snowman emblazoned on the front.

"You heard me," she said evenly.

Ian glanced over at Stella, and for the first time since he'd arrived, he looked taken aback. She had to hand it to Frances. She'd surprised them both. And she'd done it on her own terms. If she was going to sell the house, she was going to sell it to whomever she chose. She was not a forgetful old lady who couldn't handle her affairs. She could still manage just fine, and she was going to prove it.

Stella felt a distinctive warmth creep into her cheeks. She loved Frances so much, but she realized she'd been coddling her for the last few weeks. Treating her like a child. She stared at her shoes, ashamed.

Still, Ian *staying* here? And having to show him around? It was worse than him just making an outright offer. Much worse.

Taking a deep breath, she settled her gaze on Frances again, this time trying to center herself. "Frances, can we at least talk about this?"

"There's nothing to talk about. I was up half the night thinking about it, and it makes perfect sense."

Ian frowned, clearly wondering how he'd been so close to a deal, only to let this wriggle right out of his grasp. Normally, Stella would be gloating, but she couldn't even bring herself to do that. What a cluster.

"I trust your instincts, Stella," Frances said. "You might think I'm dismissing all your concerns, but it's actually because I've been listening that I'm doing this. By spending time with Ian, you'll be able to gauge his true feelings."

She turned to Ian then. "And I love you to pieces, Ian. I know you probably have a hard time believing that, but I do. However, I need to know you're not just here for the real estate. And this way, I'll know."

Ian swallowed visibly. "Frances…"

"There's really nothing you can say to make me change my mind. It's made up. If you're serious about the house you'll stay, or you won't and I'll find another buyer. It's as simple as that."

Stella watched her foster mother, impressed with her badassery, and at the same time horrified that she appeared to mean everything she'd just said. Ian was going to stay. *Until Christmas Eve.*

That is…unless he didn't. She looked over at him, wondering if Frances had called his bluff. There was always that possibility, and she felt the stirrings of hope in her belly. Maybe she wouldn't have to spend any more time with him after all.

He seemed deep in thought. His dark brows were furrowed, his jaw working methodically. He looked far away, weighing how much he actually wanted the property, no doubt. Was it really worth two weeks of his life? She guessed he already had more money than God. Why did he need more?

But right as she was thinking it, his gaze shifted to Frances, and there was something in his eyes that told Stella her foster mother might've just met her match.

"It's a deal, Frances," he said evenly. "On Christmas Eve, you'll see that I'm the right buyer for this house."

"I'm still not sure what you mean," Carter said, sounding confused on the other end of the line. "You're *staying* there?"

Ian sighed and leaned back against the motel bed's headrest. There was a light rain falling outside, and the ocean churned, grumpy and gray beyond the beach. He really didn't care to repeat himself—he wasn't in the mood. But the fact was, he was going to have to be doing a lot of that in the days to come. Telling people over and over again why he was here. His associates, his employees, Christmas Bay locals. He swallowed a groan. *God.* The Christmas Bay locals. If the front desk lady was any indication of the amount of nosiness around here, he'd have to tell everyone his business. And would any of them swallow his reasons for wanting to come back here? They'd have to if he had any hope of convincing Frances.

He felt his shoulders tighten. And it wasn't just Frances anymore. It was Stella, too. And having to convince her was what had him worried. Plenty.

"Yes," he said, gripping his phone tighter than he needed to. "It's a long story. But in order to secure this sale, I need to put the time in."

"Yeah, but two *weeks*?"

He could almost see his partner leaning back in her corner office chair, the bay sparkling behind her. She'd think this was ridiculous, of course. She'd think Ian was losing his edge if it was taking him two days to make a sale, much less two weeks. But if he didn't secure it, as far as he was concerned, that *would* be losing his edge, and he wasn't about to let that happen. Two weeks was a long time, but it would be worth it in the end. Another notch in his belt, another win for his company. And his bank account. All he needed was for Carter to take over while he was gone and deal with their clients in person. He could Zoom until the cows came home, but some of them were finicky and needed to be handled like high-strung racehorses. Zoom meetings didn't always cut it.

"Two weeks," Ian said. "Just trust me on this."

"Okaaay. Two weeks. I can't wait to hear all about it."

That was a lie. Carter didn't actually care if Ian camped out on the moon, just as long as he made them money. She was just as cutthroat as he was. Maybe even more so, and that was saying something in this business.

"Listen," Ian said. "I'm going to drive down tomorrow and pick up some clothes. So if you need me for anything, I can swing by the office before heading back. I'll call on the way down, okay?"

"Sounds good. Talk then."

Ian hung up and rubbed his temple. The headache from yesterday had turned into a full-blown pain in the ass. What he really needed to do was get in the car and head to the little market in town. Pick up a few groceries for his room. He had a microwave, minifridge and a coffee pot, thank God. He'd be living on macaroni and cheese and granola bars for a while. *Great.* This really couldn't get much worse.

But it could get worse, he knew that. He could put in the time and effort for this property, and by Christmas Eve, he might not be able to convince Stella that he was being genuine. He might not be able to convince Frances to sell to him, and then what?

He scraped a hand through his hair. He'd just have to cross that bridge when he came to it. Right now, he was going to have to gird his loins and head into town.

Lord help him.

Stella watched seven-year-old Gracie, wearing a pink slicker with the hood flopping on her shoulders, run up the beach.

"Don't go too far!" Kyla yelled through her cupped hands.

At that, Gracie turned and waved. She was so cute. Dark hair, dark eyes. Maybe one of the cutest kids Stella had ever seen. And she was about to get a brand-new stepmom. Kyla was going to marry Ben Martinez, Christmas Bay's police chief and the love of her life, next spring. She was positively glowing.

But as she walked alongside Stella now, the wind blowing her shoulder-length hair in front of her face, she looked more worried than anything.

"I'm not sure I like this," Kyla said. "It has trouble written all over it."

Stella pulled her cardigan tighter around her, watching as Gracie bent down to inspect something in the sand, then shoved it in her slicker pocket. Stella hoped it wasn't alive. "Tell me about it. I haven't liked it from the beginning."

"And this was Frances's idea? Actually, don't answer that. It sounds exactly like something Frances would do."

Stella nodded. "I know. She definitely wants to know Ian's serious, but there's also a part of her that wants to show us she's still in control. I'm proud of her. I mean, I'm super annoyed, but you have to hand it to her. It's kind of brilliant."

"So, what are you going to do?"

"What can I do? The only way to know for sure if Ian's serious is to spend some time with him, like she said. And even then, I'm not sure he'll ever be honest with us. What if he keeps up this charade about wanting to live in the house?"

"Then she'll have to trust you when you tell her it's just a charade."

Stella looked out over the water. It was gorgeous today. A little windy—the ocean was choppy and unsettled— but the sun was out, warming everything up.

"That's true," she said. "But two weeks… It seems like a lifetime."

Kyla hooked her arm in Stella's. "I'm sorry you got stuck with this."

"Me too. But Frances is worth it. The house is worth it. I'll just have to keep reminding myself of that every time I have to be within five feet of him."

Kyla laughed. "He's still that bad?"

"Worse."

"But good-looking."

Stella turned to her. "Who told you that?"

"Frances. On the phone this morning."

"What do his looks have to do with anything?"

"Nothing…but just how good-looking are we talking?"

"Kyla."

Her foster sister shrugged. "I'm just saying, you're single…"

"Gross. He's an ass.

"But a good-looking ass."

Stella raised a hand to shield her eyes from the sun, watching as Gracie drew in the sand with a stick. "I guess."

"Listen, you don't have to do this all by yourself. Ben and I can help. Bring him over for dinner or something. Take him to see Marley and the baby. Really lay it on thick. Maybe he'll decide he's in over his head and will give up. I mean, how much Christmas Bay can a person take, if they hate everything about Christmas Bay?"

Stella contemplated this, her wheels turning. "That's true…"

"I bet after a few days, he'll start wondering what the hell he's doing here and will leave early."

"Kyla," Stella said slowly. "You just gave me the best idea."

"Uh-oh."

"He'd *definitely* have second thoughts if he has a miserable time. Remember when Frances took us crabbing in middle school, and we were all hungry and cold, and Marley ended up falling in the water?"

"The infamous crabbing day. How could I forget?"

Stella smiled. *"Exactly."*

"Are you going to take him to the bay and push him in?"

"Don't tempt me. But why should we have to sugarcoat anything? Living in a small town isn't like a Hallmark movie. There are all kinds of things about it that drive you crazy. I'm just saying, I'll show him around. I'll introduce him to people. With the sole purpose of reminding him why he hated it here to begin with."

"Oh, you are *bad*."

"Not half as bad as he is." Stella lifted her chin as a flock of seagulls squabbled overhead, dipping and bobbing on the chilly breeze. "He dealt the cards," she said. "Now I'll show him I can play."

Don't miss
Their Christmas Resolution
by Kaylie Newell,
available September 2023 wherever
Harlequin® Special Edition
books and ebooks are sold.

www.Harlequin.com

#3013 THE MAVERICK'S HOLIDAY DELIVERY
Montana Mavericks: Lassoing Love • by Christy Jeffries

Dante Sanchez is an expert on no-strings romances. But his feelings for single mom-to-be Eloise Taylor are anything but casual. She knows there's a scandal surrounding her pregnancy. But catching the attention of the town's most notorious bachelor may be her biggest scandal yet!

#3014 TRIPLETS UNDER THE TREE
Dawson Family Ranch • by Melissa Senate

Divorced rancher Hutch Dawson has one heck of a Christmas wish: find a nanny for his baby triplets. And Savannah Walsh is his only applicant! Who knew that his high school nemesis would be the *perfect* solution to his very busy—and lonely—holiday season...

#3015 THE RANCHER'S CHRISTMAS STAR
Men of the West • by Stella Bagwell

Would Quint Hollister hire a woman to be Stone Creek Ranch's new sheepherder? Only if the woman is capable Clementine Starr. She wants no part of romance—at least until Quint's first knee-weakening kiss. But getting two stubborn singletons to admit love might take a Christmas miracle!

#3016 THEIR CONVENIENT CHRISTMAS ENGAGEMENT
Top Dog Dude Ranch • by Catherine Mann

Ian Greer is used to finding his mother, who has Alzheimer's, anywhere but at home! More often than not, he finds her at Gwen Bishop's vintage toy store. He admires the kind, plucky single mom, so a fake engagement to placate his mother—and her family—seems like the perfect plan. Until a romantic sleigh ride changes their holiday ruse into something much more real...

#3017 THE VET'S SHELTER SURPRISE
by Michelle M. Douglas

Sparks fly when beautiful PR expert Georgia O'Neill brings an armful of stray kittens to veterinarian Mel Carter's small-town animal shelter. Mel has loved and lost before, and Georgia is only in town short-term, so it makes sense to ignore their mutual attraction. But as they open up about their pasts, will they also open up to the possibility of new love?

#3018 HOLIDAY AT MISTLETOE COTTAGE
The McFaddens of Tinsley Cove • by Nancy Robards Thompson

Free-spirited photojournalist Avery Anderson just inherited her aunt's beach house. And, it seems, her aunt's sexy, outgoing neighbor. Hometown hero Forest McFadden may be Avery's polar opposite. But fortunately, he's also the adventure she's been searching for.

Get 3 FREE REWARDS!

We'll send you 2 FREE Books plus a FREE Mystery Gift.

FREE
Value Over
$20

Both the **Harlequin® Special Edition** and **Harlequin® Heartwarming™** series feature compelling novels filled with stories of love and strength where the bonds of friendship, family and community unite.

YES! Please send me 2 FREE novels from the Harlequin Special Edition or Harlequin Heartwarming series and my FREE Gift (gift is worth about $10 retail). After receiving them, if I don't wish to receive any more books, I can return the shipping statement marked "cancel." If I don't cancel, I will receive 6 brand-new Harlequin Special Edition books every month and be billed just $5.49 each in the U.S. or $6.24 each in Canada, a savings of at least 12% off the cover price, or 4 brand-new Harlequin Heartwarming Larger-Print books every month and be billed just $6.24 each in the U.S. or $6.74 each in Canada, a savings of at least 19% off the cover price. It's quite a bargain! Shipping and handling is just 50¢ per book in the U.S. and $1.25 per book in Canada.* I understand that accepting the 2 free books and gift places me under no obligation to buy anything. I can always return a shipment and cancel at any time by calling the number below. The free books and gift are mine to keep no matter what I decide.

Choose one: ☐ **Harlequin** ☐ **Harlequin** ☐ **Or Try Both!**
  Special Edition **Heartwarming** (235/335 & 161/361
  (235/335 BPA GRMK) **Larger-Print** BPA GRPZ)
  (161/361 BPA GRMK)

Name (please print)

Address   Apt. #

City   State/Province   Zip/Postal Code

Email: Please check this box ☐ if you would like to receive newsletters and promotional emails from Harlequin Enterprises ULC and its affiliates. You can unsubscribe anytime.

Mail to the **Harlequin Reader Service:**
IN U.S.A.: P.O. Box 1341, Buffalo, NY 14240-8531
IN CANADA: P.O. Box 603, Fort Erie, Ontario L2A 5X3

Want to try 2 free books from another series! Call 1-800-873-8635 or visit www.ReaderService.com.

HARLEQUIN
PLUS

Try the best multimedia subscription service for romance readers like you!

Read, Watch and Play.

Experience the easiest way to get the romance content you crave.

Start your **FREE TRIAL** at
<u>www.harlequinplus.com/freetrial</u>.